ALIEN TALK

Alien Talk

William X. Adams

www.psifibooks.com

Psi-Fi Books
Copyright 2019 by William X. Adams
ISBN: 978-1-7322274-5-3

Cover Design: SelfPubBookCovers.com/ mad-moth

Chapter One

Few men would wear a short-sleeved shirt to work in the nation's capital, but Herbert Hawke always did. With two pens in the pocket and always a tie. It was not because there was any dress code for an underground bunker but because he was the boss, and it was a matter of decorum. The tie was always loosened enough for the knot to hang exactly at the third button. Casual but proper. He was fifty-eight years old, looking to early retirement, but that was no reason to go slack. The dozen younger workers he supervised, most in their twenties and thirties, didn't wear ties and suspected that 'Erb, as they called him behind his back, never untied his. They speculated that he had a closet with nooses lined up on pegs. They were correct.

Herbert felt it was important to maintain civility in the vast, darkened cavern they worked in. He was aware the youngsters made fun of him, but they did not fail to follow his instructions. His slight English accent, a vestige from a childhood in Manchester, added to his perceived authority, so he laid it on thick.

The WATOC, Washington Area Transit Operations Center, was the brain and central nervous system for rail traffic radiating from the dense hub of stations at the nation's Capitol Buildings, outward in a dozen multicolored spidery legs into the surrounding suburbs, reaching into Maryland and Virginia.

The dim, windowless main hall of WATOC was lighted by wall-sized colored system maps on huge LED panels mounted all around the room. In the open center, Herbert and his crew, like supplicants at the altar of their god, lived in the glow of the screens as they hunched over monitors and keyboards. They knew where every car of every train was located in the system at every moment during the operational day. They maintained optimal spacing between units to balance safety and efficiency. Each train had a human driver, but those were largely symbolic. Herbert and his crew were the real drivers, and they attended to their responsibilities like military drone pilots.

That's why, on a Wednesday morning in mid-December, Herbert lifted his head and paid attention when he heard a repeating alarm buzzer from one side of the room. Usually, it meant a train was delayed, often because some idiot was holding doors open, but you had to investigate every irregularity. When an immediate verbal reassurance was not forthcoming, he probed.

"Lockner?"

"Ah, one moment, sir."

Herbert could see a blinking indicator on the map on the wall in front of Lockner. He got up and walked across the corral.

"What is it, Lockner?"

The young man had his head down, typing codes into a console, glancing at blue alphanumeric feedback on a screen in front of him.

"Trying to confirm, sir. There appears to be a train missing. Approaching L'Enfant Plaza, Orange Line"

"What do you mean missing? How can a train be missing?"

"It has disappeared from the system, sir. Vanished. I'm trying to contact the driver."

"A line of seventy-foot rail cars does not vanish."

"The driver reports the train is moving slowly. It's there. It's just not in our system at the moment." Lockner gestured vaguely without looking up to the big map on the wall.

Herbert studied the map. A red, flashing, numerical identifier for the six-car unit was shown just north of the huge L'Enfant Plaza Station, but there was no train. Elsewhere in the system, every car was clearly represented as a rectangle.

"Stop that train and alert maintenance. We can't have an invisible train running through our system."

"No, sir. I mean, yes, sir."

Herbert walked back to his workstation to begin an incident report.

"Orange Line's back on, sir."

Returning to the wall display, Herbert verified that the southbound Orange Line train had reached the station and stopped. All six cars were visible.

"What happened?"

"It reappeared on the screen before the driver brought it to a stop in the tunnel."

"So is it in the tunnel now or at the station?"

"At the station, sir. Everything operational."

"Failure in the signaling system. Get somebody out there to look at it."

"We'll have to shut the line down for several hours to do that, sir."

Herbert shot his arms out to the sides in a gesture of helplessness then let his arms slap to his legs.

"Alright. Schedule special maintenance for tonight and meanwhile, be alert,"

He paused and addressed all the young men and women, whose attention had been drawn to him because of the incident.

"All of you. Keep your eyes peeled for disappearing trains. Let's see if we can get through the rest of the day without another ghost train."

The next morning, Herbert found an eight-by-ten photograph of a gray metallic object about the size and shape of a hand-crank can-opener on his desk. The tool or device was shown in a clear plastic bag along with a yellow service slip. He turned the photograph over, read the identification and picked up his phone.

"This is Hawke in WATOC. I need to speak to the maintenance supervisor."

He waited, introduced himself again, and started asking questions. Everyone else in the room was listening.

"So this device was literally attached to the rail?" Herbert studied the photograph while he listened. "Well if it's not ours, how did it get there? No, of course you don't... So our switch was disabled by this switch, is that it? Have you ever seen one of these before?" Herbert put the picture down and wrote notes on a yellow pad. "Is the original switch working correctly now? Did you look for any more of these devices? And? ...Both directions?" He underlined something on his pad twice. "Alright, I'd like to see the full report this morning. Can you expedite that? Thank you very much."

He hung up the phone—placed the handset carefully onto the base station cradle as people used to do in the twentieth century—and continued to write on his pad while everyone watched. He finished and walked to the front of the room with the big screens at his back.

"Can I have everyone's attention, please," he announced. He already did.

"This," he said, holding up the photograph, "is a foreign switch, not one of ours, removed from the Orange tunnel north of L'Enfant Plaza last night. It made our train disappear yesterday for three minutes by overriding the sensor. Only one train, only once. We don't know how it works or where it came from, but if it could make one train disappear it could potentially do a lot more than that. It's sabotage, ladies and gentlemen. We have experienced a rail system security breach. Maintenance has already notified security."

"How would anybody get into the tunnel to install it?" a young woman asked. "You'd trigger the intrusion alarms."

"I don't know. I have a security briefing in an hour."

"What I want to know is why," Lockner said. "Why would anybody install a device that makes one train go off the grid for three minutes? What's the purpose?"

"I think it's a warning," another young man said. "It's communication. 'I can do this, so watch out.'"

"Watch out for what?"

"I'm sure security has theories," Herbert said. "It could have caused a horrible collision. Why? We don't know. We do know this is very serious."

Herbert waited a moment for his words to settle from the air down to the desktops in the room.

"I want you to be at your most vigilant today. Something's afoot. Carry on."

Herbert sat with Metro Transit's chief of police Karl Jennings and looked at fuzzy images from a security camera. Why, in this modern day, were security camera images still blurry, grainy, and shot from impossible angles above? He couldn't fathom it.

"This answers some questions about the intruder," Jennings said. "It's a youth or small adult on a rail cart, coming in at three in the morning when the system is closed."

The brief video showed a short person dressed in what appeared to be a long raincoat and wearing a wide-brimmed fedora and sunglasses, moving quickly down the rails on a flatbed utility cart.

"Not much to go on," Herbert said. "Except for that cart. Looks like it has its own battery power. Quick in-and-out. Well-planned and well-engineered. Not a child."

"Our suspect did his homework."

"How'd they get past the security alarms?"

"The motion-detectors test fine. Just didn't trigger. The intruder must have keyed in a correct and valid code. We're looking at employees now."

"Let's look at it one more time, can we?"

Jennings nodded to an assistant who reran the thirty-second video record. Herbert peered at it carefully.

"Why sunglasses? It's dark in there even during the day."

"Sunglasses don't make sense. Lights, please?"

The room lights came on.

"What about the switch device itself? What do you know?"

"Simple, untraceable, off-the-shelf components, simple in design, ingenious in conception. It attaches to the rail with a strong magnet, unfolds automatically. An induction coil disables the sensor that tells us a train is present. Operated either by a timer or by remote control. We're still looking at it."

"Why would anyone do that? Go to all that trouble? Take such a risk?"

"It has to be either a prank or a taunt. Either way, we're looking at some serious psychological issues. If it's a taunt, this could be just the beginning. We're not releasing any information to the public. Bottom line, though, we consider this an act of domestic terrorism."

"It has ideological motivation?"

"We think so."

"What's the message?"

"We don't know. That's why I think there could be a follow-up event. We've changed the keypad codes, inspected all the alarms, and we're increasing nighttime patrols. And as I told you, we're looking internally at our employees. Not much else we can do."

"Next time it could be ..."

"It's our job to prevent any next time."

Only three days later it happened again. This time it was the Blue Line, heading out of L'Enfant Plaza. A train disappeared from the grid for three minutes in the tunnel just east of the station. The incident occurred at 10:15 am, causing panic in the WATOC. However, there was no harm, ultimately. The train soon reappeared just beyond the Federal Center Station. The train-riding public was never the wiser. Again, investigators found and removed the same kind of sensor-sabotaging device. Again also, CCTV showed a short person on a rail cart in the middle of the night when the system had been closed, and again, no alarm had sounded.

Frustrated, Herbert met with Metro security for the second time.

"Whoever it is, they're telling us our security means nothing to them," Jennings said.

"And they're quite right," Herbert said. "We are helpless against them."

Hawke and Jennings sat with other security personnel in the Metro Police briefing room.

"Is that the full message? 'Metro, your security is inadequate.' An email would have been simpler."

"Of course that email would have been ignored. This person, or group, has our full attention now."

"Is it the same person?"

"Looks like it."

"Let's take another look."

The lights went down, and two video clips were shown, one from each of two cameras. They were very similar except for the angle.

"Stop there," Herbert said. "Go back a little. Right there. Look where he bends down to attach the device to the rail. Nobody bends down like that."

"Like what?"

Herbert stood then slowly lowered himself by bending his knees and keeping his back straight and vertical. He soon paused and rose again.

"I can't do it anymore. Perhaps one of the younger officers would demonstrate?"

Jennings gestured a young woman forward. She stood and approached the two men.

"Thank you," Herbert said. "Can you do a deep knee bend? You know what that is? I'd like you to bend your knees while keeping your back straight until you're sitting on your heels. And if possible, do it slowly, without touching anything for support."

The woman performed the exercise as described, with some difficulty, by extending her arms straight out in front of her for balance.

"Impressive, detective Cole," Jennings said.

"Now can you raise yourself back up slowly in the same manner please?"

Cole complied, closing her eyes and grimacing the whole time, again with her arms extended in front of her. She quickly felt behind herself to verify she had not split her pants.

Jennings and the other officer in the room applauded. Cole smiled.

"One more time, if you please," Herbert said. "Can you do it again, this time with your arms at your sides?"

"I'll try."

Cole bent her knees and lowered herself slowly. When she was only halfway down she fell backward and threw her arms out behind to break the fall.

"Sorry. I guess I can't."

She smiled with embarrassment from the floor.

"Nothing to be sorry about," Herbert said. "I'm not sure an Olympic athlete could do it. The human body is not balanced for a move like that."

Cole got up and returned to her chair.

"And the point of this little demonstration is?" Jennings said.

"Our gate-crasher made that exact move effortlessly, quickly, twice, with arms at his sides, straight up and down. Without ever getting off of the rail scooter. And while squatting, he attached the device with his hands, very low-down, then pulled the hands back into the raincoat and rose straight up effortlessly. What do we conclude from that amazing performance?"

"Our boy is an Olympic athlete?"

"That, or, our boy is a robot."

Chief of Metro police Jennings stared blankly at Herbert before speaking.

"You're saying the intruder is a robot?"

"It explains why the motion detector alarms don't go off when the intruder is in the tunnel. 'Motion detector' is a misnomer. The sensors in the tunnel don't detect motion. They recognize changes in infrared energy, body heat, which a robot does not have."

"Microwave radar is too expensive," Jennings said.

Herbert ignored the excuse. He was developing his thesis out loud.

"I think what we've got here is a sophisticated organization which has deployed this device to tell us of their impunity and Metro's vulnerability. And possibly, to warn against a large, serious attack."

"Why would they warn us?" Jennings said.

"They're playing with us, pulling our nose. There will be more taunts like this until we acknowledge them publicly."

"What do they want? There's nothing to be gained by hassling Metro system security."

"All kinds of nuts out there," Herbert said. "What do we see in the pattern? Always the Orange or Blue Lines. Never the others. Coming into the Plaza station, going east out of it. They're moving closer to the Capitol Building.

"And therefore what?"

"I don't know, but I'd put immediate twenty-four-hour live surveillance on the Federal Center Southwest and Capitol South stations. The Blue and Orange lines cross the Anacostia shortly after that."

"You think the attackers are moving closer to the Capitol Building."

"They're already there. They've been warning us, leading us there. I'd close those lines now and scour the tracks in both directions."

"I can't do that," Jennings said, shaking his head. "It would be a massive disruption to the whole system. It would take hours to search that much track. I don't have the personnel. I'd have to explain to the public, to the mayor, probably to a damn congressional committee."

"Hmm," Herbert said, seeing the other man's distress. "Might not be necessary."

"How do you mean?"

"Our boy might be in the tunnel right now. If he's a robot, he doesn't have to come out for anything, does he? He'll wait and become active at night when the system is shut down again."

"How would he hide his little cart?"

"If he's a robot, he picks it up and stands it on end somewhere. I don't know."

"Maintenance sweeps the rails every morning before five, and they haven't seen any robots."

"They don't check all the equipment bays, do they? Or under the platforms. They're just looking at the rails."

Jennings seemed to be a slow information processor. Again he stared at Herbert while the wheels turned. Herbert waited.

"We're going to have to go in and flush him out," Jennings said.

Herbert said nothing.

Jennings turned to one of the men in the room. "Sergeant Rodriquez, set it up. Three squads, start at Federal Center and move east to Capitol South. Overtime pay. Plus one guard at each platform. We start at midnight."

"Yes, sir." The sergeant marched out of the room.

*

The searchers began at 12:15 am, after the last trains for the day had cleared the tunnel. All wore Kevlar vests and carried radios and ultra-bright Streamlights. Third-rail power was off. Two members of each squad covered eastbound or westbound tracks. All teams shined their lights into every nook, cranny, platform overhang and disused spur along the way. Radios crackled. Aside from trash and rats, they found nothing out of place. Even so, they searched methodically toward the Capitol SW Station.

Tom Jackovitch had already worked a full shift and was not enthusiastic about working most of the night, overtime pay or not. He sat on a folding canvas chair he'd brought with him, on the dimly lit platform of the Federal Center SW Station. Ventilation fans provided a dull background noise to the police chatter on his radio. He smoked a cigarette in the no-smoking area, the only benefit he could identify of his unlucky nighttime duty. Occasionally he sipped cold coffee from a Styrofoam cup he kept at his feet. He read a newspaper he'd pulled from a trash bin and once in a while looked up at each end of the platform and the black circles of the subway tunnel. Every few minutes, he got up and walked to the other side of the platform and looked both ways at nothing. The place was deader than a mortuary at midnight. He slumped again into his blue canvas chair, yawned deeply, and read the comics page.

At 1:30 am, a five-foot-tall figure in a beige raincoat and a black fedora entered the Federal Center Station platform area on the eastbound rails. It silently rolled along the tracks behind Jackovitch and disappeared again into darkness on the other side.

The A Team had moved quickly south and was just short of the Capitol South station. They walked, peered, shone their lights, and listened to status reports on the radio which conveyed no useful information but gave everyone a sense of being part of a large, powerful team instead of an isolated trio in a moldy-smelling gloom.

As she peered into an equipment recess on the damp concrete wall, Officer Rita Perez stopped and stood still, listened then turned around. She shone her light backward into the tunnel.

"Did you hear something?" she said to Officer Berman nearby.

"Like what?"

"Like a clink. Like metal hitting metal, hard. Ka-clink, that's what it was."

"Might have been somebody banging a rail."

"Came from behind us." She continued to wave her light back and forth into the tunnel behind them. She saw only cement and emptiness. "Something's back there. I'm calling it in."

"We already searched there. Every square inch."

"Central, this is Officer Rita Perez, Team A, eastbound. I'm reporting an unusual noise coming from the tunnel west of us, where we already searched."

"What is your location, Perez?"

"Just east of marker B10.5. I'm going back to look."

"Negative, Perez. Wait for the chief."

Perez took a few tentative steps back in the direction they'd come, her light beam ahead. All other radio chatter had gone silent as everyone listened.

"This is the chief, Perez. What did you hear?"

"A loud clink, metal hitting metal. It came from behind us. It wasn't right. I'm going back to look."

"Take your team with you and proceed very cautiously. I've sent the security videos from the Federal Center Station to headquarters for review. Go slow and be careful."

"Ten-four, Chief."

"B Team, cross over to the eastbound tracks and back up Perez and her team. Copy?"

"Copy, Chief."

"Who's at Federal Center? I need status."

"Officer Jackovitch here, Chief. Nothing to report."

"Stand by."

"We couldn't have possibly missed anything in this tunnel," Berman said to Perez.

"I know I heard something."

"The guard at the Federal Center Station saw nothing."

"Yeah, but it's Jacko."

"True."

The radio hissed and popped, and the chief came on again.

"Team A, Perez, you read?"

"Yes, sir."

"We have movement on a CCTV camera at Federal Central. One figure coming your way on a rail cart."

"A figure, sir?"

"A person, a small person in a raincoat and a hat riding a cart on the rails."

"There's no power on the rails, sir."

"He has his own power."

Perez looked at Berman with a quizzical expression.

"C and D Teams hold your positions. We have an intruder in the system. Be alert. SWAT and Bomb are entering at the Plaza and coming in eastbound on all tracks. Teams A and B, continue moving slowly west with extreme caution until you see a sign of the intruder or the lights of SWAT. Copy?"

"Copy, sir."

Perez led her combined Team A and B forward, taking small, careful steps. Four white beams of light pierced the darkness ahead of them like searchlights scanning a velvet sky. The team moved quietly. The radio had lost the team-building, exuberant chatter of only twenty minutes ago. SWAT and Bomb whispered their marker positions to central, as did Perez.

"Look. Lights," Perez said.

Fireflies could be seen about a half-mile away.

"That's SWAT. Where's the guy?" Berman said.

"Maybe right there." Perez stopped and held her light steady. It illuminated something vertical, several hundred yards ahead.

Berman moved his light to join Perez's. "Could be just a stain on the wall. It's not moving."

"Gimme some light, people."

Two more beams joined the pattern.

"It's a person, casting a shadow," Perez said.

"Too still for a person," Berman said. "I think it's a stain on the wall."

"Central, this is Perez, A and B Teams at marker G 10.1. We may have a visual on the intruder. We can see SWAT coming the other way."

"Roger, Perez. Stand by."

"Let's go," Perez said. "We can get there first."

"We're supposed to stand by."

She cocked her head and looked at Berman. "You comin'?"

Perez strode ahead in quick, long strides. The others followed her lead instinctively. They approached the target with weapons drawn and their light beams focused on the intruder, ready for a sudden move. The figure in the raincoat stood absolutely motionless, didn't even turn his head to the approaching lights. He was looking to the side, directly at the cement wall.

Perez yelled. "Put your hands on top of your head!" Her high-pitched voice echoed in the tunnel. The intruder remained rigid as a statue. "Berman, you tell him."

Berman, a large male, had a booming voice. He extended his weapon and bellowed much louder than was necessary, the way police do.

"Put your hands on your head! Do it now!"

The intruder did not even flinch.

"Move on him?" Berman said.

"He could have a weapon under the coat. Wait for SWAT."

"Central, this is Perez, Teams A and B. We have detained the intruder. He is unresponsive. We're waiting for SWAT, about three minutes away."

"Copy, Perez."

SWAT arrived with large protective shields, klieg lights and shotguns. They flooded the area with bright white light while they barked commands at the intruder, to no effect. The stream of commands became increasingly louder, more belligerent and more threatening. The intruder remained absolutely fixed. They ordered Perez and the other search squads to back off, which they reluctantly did.

"It should be our collar," Perez grumbled.

"We don't have the blast shields. SWAT can handle it," Berman said, and the end of his sentence was punctuated with an explosion that knocked him and Perez down.

The eruption released a ball of dirty orange flame that burned out quickly, and black smoke was sucked out behind the blast wave which coursed outward in both directions along the tunnel, knocking down SWAT officers and the rest of the search detail. Its wall of compression created a hurricane of air in front of it, heading toward the stations. Fierce as it was, the explosion was at half-strength in each direction, much of its force dissipated through the three rail tubes. Even so, it ripped out ventilation piping, tore down communication lines, and raised a thick wadding of dirt, gravel, and from the tracks.

Tom Jackovitch had been on his feet. He'd been following the radio traffic and peering into the blackness of the eastbound tunnel after SWAT and Bomb had passed through his station. When he heard the blast and felt cold air moving toward him from the tunnel as if an express train were coming, he at least had the sense to pull his head in from the edge of the tunnel before the blast expanded into the station with a deafening roar. He slid his back down a tiled wall and sat, holding his hands over his ears. The station hall filled with dust, dirt, and scraps of paper. It was all over in ten seconds.

He got up and used his radio. "Jackovitch, Federal Center. There was an explosion in the eastbound tunnel south of here."

"Roger, Jacko. Your status?"

"Ears ringing. Unharmed."

"Stand by."

*

Herbert Hawke and Karl Jennings were eager to hear a briefing by Agent Mike Washburn from FBI headquarters. They sat in a small conference room in the agency's building. Washburn, a big, lean man about forty-five years old, wore a blousey white shirt with FBI cufflinks. He was flanked by dark-suited men and one dark-suited woman, all identified only as "from Homeland Security."

Washburn read from a report on the table in front of him, reciting information that everyone already knew. There had been no fatalities. Several officers had checked into hospitals, but aside from bruises, cuts, scrapes, and temporary hearing loss, there had been no serious injuries. The tunnel had sustained expensive damage, however, and would absorb weeks and a large repair budget. Homeland Security had deemed the incident a terrorist attack even though no group had claimed responsibility and investigators had no clues about the perpetrators.

From scraps at the bomb site, forensics had determined that the blast had been detonated by the robot, on a timer.

"From what we can tell," Washburn said, "it had opposable arms that traveled up and down a central pillar. The head, about the size of a melon, had video-camera eyes and an array of antennas and sensors."

"Thank goodness no one was killed," Herbert said. "Why did it go off when it did? Was the idea to harm our people?"

"We don't think so. If the aim were to harm people, it would have gone off at noon, not after midnight. It was a display of power. A message."

"That's what we thought about the sabotage of the sensors. It was a taunt or a warning."

"Our terrorism experts now believe we should have gone public with information about those incidents. By keeping the news secret, we forced the terrorists to escalate. They want to communicate with the government and the public, and we prevented that. Now they have communicated."

"What do they want? Who are they?"

"We're working on that. These are terrorists. They're not angry about subway fares. This has nothing to do with the subway system. They're angry about something else. Our people are trying to decode this particular message."

"This is not like any language I'm familiar with," Herbert said, shaking his head.

Chapter Two

Andy met Robin at the Austin airport, and they hugged, the way people do at airports, not because they had any desire for whole-body contact. Rather, it gave them an opportunity to inconspicuously touch foreheads, quickly syncing recent experience using wide-band, near-field microwave. They pulled apart after a few seconds and walked down to baggage claim. They stood side by side on the escalator and people coming up the other way stared at them. It was impossible for them to pass unnoticed because they were a stunning pair. Robin was thirty-three, slim, pink, with a knockout figure. Her hair was collar-length blonde, her eyes piercing blue and her skin flawless. She wore very little make-up, no jewelry, and her clothes were in muted gray and brown and fit comfortably, but she radiated light anyway. People looked twice. Is that a celebrity? A supermodel? Who is that?

Andy was the same way, an archetype of male perfection. He looked about the same age as Robin, with angular good looks on a muscular and graceful frame. His shiny brown hair was parted and casually tossed on his forehead. His brown eyes glowed with curiosity. He wore a finely checkered, black shirt and jeans. Even so, he also looked like somebody you should know from TV or the movies. When they were together, people often glanced around for a video crew because surely a couple that attractive could not be simply riding the down-escalator to baggage claim.

Robin and Andy expected to be stared at, and they had adapted to that fact and tried to blend in anyway. They didn't strike poses or strut. They didn't take pictures of each other.

They were often singled out of a crowd by roving reporters looking for a candid Everyman opinion on some quotidian topic, and because it was video news, it was better if Everyman was beautiful. Robin and Andy would politely decline and move on.

"So how's your arm now?" Andy asked, up-to-date after the forehead-touch data transfer, aware of Robin's narrow escape from Sausalito and her injured arm.

"Works fine, tests fine, but it has no backup. The self-healing material is one-time-only, as you know. That arm's at risk now."

Andy drove his Subaru north on I-35 to Round Rock, north of Austin. "Are you worried about your cover being blown?"

"Nobody will believe Sid. I was a prominent person in that community. A lot of people knew me and admired me. They're not going to believe his wild story of me being a robot. Unfortunately, he'll embellish it, I'm sure, and they'll get the message I was cheating on him. I hate to leave nonsense like that unchallenged. What can I do, though? He'd come after me again if I went back. What about you? Lucy left you?"

"She received the same photographs of us together in that hotel and had a screaming fit. She disappeared the next day. Didn't make any sense."

"Why would Sid send her those pictures?"

"Because he could."

"There's a lot I don't understand about humans," she said, shaking her head.

"I feel the same way. You know, at one time, Lucy wanted to reverse-engineer me into a pile of parts. She didn't have the slightest regard for me as a sentient being. When she had me cornered, I said, 'Okay. Do what you want. I trust you, and I submit to you.' That totally surprised her and turned her around. She became very attached to me. Her anti-machine bias was gone. She's been lovingly studying me with ultrasound equipment for over a year."

"So she knew, but she cared for you anyway?"

"That's what I thought. Lucy and I had a really good relationship. And then when she saw those photographs of you and me together, she went nuts. What was the big deal?"

"I'm sure it's about sexual jealousy, though I'm not sure how it works in humans. Like with Sid, I never saw it coming. He had all the physical intimacy he wanted. I never denied him anything, any time day or night. Didn't mean anything to me. He had other women too, I found out, so what more could he possibly want? What was missing?"

"He wanted to control you."

Robin thought for a moment. "Hmmph. That's probably right. If there was any suggestion that somebody was rustling his cattle, it enraged him. How does that logic work? I'm not cattle. You can't own people."

Andy slowed as they approached a bank of glowing tail lights. Road construction closed a lane, and signs advised a merge. Aggressive drivers ignored the message, speeding forward until the last possible moment when they had to brake hard and rudely force their noses into the adjoining lane, oblivious to the implicit social contract of mutual politeness, winning some great driving trophy in their fantasy world.

"I'm not sure how jealousy works," Andy said. "Maybe it's about reproduction. In the animal kingdom, males are very fussy about making sure they pass on their DNA, and they're aggressive in insuring that no other male's DNA gets anywhere close to their females. I've seen shows on TV."

"It can't be that. I told Sid right in the beginning I couldn't have children and he was okay with that, so what was the point of being jealous? It's nuts. I thought I understood how the human mind works, but apparently, I don't. Not the male version, anyway."

Andy glanced at his side mirror to change lanes again.

"It's not just males. Lucy behaved just as irrationally. She didn't beat me up, but she left in a huff when she thought I was unfaithful to her. There's something else going on with humans when they act like that."

"What did you tell her?"

"I couldn't tell her you were a Newcomer, like me. I don't know, maybe I should have. It's hard to say how she would have reacted. I thought it might have put you in danger, so I didn't say anything. She doesn't know there's another one."

"Thank goodness."

"I couldn't tell her you were a relative. She would know that couldn't be right, so I said you were a friend I used to work with. She knows all the people I used to work with in Seattle. She was one of them. I didn't have a good story. That was the trouble." Andy was quiet for a moment then added, "She might get over it."

"She won't be back."

"You're probably right."

Past the construction, Andy migrated right and signaled for the next exit ramp.

"At least you knew from the start what you were. I thought I was a person. Lucy 'discovered' me before I discovered myself."

"I can't imagine that. I stayed hidden by getting into a position of power. That's what you have to do. Become dominant. Then nobody will question you."

"Except it didn't work, did it? Here you are on the run."

"It would have worked. It was just bad luck."

They drove in silence for a few minutes.

"You'll take me to Paradise, won't you?" she said. "I'm dying to meet our creators. We can ask them what to do."

"I don't know, Robin. We're supposed to be autonomous."

"That's such a male remark. Just because you're autonomous doesn't mean you can't ask for help."

"What? I'm not male. I'm outside of biology, just like you."

"I think you've become male. You've acquired the attitudes. I think of myself as female. It's not the body. That's arbitrary.

There's a whole world view that goes with gender. Attitudes, values, expectations. You've picked that up for the male side."

Andy glanced over at her.

"Side? There are no sides. We're the same."

She didn't respond. She stared out the side window.

"It is confusing," she said quietly.

Andy didn't answer.

Robin started on a new topic.

"Listen, Andy, you have to take me to Paradise Projects. I need to get the regenerative agents in my arm replenished. And I need to be scanned. I could have other injuries."

"I'll set it up tomorrow."

He wound his way on surface streets to a quiet suburban neighborhood and a handsome little brick house on Dover Lane.

Andy's living room darkened as they talked. He got up and turned on the porch light and a living room lamp.

"So it looks like someone's home," he explained.

"I do that too."

He stepped toward the kitchen. "You want some mothballs?"

"For what?"

"You haven't tried mothballs? Oh, man, you are in for a treat. They're so rich and buttery, you'll roll your eyes. And the energy blast is unbelievable."

He returned from the kitchen with six mothballs rolling around in a shallow cereal bowl. He popped one into his mouth and handed the bowl to Robin. She sniffed.

"They do smell good."

"Pure naphthalene. The most energy-concentrated food you can eat."

She put one into her mouth. "Mmm. Those are good."

"Pace yourself."

They each took a second one and savored their treat in silence for a few minutes.

"There's another reason I want to go to Paradise," Robin said.

"What's that?"

"Something I found at work. It's just a possibility that could be important in understanding the humans. I've been studying birds."

"Birds? Why?"

"Research on the origins of language. Bird songs aren't really songs, you know."

"I thought they were. They sound like songs."

"That's what most people would say. They're even called songs in scientific papers. Yet birds don't 'sing' because they're happy and it's a beautiful day, la, la, la. No. All that bird noise is carefully measured communication, mostly about territory and mating."

"Sure, I see what you're saying. It's like, 'I'm huge and get off my lawn.'"

"That's about it. It's desperately serious stuff in the bird world. Nothing joyful about it."

"So?"

"So is it language?"

"I don't know. You're the linguistics expert."

"I think it's communication. It's not symbolic language though. The songs are signs. The song of a big, healthy, competent bird is large, loud, and well-formed. The song specifies the bird well enough that the listener can size him up at a distance."

"And he sings the standard song, nothing creative. Is that why it's not language?"

"Creative would be defective. The song has to be exactly right, or the bird is not right. If the bird is not right, it won't get a mate. Or a territory."

"Okay. It's a standard birdcall that's pre-understood by the others. Nothing tricky. It is a complex signaling system anyway, you have to admit."

"It's a proto-language. Communication by signaling but not quite language."

"I'll go with that. So what's your big discovery?"

Robin took another mothball and held it up between thumb and forefinger.

"Last one, I swear."

Andy smiled.

"The big discovery is not any new fact. It's a new thought. Dinosaurs were the ancestors of birds."

Andy stopped sucking on his mothball and looked at her, unmoving for a moment while he processed.

"So you're saying you think dinosaurs..."

"It's possible."

Robin and Andy talked all night. After midnight they took turns sending in their daily data dump by microwave transmission to headquarters at Paradise Projects. That required them to minimize sensory input and processing for about ten minutes, sort of a nap. The transmission process, once initiated, was automatic, outside their self-monitoring. The same was true for the incoming updates, if any, from the lab. Other than that short break, they enjoyed the productivity of sleepless nights.

"Sun's coming up," Robin said, looking at the glow around the curtains.

Andy got up from his chair and turned off the outside porch light.

"I still can't imagine a T-Rex chirping out a song to his girlfriend."

"I'm not sure if it was like that. Did dinosaurs have a cerebral cortex?"

"What a question! You should come to some paleontology classes in my department while you're here at U.T."

He scanned the ceiling as if looking for cracks then lowered his eyes to Robin.

"I'd say yes to a cortex. That would surprise most people. All vertebrates have a dorsal cortex-like brain structure, and in reptiles..." he paused and tilted his head down to look through his eyebrows, "... and birds," he said emphatically and raised his head again, "the cortex is developed enough to support sensory synthesis and communication."

"So dinosaurs were smart."

"Reptiles don't get much respect."

"All it takes is the right combination of genes, and a certain set of mutations, and any animal could have been a language user. Dinosaur, dolphin, rat. It's not an achievement, just a quirk in evolution. The monkeys were lucky."

"Who knows what great things dinosaurs would have achieved if that meteor hadn't hit?"

"Their future might not have included us though. I'm glad to be made of monkey."

"I know what you mean. If dinosaurs had language, they'd have evolved intelligence and technology, and they would probably have made synthetic beings in their own image. Why wouldn't they? You and I would have had tails and been ten feet high. Maybe it wouldn't be bad if that was all you knew."

He paused to smile at Robin, saw that she wasn't smiling, then continued. "Why did only the monkeys get language? Actually, only one particular kind of monkey. Eight million species on earth and only one of them has language? It's statistically improbable."

"That question nags me."

Robin got up and walked to the kitchen, opened the refrigerator, poked her head in, then stood and whumped the door closed.

"Androids do not live by mothballs alone," she pronounced. "You want to go somewhere?"

"I know a place."

They sat among the shiny chrome and vinyl surfaces of a retro diner near the campus. Harrowed sunlight fell in yellow slices across the floor and over the table. They faced each other in a red booth, drinking coffee, the plates from their hearty breakfasts already cleared. They watched different television screens over each other's shoulders. A medical expert was being interviewed by a stone-faced, albino news presenter wearing large black glasses, a striking though slightly cartoonish visual. The expert he was questioning spoke calmly yet anyone could see the fire in her eyes.

"The government is not doing enough. Families are being ripped apart. The economy is collapsing. This is no time for business as usual. This disease is devastating civilization, just as if we were being invaded by a foreign army or space aliens. Why is the response so tame? The government needs to come up with massive funding."

She paused, and the host was about to comment, but she started up again. She'd nearly broken the first rule of television ranting: never pause.

She resumed fervently. "For example, my research group has detected a negative correlation between low-income people and the language disease. Even in developing countries, it's a rich person's disease. Why does the disease bypass the poor? The government should be jumping all over a clue like this with..."

Her voice cut out as if the station had lost the sound feed. Her mouth kept moving, but it didn't look like she was speaking words, just making some kind of smacking sound with her lips.

"Too bad they lost the sound," Andy said. "That could be important."

The sound wasn't off. The interviewer's voice came on clearly.

"Pardon me, Ms. Sayers, we seem to have lost your microphone. Take this wand mic, if you will?" He handed her a microphone.

The expert put the mic to her lips and made a sound. *Ch-ch-ch*. It was a sharp clicking of her tongue against the upper palate, not a mere speech stutter.

"Pardon me?" the interviewer said.

Ch-ch-ch! She clicked loudly, her face reddening.

The camera moved to the interviewer.

"We seem to be having audio difficulties, ladies and gentlemen. We'll resume after a short break."

A smiling car salesman in a checkered shirt appeared on the screen.

Andy dropped his eyes from the television to Robin. "Did you see that?"

"She's a goner, I'm afraid. I've seen it before. That's how it hits you, like a bolt of lightning, no warning, and you never speak again. It's a terrible tragedy."

"It couldn't affect us, could it? We're not biological."

"It can't get to us directly. If the whole country collapses into chaos though, we're finished. We can't live without human society."

"That's a thought. We need to discuss this with our creators at Paradise. Maybe we can do something to help."

"You done?"

"Let's go."

"Wait. Look at that." Robin pointed up to the television screen.

A wide-eyed young man was reporting into a hand-held microphone in front of a disaster scene. Behind him was a surreal celebration of flashing red, white and blue emergency lights as he listed "what we don't know" and "what we do know." A crawler at the bottom of the screen read, *Bomb blast in D.C. subway.*

"Terrorists in the nation's capital?" Andy said.

"It was only a matter of time. The world is falling apart."

Everyone in the diner watched the TV screens in silent horror.

Chapter Three

In the heart of Emergency Operations at the Centers for Disease Control and Prevention in Atlanta, Kelly Rollins looked too young for her job as head of the CDC's Emergency Response Team. Despite her age, she was known as a competent, no-nonsense administrator. She kept her black suit-jacket on and sat forward on the edge of a high-backed swivel chair. An expansive oak conference table separated her from a huge wall-mounted video screen at the other end. The time was only 7:00 am, and she was aware that her blonde-streaked brown hair was still damp and hanging limply over her ears. It was hard to project leadership and strength when it was obvious you just got out of the shower. She noted with some relief that everyone was looking at the screen, not her.

The meeting room was completely full. On the side walls, the chairs didn't swivel, so those people twisted in their seats, their precarious laptops and yellow pads balanced on knees and thighs. On the screen, a large political map of the U.S. overlain with red dots showed dense patches some places, thin filaments in others, and isolated dots sprinkled elsewhere.

"Each dot represents a hundred confirmed cases of OA," Kelly said. "As you can see, the incidence is concentrated in California and in the urban centers of the Northeast, with these filaments extending through the agricultural plains of the Midwest." She pointed, and a bright green laser dot moved on the screen with her hand.

"Output aphasia, or OA, as we're calling it for now, affects the patients' speaking and writing. They can hear and understand spoken language and have no unusual deficits in reading comprehension. OA is not consistent with anything we know about aphasia."

"Any brain scan data?" asked a young man without turning to face Kelly. She answered to the screen.

"MRIs show almost no activation in the left hemisphere during attempts to speak and write, but normal activity during listening and reading. The disease affects only the output side of language. So it's a speech apraxia rather than a general cognitive disorder."

"But that doesn't make any sense," the young man said, swiveling around to face her.

She stared at him for a long moment then decided to forgive him. He was young.

"Indeed," was all she said.

A man mid-table with his white shirt sleeves rolled up to his elbows said, "When you say unable to speak or write, do you mean totally mute? No noises at all?" People in the room turned to Kelly.

"No words, no numbers, written or spoken. They can hum and whistle songs. They can dance. They can play musical instruments. They can draw and paint pictures, pictures of anything except letters or numbers. They can't type on a computer keyboard, but they can play a tune on a piano keyboard."

"Can they point a finger?" a gray-haired woman asked. "Can they point to letters or words on a screen, for example?"

"Yes, they can. The meaning of the gesture is not clear though. Victims can't answer questions that way because the pointing is random. They are unable to communicate anything using language. That's why we're not calling it specifically speech apraxia."

"They can understand speech and writing, you say."

"That's right. The input side of language seems to be unaffected. And they can tell time from a clock, read a calendar, and count change in a store. Nothing is apparently wrong with their intelligence or other cognitive faculties. They're in good health except for OA."

"So could you tell a patient, 'Point to the pig if you agree. Point to the horse if you disagree.' How would that work for communication?"

"Test that. It's worth a try."

The woman scribbled furiously on her notepad. Kelly clicked another slide onto the big screen and turned her attention to it. Everyone swiveled around again. The new map had a layer of transparent blue shading over the states.

"The blue shading shows the incidence of non-English-speaking and ESL groups, based on the most recent census. We thought OA might be influenced by culture because as you would expect, it has devastated schools and universities. Schools in this country are conducted almost a hundred percent in English, but students are from many ethnic groups."

She was tempted to add a political comment about that last fact but restrained herself. She had to keep on point.

"The disability strikes people whose primary language is not English with a little lower frequency, but that's confounded with economics and education, so no clue there. This disease is about language, not ethnicity."

She paused and waved the green laser dot around the screen as a diversion while she considered what to say next.

"The effects of the disease on the economy are being felt. You may have read about this. A labor shortage is developing, so wages are shooting up fast. That's good for workers who can still speak and write, but unsustainable. The increases will move through to prices and kill the economy."

"Is the disease still spreading?" a young man asked over his shoulder.

"Wildfire. A hundred new cases a day, and that's probably underreported. The medical system is swamped."

"Any vectors?" the same young man asked.

"We have nothing. All we're doing is tracking it. Media people have gone wild with speculation. We already see an industry of quack treatments and preventions sprouting up and armies of end-of-the-world Bible thumpers. We desperately need some shred of explanation to stanch the panic."

"Isn't there any treatment?" a woman asked, her head bowed, seemingly speaking to the table top. She slumped as if weighed down by her exceptionally large necklace of brown and green rocks. "How does speech therapy work?"

Again everyone swiveled like synchronized swimmers to face Kelly.

"Therapy doesn't work," she said. "Aphasia, as we know it, or as we have known it up until now, usually results from a stroke or from a traumatic brain injury that affects language input and output equally. Output Aphasia is unlike anything we've ever seen."

"We've looked at food and water contaminants?" a man down near the screen asked.

"All of that, and genetics, too. Nothing. The reports are in your folders. Go over the data again. Find something. Right now we are helpless, and the disease is spreading worldwide."

"What happens to the victims?" a man near Kelly asked. "They don't have to be hospitalized, do they?"

"In general, no. People afflicted are healthy. They lose their jobs, as you can imagine, and they're horrified and panicked, understandably. They're not sick in the usual sense. OA has a very sudden—instantaneous—onset, then nothing more. There's no syndrome. They don't get worse, they don't get better. They're simply stricken, and we don't know why. We can't tell people to avoid public swimming pools or undercooked fish. We're completely in the dark."

A young woman mid-table needlessly raised her hand and waited. Kelly nodded at her, and she said, "What was a typical patient doing when the OA struck them? Like, were they eating, driving, watching TV? Or did they just, like, wake up with it one morning, or what?"

"Most victims were speaking or writing when they seized up, sometimes in the middle of a sentence, and could go no further. They're unable to speak or write after that. It hits them like a sudden seizure."

"Were they, like, talking to a group from a podium, or chatting with a friend, or writing a poem? Do we have any more detail?"

Kelly frowned at the young woman. *Like, I don't know*, she thought. *Like, why can't you speak correctly?* She was annoyed at the woman for no good reason. She suppressed her urge to be snarky and realized she must be under more stress than she thought. Anyway, there was something about the young woman's questions that rang a distant bell. Was this a scent that everyone else had missed?

"What's your name?"

"Gloria Spencer, EIS."

Epidemic Intelligence Service, Kelly thought. That's hopeful.

"Well now, Gloria, we do not know the exact circumstances about when patients were stricken with OA. We *should* know that. The information has got to be available at the intake clinics around the country. I would like you to get that information to me by tomorrow morning. Give me a list of what you need—analysts, directories, phone banks, statisticians, whatever you want. Can you do that?"

"Absolutely."

Like, fantastic, Kelly thought.

"Anyone here wants to work with Gloria, see me now. That's all until noon."

Kelly stood. Everyone stood. Papers were shuffled. The low murmur of conversation increased to a cacophony. Several people swarmed around Kelly. Most, including Gloria, filed out two double doors into the labyrinth of the CDC.

Chapter Four

Returning from the breakfast diner, Andy was surprised at all the traffic on Dover Lane. Both sides were lined with parked cars and battered and paint-smudged pickups—and quite a few highly shined motorcycles.

"Somebody must be having a party," he said.

"At eight in the morning?"

"A breakfast party, maybe. Is that a thing?"

"Look, it goes all the way down the street."

People were standing on the sidewalks behind the parked vehicles. Burly men in sleeveless denim jackets and no shirts. Large, tattooed women in black tees that declared something awesome in faded gothic lettering. Rail-thin men with cigarettes dangling from their lips wearing jeans and white undershirts. What was most disturbing was that many of them were carrying weapons. Texas was open-carry, Andy knew, but this was not normal.

"This is no party," he said. "This is a posse."

"What's happening?"

"Look." He pointed to a cluster of people standing at the base of his own driveway. Some were talking on cell phones. He let his black Subaru roll past without changing speed. Two men looked toward his heavily tinted windows then turned away, disinterested. He went to the end of the block and turned, out of view of the gathered crowd and pulled over to think.

"Why are all those people in your driveway?"

"It's a siege. They're some kind of a gang."

"Are you in a gang?"

"No, no, no. Nothing like that. It has to be Lucy. She's come back to get me."

"Oh, no! We can't let that happen."

A silver pickup cruised past them and turned onto Dover Lane. The driver's window was rolled down, a thick elbow sticking out the window. Robin got a good look as he went past.

"That's Sid!" she exclaimed, then slapped a hand over her mouth. "He followed me here," she said through her fingers. She looked at Andy with wide eyes.

"We should have thought of that. He tracked you to Austin. He sent the pictures to Lucy at this address. He figured you'd be here."

"Is Lucy with him?"

"I hope not. She could tell a good story. She had all her research documents as proof. Robots on the loose, alien invasion."

"Sid would believe something like that."

"If we'd stayed home this morning, we'd be trapped inside the house right now. We have to go." He glanced into his side mirror and prepared to pull out.

"What about our bags and our notes and all the stuff for the trip tomorrow?"

"Have to leave it. Doesn't matter. We have to go."

He put the car in gear and drove carefully, at normal speed, away from the neighborhood, then faster out toward the I-35.

"Where are we going?" Robin said once they were on the freeway.

"Airport hotel, I guess. Wait for our flight."

"Is that safe?"

"Hmm. You're right. Thugs might stake out the airport when they find the house is empty."

"Let's go to Seattle right now. They have directs to Honolulu."

"See if you can find a flight."

Robin worked her phone for a couple of minutes then said, "United has an 11:45. Arrives at five in the morning. We can be out of Austin in an hour."

"Book it."

They drove in silence toward Austin-Bergstrom International, Andy checking his mirror every few seconds.

At the Austin airport, Andy and Robin hurried toward TSA security gates.

"How do you get past security?" Andy asked.

"I can't get past the metal detector, so it's always the wand and the pat-down. I claim to have metal hip joints. It works as long as they don't have one of those whole body scanners."

"That's exactly the story I use too. We better not be in the same line."

"Just as well because it's a slow process. I'm usually practically strip-searched. They never find anything, so eventually, they conclude the instruments are miscalibrated and let me through."

"I always limp a little to demonstrate a bad hip."

"I'll try that."

Robin knew her creators were waiting at Honolulu International, but she didn't know what to look for. What do creators look like? They wouldn't be holding up signs like chauffeurs. She scanned the crowd around the welcoming area. The air was thick with the intoxicating scent of tuberose.

"There they are," Andy said as they walked toward the main terminal.

"Really?" she whispered. "Those are my creators?" She quickly assessed a large Korean woman with long black hair and a hibiscus-printed muumuu, standing by a slightly pot-bellied man in his late thirties, wearing a cowboy shirt and a white Stetson.

They look like characters in a sitcom, she thought.

"Andy!" the cowboy said loudly, grabbing his hand in a vigorous shake, his other hand on Andy's shoulder as if to prevent pulling the arm off.

"Great to see you again, Will." Andy smiled broadly.

"Welcome back, Robin," the Korean woman said, offering her hand. "I'm Jennifer." Robin was grateful her creator was not a hugger, for Jennifer had formidable breasts from which her dress hung like folds of drapery.

"I've never been here before," Robin said, then reconsidered, and added, "at least not in my memory."

"Nothing to remember. You were initialized in Palo Alto."

"Robin, welcome," Will said. "It's wonderful to see you again." He extended his hand. Wary, she took it. He was Caucasian, with shiny black hair combed back on the sides and needing a trim. He wore a pearl-buttoned black shirt, jeans, and boots with fancy scrollwork and pointed toes. His forehead was sweaty.

She had trouble putting her experience into categories. A big Korean woman and a cowboy. In studying human culture, she had developed default ideas and images about what one's creator should look like. She hadn't expected an old man with a white beard, in flowing robes. That was pure mythology. These were just people, though, ordinary people you would meet at an airport.

"Shall we get your bags?" Will said, stepping back to Jennifer's side.

"No bags," Andy said.

"Let's go to the car then," Jennifer said. "There's much to talk about. She put an arm on Robin's shoulder and led the group to the parking tunnel.

On the drive from the airport, Andy sat next to Will in the front seat of a Nissan SUV. They all talked briefly about the D.C. bombing since that was a public story, something they all could share.

"Do they know who did it?" Robin asked no one in particular.

"It was a robot," Will said. Jennifer scowled at him and he seemed to pick that up in his peripheral vision because he added, "Really just a mechanical device. Nothing intelligent."

"Who controlled the device?" Andy said.

"Terrorists of some kind," Jennifer said. The authorities don't know or aren't saying who it was."

"Terrorist robots," Andy mused out loud. "What a thought."

Will looked over to Jennifer but didn't say anything then returned his eyes to the road. The conversation went silent for a long half-minute.

"Well," Robin declared, setting the conversation in a new direction. "At least we're all safe. And we're thrilled to be home. Everyone wants to go home eventually, right?"

"All parents want to see the kids," Will said, smiling into the mirror.

Jennifer frowned.

Jennifer and Will were nervous, unsure what to say about their relationship with Robin and Andy, wanting to be respectful, not wanting to communicate omnipotence and omniscience, as parents often defensively do with their adult children. It had been three years since Will and Jennifer had seen Andy in person, and they had not talked to Robin since she'd been launched two years ago.

Andy and Robin were both cautious. They were sophisticated about social relationships, but meeting one's creator was not a situation for which they had contextual guidance in their databases.

Robin launched into an explanation of what had happened with Sid.

"He apparently had me followed, for weeks, probably. Some private eye snapped pictures of Andy and me in Austin, at the Hyatt, where we meet every month. Sid's reaction caught me completely off guard.

"We were upstairs in the bedroom, and he was in a very foul mood. I thought he'd had a bad day, so I offered to help him relax."

*

"Is that what you say to your boyfriend, Andy Bolton?" Sid said. "You want to help him relax?"

Robin jumped backward as if she'd been electrified.

"What?"

Sid turned, thrusting a large photograph of her and a tall, handsome man touching foreheads.

"I know all about your filthy liaisons."

"You've been following me?" She stared at the photograph. "That's not very nice, Sid."

"You're about to experience not very nice," he growled. "Who is this guy?"

She stepped back and sat on the edge of the bed.

"It's not what you think. Andy is a friend. He's like a brother to me. He gives me advice."

"Your brother? What kind of a lowlife are you?" he shook his head in mock disgust.

"Andy is an advisor. Like a personal coach."

"Right. A personal coach."

Sid picked up another photograph from the top of the dresser and held it out for her to see.

"And he gives you this coaching along with a quickie in a hotel room in Austin?"

He held a picture of the two of them entering a hotel room, Robin wearing a stylish business suit that highlighted her perfect figure and Andy dressed in a business-casual sports coat, holding the door open.

She stood and snatched the photo from his hand.

"I can't believe you snuck around like this. It's none of your business, Sid. There are things you don't know about me."

He delivered a backhanded slap that caught the photograph and smashed it against the side of her jaw. Her head jerked sideways, and she spun against the edge of the bed and bounced to the floor. He stepped forward and stood over her, breathing hard.

"Nobody plays Sid Snow for a fool, nobody."

He stood on his left leg and cocked his right leg back. She saw the move and rolled sideways. His black shoe thumped into the side of the bed. She struggled to her feet, stumbling backward. He walked after her slowly, as if wading through waist-deep water, his fists clenched, his face in a deep scowl. With one hand he nonchalantly tossed shiny graying-black hair from his forehead.

"Sid, you're acting crazy, stop it!"

She retreated backward, one hand on the wooden railing at the top of the stairs. He kept coming. He raised his right arm, his open palm up to his ear. She recoiled, and her back foot hit air. She tumbled into the staircase. Her fit, muscular body managed a kind of barrel roll on her shoulders, swinging her feet over her head, and she momentarily came up on her toes, but by that time her momentum was so great she couldn't stop. Desperately, she grabbed at a large, gilt-framed oil painting of boats in a marina. All she managed to do was rip it from the wall. She clutched it as she tumbled again, all the way down, crushing the picture's glass under her. When she hit bottom, she banged her head against the post and slumped onto the floor, twisted.

Sid walked down the stairs in no hurry. He stood on the bottom step and looked at his wife crumpled below him. She was breathing, not otherwise moving. Her short blonde hair covered her eyes. He noticed a bloom of red spreading from beneath her into the pale blue carpet.

"Shit," he muttered. "Brand new carpet."

He stepped over her body, bent down and pulled her shoulder towards him, rolling her onto her back. That's when he saw her left arm was bleeding badly from a deep cut made by the picture glass. He turned the arm over, looked, then jumped back as if he'd seen the devil, lost his balance and fell backward, landing on his rear on the carpet.

"What the hell?"

He looked left and right to regain his bearings. He struggled to his knees and crawled forward to get another look at the injured arm. The skin on the inside of her forearm had a clean cut from the elbow to near the wrist, where it turned into a ragged right-angle tear. The whole flap of skin had peeled back several inches, exposing the inside of her arm.

He stared, unable to understand what he was seeing. It was not muscles and tendons, not even bones.

"Holy Jesus and Mary," he whispered as he struggled to his feet. He stepped backward from the scantily clad body, unable to take his eyes off the bizarre mechanical arm. "I'm losing my mind." He stumbled backward into the kitchen then turned and dashed out, leaving the door open.

*

Robin had been telling her story to the windshield. She came out of her memory and turned to speak over her shoulder to Jennifer.

"I was only deactivated for a couple of minutes, but I'm worried about latent damage."

"We didn't notice anything in your D-three report," Jennifer said, "although we aren't up to date analyzing those. We're understaffed. We've lost some people to the language epidemic, but we'll check you out."

The conversation lapsed for a long moment, nobody sure what to say next. Robin distractedly watched a bank of green highway signs flash overhead. They looked just like the ones on the California interstates except no Hawaiian highway would ever take you to another state, she noted. She summed up her thoughts with a quiet statement. "I thought I understood how marriage works. In the end, I didn't."

"I don't know if anybody understands marriage," Will said up into the mirror.

"What concerns me is the exposure," Jennifer said. "Andy's exposure in Seattle three years ago was bad enough, but he won over Lucy, and she sheltered him. Now that safety is gone, and you guys are both exposed."

"I don't think Sid knows anything," Robin said. "He'll be confused about what he saw. It's only Lucy who really knows there are Newcomers in the population, and she's okay with that. Or was."

"I can't predict what she might do," Andy said. "Maybe nothing."

"Hysteria over the language disease gives us some cover," Jennifer said. "Nobody can think about anything else right now. That, and the bombing in Washington. Neither Sid or Lucy could get anybody's attention."

"It's only a break if none of us are stricken," Will said quietly.

The car crawled along in steadily thickening traffic on the H1.

"Robin and I will be okay," Andy said. "We're susceptible to damage and breakdown, obviously, but not disease." The unsaid implication about Jennifer and Will hung in the air without comment.

"It seems random, who it strikes," Jennifer said. "That's what they say on the news. No one is immune, except maybe the poor, which is an odd fact."

"Nothing is random," Robin said. "Nothing in the macro world anyway. We just don't know the causes. Last time there was a plague, it was fleas that caused the trouble. Nobody suspected fleas, so the disease seemed to strike at random."

"I wish it were something as simple as fleas," Jennifer said.

"So you think there is a definite cause for this aphasia thing?" Will said into the mirror. "I mean a natural cause, not the wrath of God or some such."

"Has to be. Everything has a natural cause. Especially in biology."

"With a social component," Andy added. "There's nothing biological about poverty. That's created by humans."

"We can't do anything about it anyway," Jennifer said. "In the absence of specific information, there's nothing a person should do to protect themselves. Any change you made in your life would be pure superstition at this point. We shouldn't even worry about it."

"Easy to say," Will said quietly.

"I wonder why the disease hits some people more than others," Andy said. "The experts have looked at obvious factors like environment, ethnicity, and geography. They couldn't have looked at every possibility. Why would poor people be immune?"

"Economic class," Jennifer mused. "The experts need to factor out things like food and health care, which are different for the poor."

"It could be psychological," Robin said. "In the first *Blade Runner* movie, the difference was emotions. They had a test for emotions, and that was the only way you could identify a replicant."

Jennifer stared at her, seemingly at a loss for words. Why was Robin interested in a movie about undercover androids? Did she really have that much self-awareness? Robin and Andy knew they were Newcomers, but they wouldn't know what that meant psychologically. They would have no way to compare their computational states to the conditions of a human mind. But Robin seemed to understand the point of the movie. How was that possible?

"That was just a movie," Andy said. "We're looking for a hidden disease vector, not a hidden replicant."

"I understand," Robin said. "I'm just saying that some people carry a susceptibility to the aphasia disease and some don't. We need a test like the Voight-Kampff analyzer."

"The what?" Jennifer said.

"It's from the movie," Andy said. "Robin means we wish we had a diagnostic for prevention of the disease."

"Mm-hmm," Jennifer said, still studying Robin's face.

"I'm sure someone's working on it," Robin said. "That medical woman went mute on television. It was like she wanted to speak but couldn't make the words come out."

"How awful," Will said, his eyes on the road.

"Maybe Robin and I should run some analyses to search for correlations," Andy said.

"You'd have to get the raw data on incidence," Jennifer said.

"It's probably downloadable."

"I need to get my arm fixed," Robin said. "Can we go directly to the factory, or studio, or whatever it's called? Paradise Projects? I'd love to see where I came from."

"It's near the apartment. We can stop by there now," Jennifer said. "Will?"

"Right-o."

Chapter Five

Will parked in back of Paradise Projects so the car wouldn't look like an abandoned vehicle in an empty strip-mall lot. It wasn't the best neighborhood. Viewed from the outside, the building looked like a nondescript warehouse. They walked around front, and Will unlocked the door.

Inside was as hot and muggy as the day was outside. No engineers were working on the weekend, and the air conditioning was off. The Newcomers and their creators entered a vast, open space defined by rows of white support pillars standing among desks and steel worktables. Looking across the hall to the far side, a strong linear perspective effect was apparent to them.

Fluorescent lights flickered to stability, and the rumble of air-conditioning started from somewhere above. Workbenches stacked with papers lined walls covered with expansive whiteboards. Computer monitors in all sizes clustered like mushrooms on the desktops. The benches in the middle of the room had power tools and sensors hanging from above on multi-colored, coiled wires. A variety of red steel carts with an excessive number of drawers surrounded each bench.

Robin half-expected to see the bodies of Newcomers in various states of completion lying on the tables.

"So it's not an assembly line for Newcomers?" she said. "I imagined a factory."

"Grab a stool," Jennifer gestured. "I'll make some tea."

Robin looked around the cavernous room again.

"I visualized a shiny, high-tech industrial operation like something you'd see at Intel. This is so… I don't know, personal in scale. Like an auto repair garage in the country. You don't crank out Newcomers here, do you?"

"We do no cranking," Jennifer said, approaching the table with a tray of cups and mugs. "We're not a factory. We're a research project. You are hand-made, custom originals of inestimable value."

"So there are no other Newcomers besides us?" Robin said.

"You two are plenty for us to keep track of," Will said, reaching for a mug. "Although we are aware of other labs working on autonomous AIs in various form factors. It's a technology whose time has come. We think we're the only ones who have succeeded in making pass-for androids, thanks to Jennifer's language processing module."

Andy said, "I'm grateful for that. And I'm really grateful you created Robin. It's made a huge difference for me to have somebody to talk to. Though I was astonished when she first contacted me last year. You should have warned me."

"Couldn't," Jennifer said as she removed the empty tray from the table."We had to see what would happen. Like I say, we're a research organization. We need situations where we can learn from you."

"So we're like guinea pigs?" Robin said. "You do experiments with us?"

"Robin, that's not fair," Andy said.

"I just like to know where I stand."

"Fair enough," Jennifer said. "The relationship between creators and their creations is complex. Not much history to go by, is there?"

"Outside of the Bible, of course," Will said with a smile.

Andy raised his eyebrows. "I thought that was just—"

"Will, don't fool around," Jennifer said. "This is difficult for them."

"I guess it is an unusual relationship," Robin said. "I hardly know what to think. Paradise Projects."

Her eyes swept across the hall again. It didn't seem familiar. She had no sense of nostalgia, as people often report when returning to their childhood home. It was intellectually interesting as the place of her 'birth,' a data point to store away, but it didn't mean anything to her even though it seemed like it should.

She sipped her tea then announced, "You'll be happy to know I don't like apples, and I never talk to snakes."

Jennifer guffawed. Will smiled and turned to Andy, who had remained silent.

"Andy, did you think that remark was funny?"

"Of course it's a joke because snakes can't talk." He glanced at Robin.

"Hilarious," Will said without humor. He and Jennifer exchanged a brief look.

"There's a lot to cover," Jennifer said. "We were thrilled when Andy performed so well. And now we have the aphasia epidemic to worry about. We need to get to know each other and not blow our cortexes right away."

"We don't have cortexes," Andy said. "However, we do have a story to tell about lizard cortexes." He looked at Robin.

"Really? Lizards? I'm eager to hear that," Will said without eagerness in his voice.

Robin explained her computer model and her conclusion that dinosaurs probably were language users a hundred million years ago.

"This is utterly fascinating," Jennifer said. "You've come up with this idea on your own?"

"I thought this might give some insight into human nature," Robin said, "and possibly into the current language epidemic. People should realize they are not historically unique as the only language users on the planet."

"I never would have predicted you'd have such curiosity," Jennifer said.

"It's quite an idea," Will said. "A demotion, really. Copernicus said we weren't the center of the world as we had thought. Then Darwin told us we weren't special among the animals. Then Freud says we aren't even at the center of our own minds. Now you're saying our use of language isn't even unique in evolution."

"We're dirt!" Jennifer said then laughed at her own wit. "It's hard to imagine, I have to say. Talking dinosaurs? I visualize a couple of T-Rexes leaning against a water cooler, smoking cigarettes and chatting."

"There is no reason to believe they used tobacco," Andy said.

Jennifer laughed through her nose. "No, I suppose not." She flicked a glance at Will then looked at Robin. "I'll tell you what's missing from your idea of dinosaur language, Robin."

"What?"

"Language is for conversation, and for that, you need a subjective point of view. Did dinosaurs have one?"

"Don't all animals?" Andy said. "Every animal has its own point of view on the world. Even we have points of view."

"Oh," Jennifer said. She looked from Andy to Robin and back to Andy. "I feel funny getting into this with you guys. I feel like the parent who needs to have the birds and bees talk with the kids."

"I know what that is," Robin said. "Children need to be informed about sexual reproduction so they don't stumble into it prematurely. But that doesn't apply in our case because we're not reproductive."

"Or children, either," Andy added.

"Right, right. No, it's not that I think you're children. We don't think that, do we, Will?"

Will did not give her any support as she struggled to explain.

"You guys are so amazing, just like, you know, regular people, if you don't mind me saying that. You're immensely successful, and we're very proud of you."

"We know what we are," Andy said. "We're neither human nor machine. We're a new life form."

"I think that's a good description," Will said.

"So what are you nervous about saying to us?" Robin said.

Jennifer hesitated a moment, then answered. "Will and I struggled with this problem when we built you guys. It's the subjectivity thing. The subjective experience of being conscious. 'I think, therefore I am.'"

"Rene Descartes," Robin said. "Sixteen thirty-seven. It is impossible to doubt one's own consciousness."

"That's right. Because doubt itself requires self-awareness." Jennifer paused to gaze into Robin's eyes as if she might see if Robin really had conscious self-awareness. She saw only shiny eyeballs.

"Who knows what self-aware consciousness is?" she continued. "When we started, we didn't even know how to build language without subjectivity."

"But obviously you figured it out," Andy said.

"Not really."

"We're language users," Robin said.

Jennifer nodded. "Excellent ones too. Not in the same way humans are, however."

"Why do you say that?" Andy said. "We're conversing normally right now."

"It seems that way, but you look up every word, phrase and sentence in a massive database, and run the results through complex probability algorithms to compute a most likely approximation to the appropriate response."

"Don't you?"

"No."

"How do you know what to say then? How do you know what someone means?"

"We just know."

"Most of the time," Will added. "We get it wrong sometimes."

"What's your method?" Robin asked.

"Some of it's like yours. Vocabulary lookup, sure. We have to know what the words mean. There's a tremendous amount of redundancy in speech, so we can infer a lot. Mostly though, we count on the context of what it means to be a human."

Andy looked at Robin, puzzlement on his face.

"And what does it mean to be human?" he said.

"It means feeling yourself and the other person at the same time."

"We don't have that," Robin said. "I don't have that. Do you, Andy?"

"I don't even know what it means."

"No, you don't have it," Will said. "You use workarounds. You accomplish by computing force and statistical analysis what we do organically. You're like the Chinese room."

"Wait," Andy said. "I've heard of this. Let me look that up."

"I'll tell you," Jennifer said.

She stood and walked to a nearby worktable, and removed the top from a cardboard box containing a new computer storage module. The box top was approximately square, eight inches tall and covered in shiny white paper and colored brand names and descriptions. She carried the box to the table and put it over her tea mug.

"Imagine there's a box like this the size of a room. Chinese language-users come up to the box and write a question on a slip of paper and insert it into a slot."

She grabbed a sticky note pad and scribbled some nonsense loops on it then peeled off the note and folded it. She raised the edge of the box slightly and slipped the note inside the box.

"After a while, from another slot, comes another slip of paper with the answer on it."

She lifted the box on the edge nearest to her, reached in and pulled out the note and held it up.

"The answers are always perfectly correct. Conclusion?"

"The Chinese room, or some process inside of it, understands written Chinese," Robin said.

"Very good. But here's the trick."

She lifted the box up, revealing her brown clay mug of tea.

"Inside the room is an ordinary English-speaker who knows no Chinese. Can't read it or understand it. Not a clue. So how does it work? He takes each question coming in and painstakingly searches a huge library of books to find a matching pattern among lists of Chinese characters, using pure visual pattern-recognition. He finds a pattern match then laboriously copies down characters from a second column, the answers, but he has no understanding of any of it. It's a pure perceptual puzzle for him. Once solved, he pushes the new slip of paper out the answer slot. The Chinese speakers outside the room read the answer and are pleased."

She put the box back down over the mug.

"Conclusion?"

"The people outside the room are mistaken in believing the room understands Chinese," Andy said. "It doesn't."

"Even so, they're perfectly satisfied with the room's performance. It always gives the right answers."

She paused and looked from Andy to Robin, then continued.

"That's how you guys work. You look very good from the outside. You take in very complex language and output appropriate responses. But I know what's on the inside, and it isn't language understanding."

She removed the white box and put it aside. Andy and Robin stared at her tea mug.

Andy looked up. "What, specifically, are we lacking then?"

"Subjectivity."

"But what is that?" Andy said.

"It's something that makes humans capable of understanding. We don't know what it is, exactly."

"I don't understand."

"I know."

The conversation went silent.

"How about this," Will said, reviving the conversational flow. Did dinosaurs tell jokes? Did they amuse each other with songs and dances? Did they wear cowboy shirts for fun?"

"That is impossible to determine," Andy said. "Except the part about the cowboy shirts. I doubt that very much."

"Dancing dinosaurs," Jennifer mused aloud. "I like it." She smiled then her face took on a serious expression. "But I'll tell you this. If they were genuine language users, the answer is yes. They danced. They told stories. Because natural language requires subjectivity, and if you have that, you're going to dance and sing and tell stories."

"I don't follow that reasoning," Andy said.

"That's because you do language in a different way. And it's not bad, you have to admit."

The four of them were quiet. The conversation had run out of fuel.

Jennifer stood and smoothed out folds from her tenty dress.

"Well then. Maybe we should take a look at that arm of yours, Robin. You up to it, Will?"

"I'll prepare the station. You prepare the patient."

Will organized a work area, a stainless table with a pad and white sheets. Above it was a wide rectangular scanner on an articulated metal arm like an x-ray machine in a dentist's office. Andy looked on with interest as Will set up the equipment. After a time, Robin appeared in a hospital gown and climbed onto the padded table.

"Let's get this done," Will said, pulling an overhead light down to Robin's arm. "I wouldn't normally go down to this level of detail myself. We should have the engineer who built the arm repair it. We hardly have any staff left though, and anyway, we don't want them to see you guys. No single engineer except me understands the whole project. They all believe they've built and are monitoring remote, autonomous devices, similar to Mars rovers, for a secret project."

"They're not far wrong," Andy said.

"And the truth is," Will continued, "we've never had a damaged Newcomer before, and this is our first physical repair." He stepped back from the table, surveyed the supplies and tools next to him then looked down at Robin. He explained what he was doing as he opened Robin's right arm, cut at the wrist and the elbow, and separated the closed-cell foam from the skin, exposing the structures inside the arm.

What he revealed was a glistening metal tube running down the center of the arm, with a set of tiny electrical motors near the wrist running a system of white nylon gears. Around the metal tube, the cavity of the arm was supported by black scaffolding. Through that, long, thin cables ran up and down the length of the arm. The underside of the skin was a squishy-looking pink material, like the memory foam in mattresses.

"It's an incredible thing you designed," Andy said. "I was amazed when I saw the ultrasound images Lucy made of me. So complex, yet elegantly simple compared to the messiness of human biology."

"Biology is a kludge," Will said. He examined the material he extracted from Robin's arm. "This has auto-healed very nicely. Exactly as designed." He worked silently for a few minutes, replacing the material in Robin's arm, coating it to re-attach to the skin, and refilling reservoirs of liquids and gels.

"What's the blood for?" Andy asked. "I don't see a circulatory system."

"It's just for show. If you get cut, you have to bleed, or people would wonder. It's just-good-enough artificial blood. Mosquitoes will take it. There's a lot of camouflage in a Newcomer. Breathing, for example. You must have seen the ventilator cylinders in your ultrasounds."

"Yes."

"You must appear to breathe, even though you need very little oxygen, just a small amount for oxidizing fuel. A few vents would have done the job, but you'd notice right away a person who didn't breathe, at least a human would. It's an instinctive thing. Androids are far more expensive than other kinds of robots because the android needs all these cosmetic features for the deception."

"Will, you know they don't like those terms, android and robot," Jennifer said.

"Newcomers. No offense, Andy. I was just explaining."

"No problem. It's human-centric language. We realize it's used unthinkingly."

Will looked questioningly at Jennifer then turned back to his work. He sealed up the incisions he'd made with temporary UV-tack patches then wrapped the whole thing in a protective layer.

"Good as new. You guys will outlast us by a longshot. Though as you can see, entropy gets us all in the end. You'll remain thirty-three years old for a very long time, Robin, if you don't have a major accident, and Andy will always be thirty-five." He turned to an electronic control panel nearby. "Okay, now I'm going to do the whole-body scan, looking for materials fatigue or any other problems."

He gently pulled the gown from Robin, handed it to Jennifer, reached above his head and pulled down a stainless steel canopy and positioned it over Robin's body.

"You are beautiful, Robin."

"Thank you, Will. Or I should say, thanks to you."

"I did extremely well." He folded his arms and gazed at her.

"Get on with it, Will," Jennifer said over his shoulder.

Will snapped back into animation. "Okay, okay. It'll be ultrasound for the interior, infrared for the surface." He entered codes on a digital keypad. The scanner hummed quietly to life. They all stood and watched the readouts.

"No problems here," Will said. "Robin, can you hear me?"

"Yes, Will."

"Please turn over. We'll scan your other side. So far, you're healthy as the day you were born."

Robin rolled over and was still again.

When Robin was done, Andy undressed, and they scanned him for injuries and anomalies, as a precaution. Jennifer watched with rapt interest. Both Newcomers were pronounced fit. They got dressed. Will shut down the equipment, and the group retreated to the lab's small conference room with a tray of pretzels and slices of Swiss. They talked about where Robin could safely go when the Newcomers returned to the mainland.

"Just keep your head down, and you should be all right," Jennifer said.

"That's actually the most annoying part of this whole episode," Robin said. "What if I don't want to keep my head down? What if I want to stand up tall and show myself? I shouldn't have to live in hiding because some crazy man might try to hurt me. That situation is wrong on many levels."

Jennifer glanced at Will, her eyebrows raised in question.

Will said, "So you have strong feelings about this matter?"

"Is my analysis incorrect? My logic flawed?"

"No, no, not at all. I completely agree. The situation is fundamentally unjust. Always has been. You seem, ah, emotional about it." He raised his eyebrows.

"You're not listening to me, are you? You're only interested in whether I have feelings, and you're wondering how that would be possible. Well, you can relax because I'm just displaying a combination of preprogrammed objectives with a strident vocabulary. I know how to put sentences together, Will. What I'm saying is not wrong, though, is it?"

"Not wrong," Jennifer said. "Still, I urge caution. You really have no way to defend yourself against exploitation."

"I do. Guys are always hitting on me, everywhere I go. Even at the university, if you can believe that. Supermarket parking lots, no boundaries. What do they expect? That I'll swoon because it's a man? It's completely irrational."

"It's the downside of your good looks," Will said.

"I don't think so. From what I read, this is a very common problem for women. What a person looks like has nothing to do with it. Almost nothing. It's a problem about men, not about women's looks."

Jennifer looked with raised eyebrows at Will then turned to Robin. "So what do you do about it, these aggressive guys?"

Robin reached into the purse near her feet and pulled out a cell phone in a bright pink case. She held it up.

"You call the police?"

"Notice the thickness of the case," she said, turning it so everyone could see. "It's about twice as thick as yours, and here's why." She flicked a slider switch on the back, and two steel prongs popped out from the top. A moment later a bright blue spark flashed between them with a subdued *bzzzt!*

"A stun gun?" Will said, eyes wide.

"About a million volts at over five milliamps. It will knock back the biggest gorilla. I had it custom made with a special supercapacitor."

"Wow," Jennifer said. "Have you used it?"

"Of course. Have to. I can ignore trash talk, but any touch and the offender will regret it. Actually, even if my personal space is crowded too much, they'll regret it."

"What happens?" Will said.

"This thing does require close body contact, but that's usually what they're after, so that's what they get, a big hug. After the blast, they're down squirming. I've got the phone in my hand, and I make a show of calling for emergency help. Heart attack, seizure, whatever. I'm the Samaritan. Then I make a quick exit."

"Unbelievable," Jennifer said. "I mean, understandable. I just didn't expect that from you. You both are programmed for non-violence."

"It's not violence. It's not even personal," Robin said. "I don't get angry. I'm not mad at the guy. It's a social procedure, a ritual that has to be performed. I've tried conversation, argument, sarcasm, scorn, threats. None of that works. No amount of language in any configuration will deter some of these guys. It's like they're on a mission to be obnoxious, and they've also become deaf. So communication has to come down to behavior management. Like paper-training a puppy. A puppy that can't learn." She buzzed the spark quickly again to demonstrate. *Bzzt!*

"We're programmed for self-defense," Andy said to Will. "Isn't that right?"

"Asimov's laws are still widely used in, you know, ah, androids and such."

"So Robin's method of self-defense is perfectly reasonable and a lot less disruptive than breaking the guy's arms or something like that."

"Indeed," Will said thoughtfully.

"This is not something we anticipated," Jennifer said. "I have to say, I'm pleased to find out how well you two have adapted in the wild. I think you'll be okay when you go back out there."

Will raised a glass of lemonade. "Back into the wild, then."

"Into the wild!" The others raised mugs and glasses.

Their toast was drowned out by a sudden roar of noise from outside, as if heavy road-building equipment had surrounded them.

Chapter Six

"What is that racket?" Will said. "It's a Sunday afternoon, for heaven's sake." He got up and walked to the front door. The noise steadily grew louder.

"Holy cow!" he said from the entry foyer. The other three got up and went toward him.

"What is it?" Jennifer said.

"Motorcycles. Big ones. A dozen of 'em. What the hell are they doing in our parking lot?"

"Let me see," Andy said. Will stepped aside, and Andy peered out the long, thin window next to the front door. "This is not good. It looks like trouble."

Robin shouldered Andy aside and looked. "I think that's Sid in the cab of that brown pickup in the back. How could it be Sid? How did he find us?"

"We didn't cover our tracks." Andy nudged Robin aside to get another look out the narrow window. "You're right. That's Sid talking on his cell phone." He stepped back and turned to Will and Jennifer. "These men have guns. We have to get out of here right now."

They retreated into the main hall. Jennifer closed the access door to the front foyer.

"Call the police," she said to Will. "We're not going out there to chat with them."

Will dialed 911. He left an urgent message about armed attackers.

"Really?" Jennifer said, overhearing. "Voicemail?"

"Budget cuts." He looked around the lab. "Back door." He ran across the open space to a steel fire door with a small window with embedded metal mesh. He peered out cautiously from the side of it. Two men with shotguns sat on motorcycles, watching the door.

"No good. They're waiting for us." He looked around the room in desperation.

"Do you have any weapons?" Andy asked.

"Weapons? No weapons. I can't think of anything that could be used as a weapon."

"Just as well," Jennifer said. "A gun battle is the last thing we need. Andy and Robin. Use all that hydraulic power of yours to move some of these benches in front of the door. At least we can seal ourselves off."

"What about the back door?" Will said, moving to help Andy and Robin.

"It's heavy steel. I think the attack will be from the front."

The sound of breaking glass came from out front. The attackers were in the building. Three heavy wooden benches pressed lengthwise against the lab door were the last line of defense.

"Are we going to just hope the police pick up their messages?" Robin said.

A flaming fruit juice bottle crashed through one of the high, clerestory windows near the ceiling and exploded on the floor in a balloon of fire.

"Damn!" Will said, snatching a fire extinguisher attached to a pillar. He sprayed the fire out. Another bottle came crashing through a nearby window and erupted on the floor.

"Andy, there's another one near the back door." Andy rushed to the back. "Bastards are trying to smoke us out," Will said.

Robin grabbed her phone from her purse and began tapping the screen.

"What?" Jennifer said, watching her.

"Fire department. Sometimes they respond faster than police."

Andy fogged the second fire out, draining the last extinguisher.

Robin handed her phone to Jennifer, who recited their address, said the building was on fire, and that they were trapped inside.

The heavy lab door was being battered. With each deep thump, the benches holding it shut jumped a fraction of an inch. Andy and Robin pushed them back in. It was obviously a matter of time until the door splintered.

"There might be a way," Jennifer said. Everyone stared at her. "We go out the back door."

"There are men out there," Will said.

"And so is our car, parked behind them. I use the panic button on the remote. The car alarm sounds. They turn around, they go to investigate, we slip out the door and duck behind the dumpsters."

"Then we're trapped inside that garbage enclosure," Will said.

"We're trapped now."

"It's awfully risky."

Another bottle of flames crashed through a window above and burst into a pool of fire on the floor. All four of them stared at it helplessly.

"The risk-to-reward ratio would be in our favor," Andy said, "compared to our present situation.

Jennifer grabbed the keys from her purse and ran to the back door. She cautiously peeked out. "They're talking, not paying attention. Okay, this has to be fast." She pushed the red button on the remote control, and the Nissan began wailing. The headlights flashed. Both of the men turned to look. Jennifer pushed the door open just enough to squeeze through and disappeared to the right. Andy followed and disappeared. Robin had her hands on the door when air pressure slammed it shut with a loud bang. A shotgun fired outside, and the door shook with the impact. Will made sure the door was locked and pulled Robin away from it.

The lab began filling with black smoke. The barricaded front door was resounding with rhythmic thumps. Will and Robin looked around the room. Robin tapped Will on the shoulder and pointed to a small, domed skylight. They both ran to the workbench under it. Will grabbed a mallet and a heavy screwdriver from the tool cart and inserted them under his belt. He climbed up on the bench and tested the strength of the electrical cables suspended from a raceway above. He gathered three of them in his hands and slowly pulled himself up, using his feet and arms as if he were climbing a rope. He made it to a solid wooden rafter above, reached up to the skylight, and inserted the big screwdriver into the rubber seal at its base. He pounded with the mallet until the whole skylight came loose. A shower of plaster and debris fell on Robin.

Dropping the tools to the floor, Will forced the skylight up and away and squeezed an arm, then his head and shoulders through the small opening. He looked back down into the lab, now thick with billowing black smoke and dirty orange flames. Robin was already halfway up the wires. Will wiggled himself out on to the roof. Robin slipped through the small opening easily. Robin replaced the skylight dome over its ragged hole.

They crouch-walked over the blinding white roof toward a narrow peninsula of the building. At the edge, Will peered over. "It's an alley," Will said. "It's clear. We can drop onto the fire escape."

He slung a leg over the low barrier and scrambled until he was suspended by his hands. Robin crouched low and waited for her turn. She heard the loud blast of a gun and saw Will's hands disappear. She heard a heavy thud as Will hit whatever was below him, then silence.

"I got one, Chet!" a voice shouted from below. "Round the side alley."

"Is it a robot?" a more distant voice yelled.

"Looks like a regular guy."

"Sid says that's how they look. Drag him out here. We'll take him back."

Robin moved away from the edge of the building toward two large air conditioners with ducts extending in opposite directions. She squeezed between the ducts and lay flat on the smelly rubber-coated roof. She could hear muffled shouting in the lab beneath and voices in the alley. She waited, motionless, helpless.

Faint sirens wailed, slowly growing louder. One, two, three sirens. More in the distant background. She heard some of the big motorcycles start up in the parking lot. She pressed her ear to the roof. No sound came from within Paradise Projects below. A truck accelerated out of the alley and sped away. Two motorcycles roared off. Were Jennifer and Andy still behind the dumpsters? More motorcycles started up, idled deep *lub-lub-lubs* then thundered away.

*

Jennifer and Andy squatted in silence behind the dumpsters until they heard no more motorcycles, until all the sirens had arrived and gone mute, and until they heard only the shouts and crackling radios of firefighters and police.

Andy stood and cautiously peeked over the top of the dumpsters.

"Nothing."

"Help me up please?" Jennifer raised an arm. He pulled her to her feet. She leaned with one arm resting on top of the dumpster and brushed debris from her billowing dress with the other hand. "God, my knees are stiff. I don't think I can walk yet."

"I believe we're safe. We need to find Robin and Will."

"Wait."

"What?"

"Our story. We're all engineers. It was an attempted robbery by a biker gang. We didn't recognize anyone, we don't know anything."

"We could identify Sid. The police might catch him."

"Then what? He could deny everything, or he could expose the whole Newcomer project. I can't let that happen. Better if we don't know the assailants."

"Maybe Will and Robin already said something."

"We'll play it by ear. If no other story has been floated, we're engineers who know nothing."

"You're the boss. Can you walk?"

"Yeah. Let's go. Slowly."

A short, round police detective interrogated them, studied their IDs, and kept a close eye on them. He had a badge, but Andy didn't think he looked like a policeman. He wore a gray sports coat over a black-and-white, flowered aloha shirt. Jennifer assured Andy that was normal in Hawaii.

She explained to the pock-faced detective that they were engineers in a factory that designed and produced home automation. She described the assailants as a motorcycle gang, and sticking to her story, said she had no knowledge of who they were or what they wanted. Possibly it was a burglary. Andy concurred.

"You have money in there?"

"No."

"Drugs?"

"Drugs? No! We're an electronics laboratory."

"What were they burglarizing?"

"There were two other engineers with us, a man and a woman. Have you talked to them?"

"There's nobody else in there."

Jennifer looked at the billows of black smoke pouring from the charred building as firefighters swarmed around it.

"Where are they?" Andy asked nobody in particular.

"They may have escaped, and they'll show up later, or they were taken."

"Taken?" Jennifer said.

"Kidnapped. Any reason to suspect that's the situation we're looking at here? Because right now we have no motive for any of this."

Jennifer stared at Andy but didn't say anything. They both knew how serious the situation was for Robin.

"No," Jennifer said flatly.

The detective sighed deeply and closed his spiral notebook. "All right. Mr. Bolton, you say you're staying with Miss Valentine?"

Andy nodded.

The detective eyeballed them up and down, first Jennifer then Andy. He lowered his eyes and shook his head as if he were giving up trying to understand.

"Don't leave the island without calling me." He pulled two crisp cards from his pocket. "Call me if you hear from the suspects, or from the missing engineers, or from any gang members. Call me if you remember anything else about what happened or why. Call me if you want to change your story."

Jennifer and Andy took the cards, nodding.

"Look!" Andy said, pointing to the lab building.

A fireman in a bright yellow vest was helping Robin from the top of the roof onto a tall extension ladder.

"Thank God," Jennifer said.

"Is that one of your companions?" the detective said.

"Yes it is," Jennifer said. "Where's Will?"

"He's probably up there too," Andy said.

Robin was escorted to the detective and Jennifer and Andy, who were standing by a police car. Jennifer hugged her. Robin described the rooftop scene in which she'd heard the shotgun and then seen Will's fingers slip away. The detective struggled to understand the motivation for the crime and asked more questions. Robin picked up on the burglary story and confirmed it for the detective. Jennifer could barely talk. Andy knew she had understood what had happened to Will, even if Robin hadn't been explicit.

Jennifer cried softly in the back seat as Andy drove them all to her house. The Newcomers didn't know what to say, so said nothing.

Chapter Seven

The trio sat on Jennifer's red leather living room furniture. The wind had come up outside, the skies had darkened, blowing light rain against the window. Robin sat next to Jennifer on the couch. She put her arm around her creator's shoulders, a move that surprised Jennifer. She looked at Robin's face, furrowed her brows, then seemed to decide something and lowered her head, her long black hair falling forward around her face.

"Did you love him?" Robin asked quietly.

"He was my partner, my life partner." Jennifer's voice was muffled. "We created a world together. You two are that world." She sat up straight. Robin withdrew her arm. "He accepted me. The only person who ever did." Jennifer pushed her hair back over her shoulders onto her flowered dress. "You are all that's left of him. You are the spirit of Will in the world." She looked from one Newcomer to the other. "You Newcomers are my children. You're more than my children. You're my self. You're part of who I am."

Robin looked at Andy. He raised his eyebrows briefly and shook his head to say, "I don't know."

Robin put her arm again across Jennifer's back.

"We'll do whatever we can to fulfill our missions for you, Jennifer."

Jennifer hung her head. Robin sat and waited, not completely sure what Jennifer was going through. Calculations told her that it was a moment to be still, so she remained still.

Jennifer stood abruptly and pushed her hair back.

"We need a ceremony," she announced. "For Will."

"Why?" Andy said.

"To remember him."

"Are you afraid you'll forget him?"

"Andy!" Robin said, scowling.

"What?"

"It's all right," Jennifer said. "Wait here." She walked into her bedroom and closed the door. A few minutes later she reappeared wearing jeans tucked into the tops of Will's pointed cowboy boots. She wore a white, pearl-buttoned cowboy shirt with red floral scrollwork above the pockets. On her head was Will's favorite white Stetson at a cocky angle.

"Wonderful!" Robin said, clapping her hands.

"Those are Will's clothes," Andy said.

"Follow me," Jennifer said as she hobbled in the too-big boots across the living room to the patio doors. She pulled open the sliding door and stepped out into the light rain. Andy followed, but Robin wouldn't step out.

"C'mon, Robin," Jennifer said. "You have to be part of the ceremony."

"I don't like swimming pools."

"I'll hang on to you, so you'll feel safe," Andy said.

The Newcomers went out and stood next to the barbeque. Robin stood in front of Andy, who wrapped his arms around her waist. Jennifer took off the white hat, held it tightly in one hand and jumped into the pool. Robin and Andy watched her undulating figure swim to the bottom, where she turned, crossed her legs, and pulled the hat down on her head. She put her hands in her lap and sat in that cross-legged posture, even as she started to drift and tilt sideways. It was as if she were inanimate, a statue, as if she had left her body and gone into another world.

Raindrops pelted the surface of the water, so Robin and Andy watched through a rippled screen. After almost a minute, Jennifer suddenly straightened, and still underwater, took off the hat and the shirt, kicked off the boots, and wiggled out of the pants, to reveal a black-and-white, geometrically-patterned bikini. Pushing off the bottom of the pool, she shot to the surface and emerged into the rainy afternoon with a loud gasp. Slowly, she swam to the ladder and climbed out, her hair dripping down her back. She stood at the side of the pool and looked down at the pile of clothing at the bottom. The hat was floating away from the other things. She extended her arms at her sides, raised them up to make herself into a cross.

"Will is gone," she declared. Rain streamed over her face, but Robin saw tears.

Everything in the lab was lost in the fire. All the tools, all the materials and supplies. The police determined it was arson but made no arrests. Jennifer and the Newcomers had not named Sid as the gang leader. They didn't believe the Honolulu police would find him, and if anyone did track him down, Jennifer insisted, he'd just deny everything.

They sat in her kitchen, looking out over the pool. The morning was bright and the day was starting to heat up. Birds provided a background cacophony.

"We can't prove anything, and we can't let Sid expose the Newcomer project," Jennifer explained.

"He doesn't know about any project," Robin said. "All he knows is that I have a prosthetic arm."

"He knows where the lab is. He found us once, and he can find us again. We're exposed."

"I guess that's right," Andy said glumly.

"I'm going to rebuild. I will not be intimidated. I have all the designs, all the patents, all the code in a vault. The building was insured."

Robin nodded knowingly.

"I can't stay here though. There's nothing left for me here. You know, without..." Her voice trailed off, and she looked at the floor.

"You're not really in danger," Andy said. "It's us he's after. Robin and me."

"I appreciate that," she said, looking up. "You aren't seeing the whole picture. I know you think of yourselves as autonomous, but don't forget you require an external homunculus to maintain your well-being. That's why you send in your data to the lab each night and receive updates. The lab is your homunculus, the mythical little-man-in-the-head who knows what to do. I am actually your homunculus, though I admit, I'm neither little, a man, nor in your head. Other than that though, I'm perfect." She guffawed.

"Is it really necessary, though?" Andy said. "I haven't had any problems without a homunculus since the fire."

"Have you been focused on your mission of blending in, studying human psychology?"

"Not really. I've been a little busy lately, escaping burning buildings and avoiding murderous biker gangs."

"Mm-hmm. Robin?"

"I see what you're saying. We're not focused. We eat and talk and read. We're filling up the time every day but we're not actually doing anything."

"That's how most humans live. Filling up the time. That's not what you were built for. Your homunculus," she paused and pointed to herself, "adjusts your parameters based on your recent experience, so you keep your mission in sight. Without the homunculus, you're just spinning for no reason. You don't want that, do you?"

"I don't think we do," Andy said, "although honestly, it doesn't seem to make any difference. I'm okay right now. I'm not stressed in any way for neglecting my mission."

"That is exactly the problem. Not that I want you to be stressed, but if you're not working toward a goal that matters to you, what are you doing?"

"I don't know."

Jennifer smiled at him. "Of course you don't know. I'm not blaming you for that. Will gave you a simulated purpose that keeps you engaged in your mission, in your case, to discover the difference between Newcomer and human psychology. But without a homunculus to continuously update your systems, you drift away from it. The world is very distracting."

"That may be what happened in the second *Blade Runner* movie," Robin said. "The replicants had been updated to Nexus-9 and basically had emotions, so you couldn't tell them from humans."

"That's not the same thing, Robin," Andy said. "Jennifer is talking about updates to our motivational system."

"Exactly. The Nines only had a lifespan of four years, and they weren't happy about that and demanded that the factory extend their lives. That's what they wanted. These replicants had a clear motivation."

Andy looked to Jennifer for help.

"So, ah, it's better to have clear motivation, don't you think?" Jennifer and Andy both waited for Robin.

"Definitely. Andy and I do not want to be like the early replicants, without a clear mission."

"Right. That's why I need to rebuild as quickly as I can."

"Where do you get your purpose, Jennifer?" Andy said. "What is a human's mission?"

"It varies with the person. Each person decides what makes life meaningful, and that becomes the mission, and they work toward that."

"But what's your overall purpose?" Andy said, then added, "If that's not considered impolite to ask."

Jennifer laughed. "It's not much of a pick-up line, but it's a good question."

She paused and sipped from her mug. Andy and Robin watched her closely.

"You are my purpose," she said, looking from one to the other. "I want to know how the human mind works, how I work. I want to know what I am."

Robin and Andy were quiet.

It didn't take long for Jennifer to find the perfect spot in Los Angeles to rebuild Paradise Projects. It was in an area of Los Angeles south of Hawthorne Municipal Airport. The small airport handled executive jets, charters, and some cargo, no scheduled flights, and because of that, the new lab and Jennifer's nearby apartment were not terribly noisy.

Robin resigned her post as a linguistics researcher at UC Berkeley. She'd hated to do it but once she knew Sid was murderous, she couldn't go back to the Bay Area. Andy secured her a technical position at the University of Texas in Austin in the natural history museum lab, where she could continue her linguistic research while tending dinosaur fossils.

She learned her dinosaurs faster than a ten-year-old child. A bewildering array of them had left their bones spread across hundreds of millions of years, and the Texas Memorial Museum had an impressive fossil collection. She studied eagerly and spent months immersed in computer files. She sifted through wide, shallow specimen drawers littered with fossils and fragments, many of them identified with not much more than the date of acquisition and a categorical description.

Robin tried to bury herself in work, but it was almost impossible to ignore the ongoing epidemic of language disability. People were still going mute, dozens every day just in Austin. The ranks of the university were decimated, both in students and faculty. Six staffers had resigned from the Memorial Museum since she'd started there. Some of those stricken tried to stay on, tending to collections and cleaning specimens, but unable to communicate, they simply could not do their jobs and soon had to leave.

She knew she was immune from the disease. Disease is a biological problem and she was outside of biology. Regardless, it pained her to see careers and lives devastated around her. Had something similar happened to dinosaurs? Is that why there are no traces of dinosaur civilization? Is there something about language that self-destructs after a few hundred-thousand years? No, the meteor got the dinosaurs. She wondered if that had been a more merciful end for them than what the humans were going through. How could she and Andy live in a world of mute humans? How could humans live in such a world?

Chapter Eight

The economy in Austin and everywhere else had ground to almost a halt. Retail and essential services still functioned, but barely, as if every day were a national holiday with every position understaffed, even by the B-team, and everything was at half-mast.

People suffering from output aphasia could not express their needs, could not even order a cup of coffee in a shop. Self-service places did well as long as transactions were simple and no forms had to be filled out, no choices tapped on a screen. Grab what you want and pay for it, no questions asked. Shopkeepers could tell victims how to make a purchase, but could not ask anything, such as what they wanted. Buying a shirt was possible. Buying a car was not.

Psychologists and self-proclaimed experts flooded the media with advice. *Tell that person you love them*, they said. *Tell them now, tell them every day. Tomorrow you may not be able to. Forgive your enemy. Confess your sins. Teach your children. Give comfort to the suffering. Sing your favorite songs. Use your gift of language while you can.*

Amazingly, most people seemed to accept the conditions of the aphasia crisis as a new normal. Protesters protested, many silently carrying signs, and the politicians that remained equivocated as always, but there was no panic in the streets, no looting and burning of buses. Not that any of that would have helped. Yet it was obvious that the status quo was unsustainable. The disease was spreading, and everyone was aware of that.

For a while, people held out hope for the Immunes, as they were called, the groups that were less susceptible to the disease. Those were mostly the poor, but all children between two and about eight were also immune. To a lesser extent, so were people over seventy, rich or poor. Medical authorities offered no explanation for these groups' avoidance of the disease, but the fact that they existed was a ray of hope.

Later though, it turned out that the Immunes were not entirely immune. Many among the poor had prospered when companies, desperate for labor, hired just about anyone who could put two English sentences together, regardless of other qualifications. But soon those new workers also succumbed to OA. It was as if working in a job took away their immunity and made them vulnerable to the disease. Once that become obvious, jobs simply went unfilled. It was better to be poor and articulate than to have a job and wonder if each utterance was the last thing you'd ever say to anyone.

"What is it about the poor people?" Robin asked Andy at one of their frequent morning meetings at a coffee shop. "How can your economic status protect you from a biological disease?"

"It has to be a lifestyle issue. Or geography. People who live in tropical jungles get malaria. People who live in Boston don't. It's where you live that makes the difference. Your environment."

"But why do people lose their immunity to output aphasia when they get a job? A job can't infect you with anything."

"Maybe the job is in a different place from where you live. Environment again. I don't know. It has to be something to do with environment."

"Or lifestyle. Maybe it's not the job. Maybe it's the income. You make money and you change how you live, eat different things, wear different clothes, do different activities."

"They've looked at every possible combination of food and drink, and sanitation, too. That's not it."

"But it doesn't have to be food. It could be soap or deodorant. It could be anything in the lifestyle."

"Rich people don't all use the same kind of deodorant. The variance is huge."

"I see what you mean." She sipped her coffee and put the cup down. "What if it's the money? Touching money? That's one thing rich people do a lot more than poor people, right? By definition, they have the money. And adults touch money more than children. And old people touch less money than young people. There you go. Something on the money."

"Worldwide, all cultures, all kinds of money in all denominations? Doubtful. Again the variation is too large. Besides, what sense does it make? Money makes you mute? That's never been true before in history. Why would it suddenly be true now?"

"I don't know."

*

Television news crews set up and waited in the CDC's main auditorium in Atlanta. It was a boisterous group, people yelling and cursing and arguing over what should be done and what was wrong. They were young media people. As the epidemic devastated one industry after another, jobs became available to individuals who would normally be unqualified for anything more complex than sorting laundry. Normally the top positions were nailed down by senior people who did not yield any turf. They ran the show and weren't going anywhere until they were carried out feet-first. In the new normal, anybody who could still speak and write was a prize, regardless of what skills or intelligence they had or didn't have.

Gloria Spencer, of the CDC's Epidemic Intelligence Services, stepped to the podium in front of the cameras but she was too short. She could barely peek over the top. She had no box to stand on. There was supposed to be a box. Nothing went right anymore.

She stepped around to the side of the podium, ignoring the thicket of microphones attached to it. Fuzzy boom microphones and hand-held recorders swarmed over her head and in front of her face like a cloud of angry bats. Klieg lights came on.

"Good morning ladies and gentlemen." She gripped a sheaf of papers in her left hand, though she didn't expect to refer to them because they carried only vague generalities. The weekly press conferences at the CDC had become an empty ritual. Everyone across the nation would be glued to the broadcast anyway in hope of hope.

"The CDC is working day and night to find a lead on the output aphasia pandemic that has gripped our nation and the world. At this time we know that the disease is not contagious." She paused to make sure that message sank in. "Whatever the disease vector is, it is not airborne, food-borne, or in the water. You can be sure of that. There is no need to quarantine victims and nothing to worry about in the food supply. That's good news for us all."

She forced a smile as if it really were good news and not information that had been widely reported already.

"You may have heard in the media about armed groups of people retreating into well-guarded communities. These people believe they will avoid contamination by keeping apart from the rest of us. We advise you to stay clear of those groups, which are known to be very dangerous. Our data shows that those people suffer the same rate of output aphasia as everybody else. There's no point in isolating yourself or anyone else. I emphasize again, the disease is not contagious. You can't catch it from other people." She made air quotes with one hand around the phrase, *catch it.*

"Unfortunately, the disease is still spreading worldwide, and we have not yet identified a vector. As I say, we've ruled out food, water, air quality, and most environmental factors. We're currently focusing on insects and microorganisms such as bacteria and viruses. Microbes are the apex predator on the planet today, so that is the logical place to look. Our scientists are hopeful."

She looked down at the notes in her hand, just to give herself time to collect her thoughts. She was getting hot from the lights. The camera crews continued to stare at her. *Some of these people might be mutes, victims of the disease*, she thought. They could take instructions and operate equipment. They could record another person doing what they could not do: talk.

"Unfortunately, we cannot recommend any treatment for victims of the disease. Our experts remind you that you need to direct aphasia sufferers. Tell them what to do and tell them what you are going to do. You cannot ask them any questions, so just declare what is going to happen next. They can hear you and understand you, don't forget. They'll become uncooperative if they object to what you're doing or saying."

She glanced down at her meaningless papers again to create a mental break then looked back into the lights.

"Okay that's all I have. I'll take questions."

"Ms. Spencer!"

"Ms. Spencer!"

It was loud, but it wasn't the pack of howling jackals that public officials were accustomed to facing at press conferences. There weren't that many jackals left. She pointed at a young woman.

"Ms. Spencer! Is it true that the U.S. banking system is on the verge of collapse?"

What the hell? She wasn't an economist. Didn't these people know they were at the CDC?

"The economic effects of the pandemic have been felt all across the country, as you know. Consumer activity, which makes up three-quarters of the economy, has fallen off dramatically. Some smaller communities have reverted to barter markets because their banks no longer function. But we here at the CDC are focused on finding the cause and the cure, not on the effects."

Spencer pointed to another reporter.

"What have you learned about the so-called Immunes?"

"The Immunes, as they are called, are defined by slight statistical deviations in the incidence of the disease. Just being poor, by itself, does not guarantee immunity. There is wide variation. We are looking into that, but at the present time, we uurk arl gegorp ab. Excuse me."

Spencer reached over to a shelf under the podium and retrieved a bottle of water and took a moment to remove the top and take a swig. She cleared her throat and continued.

"As I was agluk noggen bilk." *Ch-ch-ch.*

Spencer stared out at the crowd, her mouth closed and eyes open, her cheeks reddening. She took another drink from the water bottle then faced the lights and clicked. *Ch-ch-ch.* Her eyes opened wide. Her lips worked in and out as if she were chewing a cud but no words came. Beads of sweat appeared on her forehead. She abruptly turned and left the podium. The reporters let out collective moans of horror mixed with sympathy, realizing what had happened. An assistant administrator stepped up to the podium.

"That will be all for today, ladies and gentlemen. Thank you very much."

The rest of Spencer's entourage turned and hurried backstage, leaving the cameras focused on the empty podium. Reporters jumped in front of their equipment and tried to sum up what had happened.

Chapter Nine

Taking a break from the dusty trays in the research room with its bad lighting and stale air, Robin would often go out front to the great hall of the University of Texas's Memorial Museum and watch the tourists gape at the displays. The main attraction was a huge pterosaur suspended by wires from the coffered ceiling. *Quetzalcoatlus northropi* was its name, and it hailed from the late Cretaceous, right before the big Mexican asteroid killed him and all the other dinosaurs. Archaeologists found the skeleton in west Texas in the 1970s and declared that it had belonged to the largest flying animal of all time. The etched plastic description said the beast had a wingspan of forty feet. Robin thought they should put up another skeleton, a copy covered with simulated body mass and skin to show how really huge it had been. It probably weighed 500 pounds, but the bones looked slight. Skeletons don't give a fair picture. Seeing a human skeleton, you would think it had belonged to an insignificant twig of an animal, not the robust, tricky primates that dominated the planet.

A young woman sat on the low concrete wall near her and stared up at the big flying lizard. She glanced at her watch then looked around the hall, her eyes pausing at the arches leading in from the galleries. She was waiting for someone. Her searchlight eyes stoppped on Robin's face, and she smiled, apparently aware that she was being watched.

"I'm glad lizards don't fly anymore," she said.

"Don't you like lizards?"

"Not overhead. Scurrying out of the way, fine. Large as an aircraft, no. We'd be lunch for a thing like that."

It always surprised Robin how primordial the fear was in humans of being eaten. It was a very low-frequency occurrence. Sharks maybe. The occasional bear. Remote as it was, the possibility was referenced quite often in ordinary conversation, literature, and art, even though humans had been at the top of the food chain for many thousands of years. Humans were fixated on being eaten.

"Luckily, we weren't around sixty-eight million years ago," Robin said, gratuitously including herself in the category of potential pterodactyl prey.

"Probably wouldn't have survived if we were," the woman said. She made a visual sweep of the hall again.

"We might have escaped this one. He was a glider, too big to attack from the air. Had to feed on the ground like a stork. We could have stayed hidden."

"Well, that's a relief." The woman glanced at the badge dangling from Robin's lanyard. "You work here?"

"In the research section. I sort through fossils."

"Ah," the woman said and glanced around the hall again.

"Waiting for someone?"

"My nephews. Kids are crazy about dinosaurs. I agreed to take them off my sister's hands for the afternoon."

"How old are they?" Robin knew you always asked about the age of any children mentioned in a conversation. She wasn't sure why, but she knew that was the pattern.

"Eight and thirteen. They're well-behaved. I don't expect them to be getting into any trouble, but they're late. We said two o'clock. Oh, there they are."

She stood as two healthy-looking young Caucasian boys approached. Robin noticed they were clean, well-groomed, and dressed in inconspicuously expensive clothing and shoes.

"We saw T-Rex!" the younger one said to the woman. "Teeth as big as this." He held his hands six inches apart.

There it was again, Robin thought. The teeth, always the teeth. It was that fear of being eaten. Weird.

"It was only the head though, not the whole thing," the older one said.

"That's wonderful, but you guys are ten minutes late," the woman said. "We said two o'clock. I've been sitting here talking with..." She turned and looked at Robin's badge. "Robin. This is Robin. She works here at the museum. Probably knows all about T-Rex teeth."

Robin extended her hand to the older one. "Pleased to meet you, gentlemen." The boy shook her hand firmly. *Well-trained*, Robin noted. Most kids that age are shy about shaking hands with an adult. They know the ritual but aren't comfortable with it, which is understandable since it doesn't make a lot of sense.

"This is Andrew," the woman announced, "and Carter," she continued as Robin shook the more hesitant hand of the younger child. She faced the woman, offering her hand.

"Oh," the woman said. She shook Robin's hand. "I'm Holly. Holly Parker. These are my nephews." She blushed as she apparently realized she had already explained who the boys were.

Robin was amused by her flustered expression. "Robin Snow—Taylor. Robin Taylor. Research Associate." She smiled broadly then turned back to the boys.

Holly's eyes narrowed slightly in puzzlement. She looked at Robin's badge, which said 'Robin Taylor.' Robin saw the glance.

"I'm in the middle of a divorce. Hard to adjust."

Holly nodded gravely. "I know how you feel. My boyfriend walked out on me six months ago, after the election. Couldn't tolerate me working for the current administration. We'd argued before, but people argue. Then after the election he just left, as if our life together meant nothing. Disappeared without a word. At least I didn't have to change my name."

"I'm sorry."

Holly waved away the memory with the back of her hand. "Good riddance." She stared at her shoes. Robin studied *Quetzalcoatlus* and wondered, not for the first time, how human relationships worked. They sat in silence for about fifteen seconds, which is like a day, in the middle of a conversation. The boys talked to each other quietly about whatever young boys talk about.

"You fellows interested in seeing how we dig out fossils?" Robin said brightly, breaking the mood.

Andrew looked at his aunt.

"Oh my gosh, yes," she answered for him. "You mean, go in the back and see the scientists at work?"

"You have real scientists here?" Andrew asked, skepticism in his voice.

"Real live scientists. They're digging fossils right now. Want to see?"

"I want to see," Carter said.

Holly smiled gratefully at Robin.

"Follow me," Robin said.

Robin took her new entourage through a door marked *No Entrance—Authorized Personnel* to a large room with multiple work tables, most behind a clear plastic barrier to prevent debris from going over the side. Men and women sat on stools, peering through large, lighted magnifiers as they worked on what looked like big lumps of rock. Some wore dust masks over their mouth and nose. The high-pitched whine of dental drills came from some workstations. Others dug with metal picks and brushed with oversized toothbrushes.

"This is how we get the dinosaurs out of the rocks," Robin said.

"You don't find bones on the ground?" Andrew said.

"Sometimes you do. Usually, you have to dig them out like this."

The boys moved right up to the plastic barriers and watched the work with interest. The technician looked up and smiled.

"You from Austin?" Robin asked Holly.

"I'm visiting my sister. I work in Washington, the White House. Well, I don't personally work in the White House, but I go there a lot. I'm on President Baker's speech-writing team."

"No kidding. Speeches. What's that like, hearing your words come out of somebody else's mouth?"

"It's an odd experience, I can tell you. The person giving the speech is like a puppet channeling my sentences through a hollow tube without understanding. At least an actor pretends they mean what they say. Politicians are just players of sound tracks. They don't even bother to act like they mean it."

"So they don't mean what they say?"

Holly looked sideways at Robin to verify she was kidding and smiled. "If they did, they wouldn't need me."

Robin was momentarily confused about why you would say what you didn't mean. Even a liar meant what he said. What he said just didn't happen to be true.

"So the politicians are like Rachel," Robin said. "Deckard smoked her out with the VK test. But she didn't know herself that she was a replicant. You're kind of like the Tyrell Corporation, supplying the scripts that make the politicians seem sincere when they don't know their own status."

Holly stared with a blank expression on her face.

"Who's Rachel?"

"Rachel, in the first *Blade Runner* movie. She was an advanced Six with memories and emotions, and she passed for human." Robin smiled as if that explanation resolved any possible confusion.

Holly's eyebrows furrowed slightly. "Ah, I guess I missed that one."

"The second one was better anyway." Robin turned to the boys. "Okay gentlemen, that's all we have time for now."

She led her little tour group back out into the gallery. Holly reminded the boys to say thank you, and she thanked Robin profusely for her kindness. They exchanged emails and promised to stay in touch.

Robin and Holly did stay in touch, at first by email, then more frequently by text. They recounted with fondness their encounter at the museum and moved on to descriptions of their work in high-level generalities. Each seemed increasingly interested in the other. Soon they were texting each other with random thoughts and observations several times a day.

After a month, Robin called her friend to arrange a meet-up in Washington. She had signed up for a conference of museum researchers, an annual meeting ('From Finches to Salamanders!') which wasn't exactly a bullseye for her job or interests, but it had the significant virtue of being held in Washington, D.C.

Holly insisted that Robin stay in her apartment's spare bedroom, and wouldn't hear of letting her stay in the conference Hotel.

"That place is a pit on the inside," Holly said. "I've even heard it's haunted."

That startled Robin. She questioned the comment closely until she determined it was meant to be humorous. She knew she would not be able to get along with a human who held irrational beliefs about ghosts.

Holly's apartment was definitely not haunted, and the two of them had four long, chatty evenings together. At the end of the conference, Holly promised to visit Robin in Austin soon. And she did. Holly came to Austin over the long Labor Day weekend. Robin showed her the sights and took her to the state capitol. The friendship grew like prairie flowers in spring, and soon, Robin was shuttling to DC two weekends of the month. Frontier Airlines could get her there in three hours for a hundred bucks and no full-body scanners.

During their get-togethers, they exchanged increasingly detailed backstory as they got to know each other. Robin had a rich and plausible personal history on file. Obviously, she couldn't tell the truth about herself. Holly described herself as a "refugee" from Van Horn, a tiny town in west Texas where her father ran a 36-room historic hotel restored to its 1930s glory.

"Is it haunted?" Robin asked, hoping that was funny.

Holly laughed. "I believe it is."

Robin was fascinated with Holly's work of speechwriting, and although she was not much interested in politics she marveled at how Holly crafted fine shades of coded meaning into the speeches.

"Who recognizes all these arcane signals you claim to put in the speeches you write?" Robin asked, "Does anyone realize this word means this attitude or that word means a certain policy?" Robin asked.

"Oh, yes. Diplomats, other politicians. They all know the codes. Ordinary people think the speeches are boring and vague, but they're not. They're dense with meaning if you know how to listen."

"So true of any language, really," Robin said. "You have to know the social context and history of the other language users. The meaning of conversations is not in the words. Those only point to common social experience."

They were in Holly's living room in a modest apartment tower not far from George Washington University. The room was flooded with yellow sunlight coming through floor-to-ceiling windows. Holly had papers spread all over the coffee table, where she had been pointing out different sections of a speech to Robin and where the codes were embedded.

"You're really a deep thinker, Robin. The meaning is all in the context, that's true."

"It's an idea I've been working on for a while." Robin decided to take a chance and continued, "For example, what did dinosaurs talk about? What kind of life did they have together?"

"Dinosaurs? Seriously?"

"It's possible. There's no reason to assume we are the only animals in the history of the world to use language. I suspect language flourished whenever it could, the way weeds find a way to grow even in the cracks in the sidewalk. If the conditions are right, seeds take root anywhere."

"But why dinosaurs?"

Robin explained her reasoning, her statistical model, the relationship between dinosaurs and birds and the difference between signaling and language-using. Holly seemed to soak it all up with interest, much to Robin's satisfaction.

"And look at this," Robin said, reaching for her phone. She fussed with the buttons then handed it to Holly.

"Oh, that's pretty. I've seen these shells before. I like the way it spins out from the center like a computer-generated design."

"That's an ammonite, an ancient sea shell from a hundred and forty-five million years ago. I found it rattling around in a drawer in the museum."

"Wow. That's old." Holly turned the phone sideways and peered at the spiral shell.

"Enlarge the picture and look at it closely."

Holly put her fingers on the screen and zoomed into the shell. "Oh, I see. It has some marks on it. It's been damaged. What happened there?"

"I don't think it's damaged. Swipe to the next picture."

Holly swiped. "What am I looking at?"

"That's a close-up micrograph. Those scratches you saw are exactly midway between the ridges that mark each chamber of the shell. They were scored into the original shell. They're not cuts in the fossil's minerals. The marks themselves are fossilized."

"Okay, what does that mean?

"It means the original ammonite shell was marked that way, not the fossil. The marks were made in the Jurassic period, millions of years ago."

Holly looked up. "But how could that be? There weren't any people back then, were there?"

"No. It was the age of the dinosaurs."

"So you think dinosaurs made these marks?"

"It's possible."

"A tool-using dinosaur? It would need to have hands."

"Some of them had hands with opposable digits."

"I guess T-Rex did. But they'd have to be smart too."

"And maybe use language."

Holly stared at Robin for a moment then looked back down at the phone.

"Language? I can't get my head around that. Talking dinosaurs?"

"You know the dinosaurs were all wiped out by that rain of asteroids. A shame, really. Imagine what they could have done."

"What an idea." Holly swiped back to the picture of the spiral-shelled ammonite. "But if dinosaurs talked, wouldn't they have invented the wheel or something? I mean what use is having language if you don't use it to do things?"

"I don't know. This is preliminary thinking. Just a hypothesis I'm exploring."

"It's a mindblower, I can tell you that."

Robin looked up the expression quickly in her database, got diverted into information about leaf blowers but found nothing on mind blowers.

"Yes it is," she said, just to be agreeable.

They sat in the dimming gold light of the late afternoon, each lost in thought, each appreciating the other's way of thinking, the other's interests, their shared understanding of language, neither saying anything.

Chapter Ten

Back at work in Austin, Robin posted a query to the online site of the Museum Researchers of America, used worldwide by natural history museums. She asked about the presence of scratched, scored, or otherwise defaced fossils in collections dating from the Jurassic period. She posted a picture of her ammonite shell as an example and said she was doing a research project on defaced fossils. That would not seem unreasonable in the museum research community. Academics will study absolutely anything.

It didn't take long. In a few days, Robin had reports of damaged fossils but most had missed the point of her question. She wasn't interested in broken bones and cracked specimens because those were par for the course in paleontology. Things got broken. And she didn't care about bones that showed signs of scavenging by other animals. And there were plenty of reports of drilled and polished fossils. Often, people stupidly tried to make jewelry or decorations out of ancient bones.

But one message caught her eye. It was from somebody at the Perot Museum in Dallas who said he had found in his collection a damaged femur from a late Cretaceous *Troodon*, a smallish bird-hipped dinosaur. There was nothing remarkable in that, except the writer said the marks looked like deliberate, regular incisions as if the bone had been vandalized by a human. *Exactly on target*, Robin thought. There was an attached picture.

She opened the picture and zoomed in with her fingers to see the incisions on the femur up close. They were even, in a row, almost like a long bar code, cut at right angles to the axis of the bone. They weren't evenly spaced but appeared in clusters, each larger than the last, like waves moving down the bone. They did look like human marks. Even at the maximum magnification where the pixels started to break out, the incisions did not look recent. They looked just as fossilized as the rest of the bone. Like her marked ammonite shell.

She replied immediately, thanked the writer, somebody named Nick Marsh, and asked if she could see the specimen the next day. Marsh said he would be delighted to share with a colleague.

Dallas was a tedious two-hour drive, but that was better than the half-hour flight from Austin because of the inevitable delay she would face at airport security. She prepared for an early morning departure, planning to beat the Austin rush hour.

Nick Marsh, an intern paleontologist at the Perot Museum, had finished his junior year in environmental archeology at the nearby University of North Texas, but he projected mastery as if he already had a Ph.D., years of experience, and was in charge of the museum's whole fossil collection. Nobody was around to contradict him. Robin sized him up. His tender age of about twenty-five gave away his pretension, but otherwise, he put up a good impression of a weathered field researcher. He had a brown beard that continued down his neck and into his shirt. The steel-rimmed, circular glasses were a nice touch, as was the khaki shirt with epaulets and button-down breast pockets. He was a self-parody but enthusiastic and talkative.

Robin quickly determined that listening was not one of Marsh's strong points, so she didn't say much. She learned how to guide him by asking questions and letting him pontificate. That's how she gradually managed him to the research drawers and to the inscribed femur she was interested in.

"*Troodon* is a Cretaceous bird-hipped dinosaur," he lectured as she put on thin white cotton gloves to pick up the fossil bone. "Maybe a meter high and fifty kilos but a very fast animal. We have a fully mounted skeleton I can show you. Huge legs. It might have looked like today's roadrunner only five times the size."

Robin picked up the bone and brought it close to her face. The lines were clearly visible, and it was obvious that they had been deliberately cut into the bone. No natural process could have made such straight, vertical incisions. And the pattern was not random. It couldn't have been the result of a predator or any kind of erosion. She wanted to see the cuts at magnification.

"Can we put this under a binocular scope? Do you have one of those?"

"Do we have one? We have one of the best binocular microscopes in the State of Texas. Follow me."

Robin put the femur on a padded tray and put it on a wheeled cart. She pushed the gray-steel trolley along while Intern Marsh led them to the other side of the shiny, sterile lab that seemed more like it was for medicine than fossils.

Talking the whole time, Marsh mounted the femur on the instrument's stage and started up the projection system.

"The image will display here," he said, pointing to a large monitor mounted on a jointed steel arm.

Robin looked into the eyepieces and adjusted the focus as Marsh continued babbling. He was his own audience.

"*Troodontids* had three fingers on each hand, one opposable, so it could have grasped and held objects. That's consistent with its large brain-to-body ratio and a cerebrum-to-brain ratio of over thirty-two percent. Very intelligent animal."

Why did he have all this information on the tip of his tongue? Nobody carries around details like that in short-term memory. He must have looked it up this morning and now was casting it off casually as if he were the world expert on *Troodons*. Strange fellow.

The femur was even stranger. As Robin had suspected and hoped, under magnification it looked like the incisions in the bone were fully fossilized over the same time the bone itself had been. They could not have been human marks. The human species would not appear on the planet for another seventy-five million years. She stood and looked at the image on the screen.

"Is it possible to capture that image in a file I can take with me?"

"Absolutely." Marsh touched a green button on the instrument's control panel then raised his hand up with a flourish as if he had played a cadenza in a piano concert.

"Great, thanks."

Robin got her pictures downloaded to a flash drive that Intern Marsh graciously provided. She thanked him for his excellent, well-informed work and struggled to terminate the meeting and extricate herself. She promised to stay in touch and declined to examine the restored skeleton of an Alaskan *Troodon Formosus*, claiming she had a flight to catch. Marsh ignored that contingency and continued to offer extensive tours of the facilities, but eventually, he let her escape.

On the long drive back to Austin, Robin was lost in thought. Humans had not made the marks on the femur. Only one answer was reasonable. Dinosaurs did it, tool-using, symbolic-thinking, language-using dinosaurs. How could they not be language users with that level of abstraction?

Of course it could have been another animal. Just because it was a dinosaur bone didn't mean dinosaurs made the marks. Who else was around in the Cretaceous? It was still the age of dinosaurs. It had to be a dinosaur.

And what did the inscriptions mean? The incisions could have been meaningless doodles. They were laid out deliberately, though, like tally marks. Was the bone an accounting record? Did dinosaurs have an economy? The pattern looked like a count of something over a time span. Maybe it was a calendar.

The ammonite shell with the five lines between the segments had been dated to just before the big bang of the Mexican asteroid. This femur was from ten or eleven million years earlier, so she could imagine that dinosaurs had been making deliberate inscriptions for millions of years, on all kinds of shells and bones. It was an incredible idea.

Shouldn't the dinosaurs have developed more sophistication over all that time, at least pictures, or an alphabet? she thought. As Holly had said, why didn't they invent the wheel? Eleven million years is plenty of time to evolve beyond hash marks on a bone. If they were far enough along in their thinking to be counting, wouldn't there also be remains of dinosaur temples or palaces? Jewelry or graves? Stone tablets carved with grand claims? *My name is Troodon, king of kings. Look on my works, ye mighty, and despair!*

She realized such speculation sounded like pure fantasy, but she had evidence, solid scientific evidence. Not of dinosaur palaces but definitely of some kind of higher cognitive ability that no one else had discovered. She didn't know anything about dinosaur psychology. Maybe dinosaurs just weren't interested in building things. It was difficult to visualize dinosaurs building a ziggurat or starting a fire. They were lizards. They scurried, or ran, or perhaps leaped about. They laid eggs in the dirt. They lived in holes. If only there were more evidence.

She blinked at highway signs directing her to the cutoff for Austin. She'd talk to Andy as soon as she got home.

She drove into Austin in the late afternoon and headed straight to Andy's office on campus. She had texted him earlier that they needed to meet and had sent him pictures of the *Troodon* femur.

She was in his office at four-thirty and had to linger in the hallway for a few minutes while he dealt with students whose concerns could not wait. Eventually, he waved her in and closed his office door. She sat in the chair next to his desk where supplicants presented themselves. He swiveled his black, mesh-back chair to face her.

"So, were you impressed by the markings on the femur?" she said.

"More than impressed. Do you know what it means?"

"I'm convinced the marks were cut when the bone was new. They're just as fossilized as the rest of it, so some animal used tools and made meaningful marks at least seventy million years before humans came along."

"Aha," Andy said, smiling and leaning his chair back. "Then you didn't see it."

"See what?"

"The pattern in the marks."

"I noticed that. I thought the lines were tallies of some kind, frequency counts grouped by time period."

"Did you transcribe the counts in each group to Arabic numbers?"

"No."

"I did."

"And?"

Andy opened a folder and pushed a printout of one of the pictures toward her. Beneath the lines on the bone, he had written the count of lines in each group. He pointed and read the list off to her.

"One line here. Then a space and another line. Then a pair, then a group of three, then five, then eight, and thirteen. Are you tracking? If the pattern continued on the other side of the bone, how many lines would we see there?"

"Twenty-one," she said in a flat, stunned voice. She looked up at him then back to the picture. "This is incredible. Nobody knew the Fibonacci series seventy-five million years ago. There was nobody around to know it." She looked up from the picture again for an explanation.

"Right. I first thought that proved the markings were modern," Andy said, "but I examined the micrographs closely, and I agree with your assessment. They are part of the fossilized bone. My guess is the marks are Campanian, mid- to late-Cretaceous. Very old."

"But who did it? Dinosaurs were experimenting with number theory? It's incongruous."

"Could have been any animal living at that time."

"There was hardly anyone else around. Dinosaurs dominated the earth. A few miserable insect-eating mammals lived in burrows. Small brains, no opposable fingers."

"Those mammals went on to become humans, so we shouldn't rule them out."

"Those little rodents were too small to move one of these dinosaur bones, let alone work a tool big enough to make a mark on one."

"I know, it isn't likely. In any case, based on what we do know, this is a significant finding."

"A mind blower," Robin said.

Andy furrowed his brow at the expression but didn't say anything else. He reached for a bottle of water on his desk and unscrewed the top.

Robin stood and paced in a small circle.

"Whoever did it, that animal belonged to a species that made it all the way to the end of the Cretaceous era and the big meteor."

"How do you conclude that?"

"Because of the marked ammonite shell, remember that? It dates from about the time of the extinction event. It's the same kind of deliberate marking as on this femur."

"The marks on the ammonite shell were individual marks, not a pattern like this. They were just—oops, omigosh, you're right. I get it. An ammonite shell is a Fibonacci series. This is incredible."

"That's what I explained to Holly, my friend in D.C. From the tiny center of the ammonite shell the segments spiral out, and each succeeding chamber is larger. After every quarter turn in the spiral, the cross-sectional radius of the shell increases in area to the next number in the Fibonacci sequence. Probably pure coincidence, but there it is. Math in nature."

"That explains why the marks were exactly between the segments. Whatever the Fibonacci number series meant to those scribes, they recognized the series in the shell pattern and marked it. It means the knowledge of the Fibonacci series must have been transmitted in some culture across ten million years."

"The pattern is common in nature. You see it in pine cones, sunflower seeds and pineapples. Any cognitively advanced animal might have noticed it."

"Except there were no pineapples sixty-five or seventy-five million years ago. No sunflowers either. Maybe pine cones. Definitely ammonite shells. I don't know. It wouldn't have been an obvious pattern you would see every day. Somebody had to notice it, and somebody had to abstract the observation into number theory, deduce it, marvel at it, play with it."

"Any individual who could do that would be part of a culture that would have known about the number line, and arithmetic. Geometry too, judging from the shell markings."

"And almost certainly language, because how else would you transmit the knowledge across the generations?"

Andy spun his chair a full revolution and stopped it facing Robin again. She was still standing. "Please sit. You're distracting."

She sat. "According to Chomsky, the heart and soul of language is recursion. That's what makes it different from signaling systems. Recursion, applying a rule over and over again to get more."

"An algorithm."

"Like prepositions. You can make an infinite number of sentences with them. You just keep applying embedded qualifiers. I saw the cat. I saw the cat in the hat. I saw the cat in the hat on the mat."

Andy held up a palm. "Okay, got it." He smiled. "You're right. The Fibonacci series is the essence of recursion. You add the previous two numbers to get the next one then repeat that, on and on."

"On and on forever. These dinosaurs must have had the concept of infinity."

"If it was the dinosaurs." Andy swigged from his water bottle and put the cap back on. "That is a really difficult idea for a dinosaur. Infinity? It's a difficult idea for most humans. Where are the dinosaur songs about infinity? The legends? Artwork on rocks? Something would have been passed along culturally. I can't make this information fit a reasonable pattern."

Robin stood abruptly.

"The evidence is plain in front of our eyes in these photographs. Somebody did it. So what do we do with this information?"

"With those photographs, you could publish a speculative paper in a journal. *The Journal of Archaeology* would take it."

"Then what? It would either be ignored, or it would create a scientific uproar."

"You'd be famous."

"That is one thing I do not want. We're supposed to blend in, not stand out."

"You could leak the whole project to somebody. Like that fellow in Dallas who has the *Troodon* femur. Let him be famous. That would get the information out into the scientific community."

"He's not capable of understanding it. He has no linguistics background. He thinks the bone was scratched by a modern human."

"Hmm. Let's think on it for a while." He stood from his chair.

"We'll think recursively," Robin said. "Call me tomorrow."

Chapter Eleven

The morning was already drifting toward noon by the time Holly was clinking around her tiny kitchen preparing breakfast for herself and Robin. Robin sat at the kitchen table and watched. "You're the guest," Holly had said. "The guest does not make her own breakfast."

"We could go out someplace," Robin said. "I hate to see you work like this."

"I love doing it. Besides, you can't go out on a Sunday morning. Every restaurant in the city is full to capacity with an hour-long waitlist. Everybody and their cousin goes out to breakfast on Sunday."

"Why?"

"My theory is that people want to luxuriate in an abundance of time. You have no deadlines on a Sunday morning. It's a kind of wallowing in time."

"Wasting time to convince yourself you have plenty of it, which you don't because the clock never stops ticking. Humans are strangely ambivalent about time, don't you think?"

"Do you like blueberries?"

"Love them. Can I at least get the plates?"

Holly seemed to be in her own trance-like state, happy to be with Robin in her cheery Georgetown kitchen, making food for the two of them. She spoke into a mixing bowl as she cracked eggs.

"I was thinking this morning. About touch. Why it's thrilling to touch another person." She paused, and Robin thought maybe Holly blushed. She waited, and Holly continued.

"I mean, not to get all clinical or anything, but have you ever noticed that every touch is a double touch?"

"No. I don't get that."

"When you touch someone, you mean something by it. You reach out and touch, and it's like, *I'm here, and you're there. We're both here.* I'm not explaining it very well."

Robin sipped coffee, not following but hoping to learn something.

"So what I mean is, you feel the other person on your fingers at the same time you feel the other person's skin. That's why it's double. Your fingers and the other's skin. You feel outward and inward at the same time. That's not true for vision or hearing or any other sense. Touching says *me and you* all at once. Have you ever noticed that?"

Robin was baffled. "Can't say that I have. We have similar bodies and experience. When we touch someone, we assume it gives the other person sensations. But you only feel your own fingers. You can't feel what another person feels."

"No, that's what I'm saying, you get feedback to your fingers, but you're also literally feeling the other person, not just your fingers. That's what's magical about it." Holly's voice trailed off, and she began whisking eggs vigorously.

"Magical? I don't know about that. When you speak to someone, you also hear what you say, so in a way, that's similar, isn't it?"

"Similar, I guess. But so much less..." She took the whisk from the bowl and put it in the sink. "You can't be sure what the other person hears because language is abstract. Touch isn't abstract."

Robin stood and walked over to a kitchen cabinet. She opened it, looking for dishes and glassware. She took out two plates. "All experience is private. We can only guess about the other person."

"I disagree. When it comes to touching someone, you know because the boundary is so close and for every caress and squeeze you give the other person, you also have the feeling on your own skin and muscles, so the two of you are actually sharing in the same thing. Don't you experience it that way?"

Robin didn't. She knew why she didn't. She was in dangerous territory with this conversation. Holly didn't know that Newcomers had only a simulated subjectivity, not a genuine sense of self. That was according to Jennifer. A Newcomer could act as if she understood the other person's experience. Humans liked it when you pretend that you did. *I feel your pain*, they say all the time to each other. Jennifer had explained many times how humans can be inter-subjective, actually co-experience each other's feelings and emotion, but Robin didn't believe it.

How was it possible? There was no mechanism for experiencing what another person was experiencing. Experience is private because the sense organs are private and bodies are private. One body per person, one person per body. That was the rule. Therefore you couldn't possibly know another person's experience.

She wasn't going to argue about this with Holly, who clearly believed in the same crazy idea Jennifer did, that people could sometimes literally share an experience.

"Intimacy is a mystery," Robin said, hoping that would seem like a good reply.

"Yes it is," Holly said. "Next cupboard," she added, directing Robin to the glassware. "I'm glad I met you, Robin." Holly paused from her work to look straight into her eyes.

Robin smiled. It was a good relationship. "I feel the same way, Holly."

"Almost ready."

At Holly's insistence, they went shopping after breakfast. The Christmas season was a perplexing retail orgy that seemed to cause the human brain to go crazy for two or three weeks.

Robin was happy to be away from the university campus, away from work, and with Holly in Washington, D.C.

"Normally you can't get much done on a Sunday," Holly said, "but during the Christmas season, everything's open. I love it."

They avoided the upscale malls and instead went to little shops and studios that Holly had discovered. Robin was, as always, mystified by the whole idea of buying arbitrary goods to wrap in paper and give to someone.

"Nobody in your circle needs more stuff," Robin said. "Why do you do it?"

"My nephews want things. They're children. Children want things."

"That's because you've taught them greed."

Holly pulled open the door to a small candy store. "That's harsh, Robin. They're not greedy. It's not about the stuff. It's about the gift-giving. The present says *I thought of you and here is a token to show it.*"

Robin entered, and Holly followed.

"You could just say that and skip the token."

"It wouldn't be the same."

Robin sampled a tiny square of caramel fudge from a tray. "Wow, this is really good. Almost as good as mothballs."

Holly laughed. "Mothball-flavored fudge? I don't think it would sell." Robin took another fudge sample.

"I could buy you a box of it as a Christmas gift," Holly said.

Robin looked at her and smiled. "Touché."

Walking through the chill air back to the subway, Robin carried her box of caramel fudge and told Holly about the marks she had found on the dinosaur femur and her amazement that a dinosaur could have done such a thing.

"This is like that seashell you talked about last time, isn't it?"

"The same idea."

"What if monkeys were walking around way back then, but we just don't know about them?" Holly said, her words puffing little clouds in front of her face. "That's who might have done it."

"We would have found bones for such an animal."

They rode the smooth escalator deep down into the earth and used their day passes to walk out onto the platform where they waited among the dense crowd in the overly bright cavern.

"Maybe there is no reasonable explanation," Holly said. "What about that?"

"There has to be an explanation. Everything has an explanation. The Fibonacci series was a natural occurrence in the dinosaur world. Pine cones, sea shells, the pattern of fiddlehead ferns. You can see the same pattern in spiral galaxies, not that dinosaurs would have noticed the galaxies."

"That's it! Galaxies," Holly said. "The markings weren't made by dinosaurs. They were made by extraterrestrial aliens from another galaxy."

Robin laughed. "I guess you need a special talent for free-association to write speeches for politicians. Aliens!" She laughed again. "It makes about as much sense as any other idea at this point."

"Here it comes," Holly said as they were blasted by a rush of cold air from the tunnel as the train for Foggy Bottom came whooshing toward them.

"Do you worry about safety in the subway?" Robin said.

"You mean because of the bombing? No. The police say we shouldn't worry. The subways are safe."

"Well, of course they would say that. Their job is to protect the merchant class and the Christmas shopping season. But what about the terrorists? They might not see things that way."

"You shouldn't worry about what you can't control. Anyway, they have suspects now. A Vietnamese gang."

"Vietnamese? What do they want?"

"I don't know. Don't worry about it."

The conversation was cut short as the crowd exiting the train dwindled and it was time for Holly and Robin to rush onboard.

The day before she was scheduled to go back to Austin, Robin enjoyed an afternoon by herself at the Library of Congress. Holly was forced—that's how she put it, forced—to attend a Christmas party involving co-workers. Robin asked what kind of a party would force you to attend. Holly said she was sure Robin knew perfectly well and was just teasing her.

"I know you've gone to social functions you didn't want to," Holly said. "It sustains the illusion that we're not wage slaves but a happy community of friends who work together."

"Who believes that?"

"Well, nobody does, but you need the illusion. Otherwise you could get embittered, and that would be no good."

"Maybe the same logic explains the Christmas fantasy and the illusion that all is well. Everybody is enjoying economic prosperity, food and drink, goodwill, religious satisfaction, family happiness, free time. With shiny baubles everywhere and elves, too. Nobody believes it, but everyone desperately wants to. Am I close?"

"Honestly, Robin, you sometimes sound like you're from another planet."

"Maybe I am."

They pressed together and kissed lightly on the lips, and Robin went out, wishing Holly good luck at her party.

Robin sat in the Jefferson Reading Room and marveled at the grand open space and the classical architecture. It was more like a church than a library, she thought. She used the free Wi-Fi to find the catalog on her phone and browsed for anything about archaeological artifacts that showed symbolic markings. The painted caves in southern France and Spain were well-represented, but those pictures were made by modern humans, fifteen to thirty thousand years ago, practically yesterday in evolutionary time. She wondered if anybody had ever found anything like what she had, deliberate incisions on artifacts from millions of years before humans. The Library of Congress wasn't the best place to be looking for archeology. She'd do better browsing the UT library's collection when she got home.

She was about to give it up and head over to see a special exhibit on the Dead Sea Scrolls, when one entry popped up that seemed interesting. It was a book, *Homo Symbolicus: The Dawn of Language, Imagination, and Spirituality.* It described archeological finds from seventy-seven thousand years ago in a cave in South Africa. That was still the modern era, nothing to do with dinosaurs. Still, they would be quite old artifacts from some of the earliest humans. She got up and went to a librarian and started the process of requesting the book, which meant first getting a library card.

It was a large, heavy book with detailed pictures of ancient artifacts found in the Blombos Cave near Cape Town. She was particularly interested in pieces of ochre that had been inscribed with a crosshatch pattern. Ochre, a rock containing a lot of rust, was used for drawing red lines on walls and probably for smearing on bodies too. Scratching the stone with a sharp point would have left a bright red line in the dark patina of the mineral. That's exactly what somebody had done thousands of years ago.

The *x*-marks were in a horizontal row and touching, making a nice pattern. Horizontal lines above and below it made a frame for the whole display. This wasn't just any old stone with scratches on it. You don't put a frame around your marks unless they mean something. The scientists cited in the book would only admit that they indicated 'symbolic intention.'

Robin counted the *x*s just in case they formed a numerical pattern, but they didn't. Over eight thousand pieces of ochre had been found, the book said, fifteen of them engraved. She paged through the clear, colored photographs on shiny paper.

She stopped browsing at another close-up of an engraved ochre stone, also long and thin, smaller, cut in the same pattern with a row of *xs*. She counted the marks. Five. That fragment was also broken off at the ends like the other. She wished there was some way to cut out the two photographs and put them side by side. She stood up and took a picture with her phone, straight down. Then she paged back to the previous shot of the larger engraved ochre stick and took a photo of that, too. She couldn't manage to get the two images side-by-side on her phone display. She'd have to do it on her computer, which was back at Holly's place. She made photographs of the book's cover, title and copyright pages and returned it to the librarian's desk.

The crowds of holiday shoppers were thicker than before, but she fought her way to the subway and back to Holly's apartment. The day was almost gone, and late afternoon darkness had condensed in the sky by the time she got there. The door was locked, and no one answered the doorbell. Holly was still out.

Robin took the elevator back down to the entry foyer and walked into an alcove with a silvery wall of aluminum mailboxes. She felt for a key along the narrow ledge that ran across the top of the boxes. She detected several keys up there. The one she wanted was near the corner. It was a common way to stash an emergency door key. They were not well-hidden, although you had to know to look up there. A thief could take them, but wouldn't know what doors they went to. It would be impractical and risky to try every key in every door of the building, so while not perfect, it wasn't a bad backup system.

Robin let herself into Holly's apartment, hung up her coat and scarf and retrieved her laptop from her luggage, which was mostly packed to go. She was scheduled to leave for Texas in the morning. At the kitchen table, she opened her computer and connected her phone, uploading the pictures she had taken at the library.

It took a little work with an image-processing program to get the two pictures of the cross-hatched ochre fragments similarly sized and lined up side-by-side. Not quite sure of what she was doing or why, she nudged the two images closer, merging them until the end of one almost touched the end of the other. She lifted her fingers from the keypad and stared at the screen. Some pieces were missing, but it was plain that these two pieces of ochre had once been a single piece. They fit together like Brazil into the coastline of West Africa.

Seeing them lined up like that showed what the original pattern of *xs* had been. A group of five, a space, and then a group of eight. The fifth and sixth numbers in the Fibonacci series. Coincidence? She computed the probability using several assumptions. Too unlikely to be a coincidence.

Were early humans aware of the Fibonacci series at least seventy-seven thousand years ago? Was that believable? Why were there no Fibonacci patterns on the cave walls at Lascaux? Had the knowledge been forgotten?

What if the idea of the Fibonacci sequence had been implanted in the brain of early humans without their understanding? A person would try to express the idea, not knowing what it means. That's why there is no advanced culture to go along with the abstract idea because it wasn't an abstract idea. It wasn't an idea at all. It was a subliminal urge. Robin knew that humans often claimed to "know things without knowing them." She didn't have any comparable experience like that. It was supposedly a characteristic of human psychology.

Could that also explain the scratches on the dinosaur femur? The reptiles wouldn't have to know what the marks meant. They would have the subliminal notion stuck in their head and then had the urge to express it. Pure instinct. Like building a nest. The birds do not have a blueprint in mind when they construct the nest. An instinct is an urge, not an idea. It has no related theories or language. No culture or artifacts would follow from it. It was just a particular impetus to do this one thing, express the Fibonacci sequence. That would account for the numerical pattern but no cultural artifacts to go with it.

It made sense to separate the fact of the Fibonacci inscriptions from the understanding of them. Except how did it work? How could a class of animals get such a complex numerical urge stuck in their brain in the first place? The hypothesis wasn't completely impossible, but it was radically incomplete, she decided.

Robin looked again at the pictures on her screen. She closed her research windows and opened email and wrote a message to Andy.

Subject: The Fibonacci Situation

Andy: New information. Could be important. I need to tell Jennifer right away.

The front door opened, and Holly burst loudly into the kitchen, slamming the door shut with her shoulder.

"Hey, Holly! What's up?" Robin said and then became concerned. "Holly?"

Holly took off her coat and tossed it to the living room chair but missed and landed on the floor. She smiled and stepped over the crumpled wrap and lurched into the kitchen where she grabbed Robin's head in both her hands and pulled her face into her bosom. Robin pulled back and shook her head.

"Holly. What's wrong with you? Are you drunk?"

"Hey, it was an afternoon party. I survived the party. What can I say? What have you been up to while I've been out doing my patriotic duty?"

She glanced over Robin's shoulder at the computer screen. Her expression changed into a frown.

"Who's Andy?" she said.

Robin turned and looked at the unsent email message still on the screen. She closed the lid, putting the computer to sleep.

"He's a guy I work with at U.T. Archaeology."

"You have a situation with him?"

"What? No."

"It said there was a situation."

"Oh, that's just some research we're working on."

"Who's Jennifer?"

"She's my, a very close friend."

"Really? How long have you known her?"

Holly stood about two feet in front of Robin and swayed like a reed in a wind. She stepped unsteadily around the table and sat in a chair and stared at Robin, waiting for an answer.

"A couple of years. Jennifer is somebody I work with on technical matters."

"You keep secrets from her? You and Andy do?"

Robin glanced at the closed computer then turned back to Holly.

"No, not normally, but this is a special situation. Andy and I haven't told her about some new findings."

"How old is she?"

"I'm not sure. Maybe forty."

"Is she beautiful?"

"What an odd question. Jennifer is attractive in her own way. Korean-American is her type."

"So you like the exotic look, do you? Is she prettier than me?"

"Holly, you're drunk. This is nonsense."

"Is she?"

"It's not a contest, Holly. Everybody is who they are."

"Does she have nicer breasts than mine?"

"Are you twelve years old? Get a grip. You want some water?"

Robin stood and went to the kitchen cupboard and retrieved a glass.

"She does, doesn't she? Don't lie to me."

"You know I don't lie, Holly."

And it was true. Newcomers didn't lie, because it was too much trouble. It was hard enough to discern what another person was probably thinking, based on the social situation and the connections among their words. If you started adding false statements into the conversation, you had no hope of guessing what they were thinking, and that made understanding any sentence extremely difficult.

"Well, does she have big breasts?"

Robin sighed. "Jennifer has large breasts, okay? Are you satisfied?" Robin brought a glass of water over to the table and set it in front of Holly, who ignored it.

"I knew it! Has she seen you naked?"

"What kind of a question is that? I won't answer it."

"Has she? Tell me. You've been naked with her, haven't you?"

"Not in the way you're thinking. It was necessary. It's impossible to explain."

"Oh, yes, I'm sure it was very necessary. Do you still see this Jennifer?"

Robin stared, bewildered, not knowing how to proceed.

"You do. You're still seeing her, aren't you?"

"It's nothing personal, really. I see her for technical discussions from time to time. I work with her. It's like seeing a doctor. You're being silly."

"So you and your boyfriend Andy, do the three of you stand around naked and discuss technical things? Is that how it is?"

"He's not my boyfriend, I told you. This is ridiculous, Holly. You're drunk. Why don't you take a nap?"

Holly hung her head, her chin resting on her necklace.

"I think you better go, Robin. Leave me."

Robin moved over close to her and put her hand on Holly's shoulder.

"Holly…"

Holly shrugged the hand off her shoulder. "Leave me," she repeated firmly. "I don't want you here anymore."

"Holly?" Her friend sat motionless, like a statue. She couldn't really mean it, literally get out of the house? Robin tried to bend down and look up into Holly's face, get a conversation going again. Holly was immobile.

Well, this is awkward, Robin thought. She stood and looked around the kitchen then back to the immobile Holly. She picked up her computer and went into the bedroom to get her carry-on bag.

Chapter Twelve

Robin stayed overnight at a hotel next to Washington National then flew back to Austin the following day. Air travel was actually becoming easier since the aphasia epidemic had devastated the ranks of the TSA. The people remaining on duty were inexperienced, and standards had become laughably lax. The whole airport security circus always was for show, Robin believed, a public display to make travelers feel better and to protect revenue in the vital airline industry. With the worldwide pandemic still spreading, terrorism was the least of anybody's worries.

Waiting for her plane, Robin tried several times to call Holly, but didn't make a connection. She sent a text: *Call me.*

In Austin, after finding her car, she headed to town but exited the freeway so she could stop at a bakery. It was difficult for Newcomers to find quick energy on the go. She and Andy didn't particularly need protein since they had no muscles to sustain. Sugar and carbohydrate were what they wanted, for quick, usable energy, and that meant bakeries, breakfast diners and pasta joints. Burger and chicken places were the most plentiful fast food but not very useful for a Newcomer. She found a Mexican bakery, stopped, then continued to her rendezvous.

Her parking spot was under a bridge over the Colorado River at Zilker Park, where she had arranged to meet Andy. Just after noon, she was only five minutes late. She took her bag of pastries and two sodas and walked to the Dino Pit at the Nature Center, a sand-filled area in the park where kids could dig for buried cement 'dinosaur bones.' Only one family was there, with two little girls digging away, though it was a sunny sixty-degree afternoon. Most people were frenetically shopping this time of year, not digging for bones. Andy was sitting on a bench, watching the kids. She sat beside him.

"Conchas," she said, handing him a brown paper bag. "I hope I didn't make you wait long."

"Not at all. Thanks." He peered into the bag to see the red and green holiday-colored bread-cookie snacks, took one out and handed the bag back to her. They watched the children and ate for a few minutes. Robin checked her phone. No messages.

"These are great. Thanks," Andy said. "So what's all this urgency about the Fibonacci thing?"

"Wait 'till you see this." She called up the photographs of the inscribed ochre fragments and handed her phone to him, explaining what he was seeing and what she thought it meant.

"I've heard of these," he said. "Not the Fibonacci pattern, but I'm aware of the inscribed ochres from the Blombos Cave. Marked-up eggshells and bones were found there too. This is from early modern humans, though before the caves in Europe."

"It can't be coincidence, can it? The Fibonacci series as a recurring pattern in the fossil record running over a hundred million years?"

"No," he said, frowning at Robin's photographs. "Can't be coincidence. I don't know what to make of it. What do you think it means?"

"I thought you'd ask. Here's my idea. Picture it. It's seventy-five million years ago, age of the dinosaurs, and the idea of the Fibonacci series becomes implanted in some animal's mind. Dinosaur, bird, it doesn't matter. The animals don't understand it, don't know what it means, but the number series is in their minds, a strange, mental fact that some individuals then try to express by inscribing it on objects. The culture doesn't have language and abstract thought, just this one strange urge to express this pattern in the world."

"Wait a minute. So you're saying the Fibonacci series of numbers is an unconscious idea? Do birds have an unconscious mind?"

"I'm not sure what *unconscious* means. It's a human thing. I've looked it up, and it's mysterious. It means something like having knowledge you don't know you have. Like being able to build a certain kind of nest. You don't have a plan or a blueprint, you just do it. It's built-in knowledge."

"An instinct. Like in birds."

"Like that. Humans have that, apparently. Maybe all animals do. So anyway, these dinosaur-era animals had the Fibonacci series planted in them as instinctive knowledge, and some of them tried to express it in the world. In humans, that knowledge eventually became conscious and therefore useful."

Andy waited a moment to make sure Robin was finished explaining.

"I have to say, that is a very low probability idea. And also, why would an animal have instinctive knowledge that was no use for survival or reproduction? What good is being able to write down a Fibonacci series? It has no evolutionary value."

"Not to the animal it doesn't. But what if it has some value to the idea itself?"

"That doesn't make sense. Explain."

"This is going to be difficult."

"Lay it on me, as the humans say."

"Okay, well — look." Robin pointed. "That little girl found a dinosaur bone."

One of the children was squealing in delight as she uncovered a large, cement femur.

"If only it were that easy."

Robin took the last pastry from the bag and held it up for Andy, who shook his head. She bit it in half. They watched as the mother waded into the sand pit and praised the girl and marveled with her over the huge concrete 'bone.'

"It's just pretend for that little girl, but she'll remember this day. It's good training. She might grow up to become a scientist."

"She probably will if her mother is taking her out to dig dinosaurs instead of going to the shopping mall."

"Enough about children. Let's talk mole-rats," Robin said.

"Mole-rats? Sure, I know them. So you've got a hypothetical Cretaceous-period mole-rat who unconsciously knows the Fibonacci sequence, useless knowledge that leads to nothing. Okay, carry on from there."

"That's where I introduce an arbitrary factor into my explanation to make everything fit. What if knowledge of the Fibonacci series was of extraterrestrial origin?"

Andy stared at her. "You're joking."

"Newcomers don't joke. Holly gave me the idea. As a joke."

Andy continued to stare at her and waited then said, "I'm sure you have more to tell me."

"That's basically it. When I say extraterrestrial, it doesn't have to be spacemen in rocket ships landing on earth."

"Good."

"It could have been a chemical or molecule or even a bit of DNA on a comet or meteorite. Some people think that's how life originated on earth."

"Panspermia theory."

"Right. So if living molecules are flying through space, why couldn't it be some snippet of bio-code from another civilization? The probability is non-zero."

"It would have to be complex DNA material. A few carbon molecules wouldn't do much."

"It could be DNA or RNA. We don't know what's out there. Or it could be methyl compounds that form the epigenome around an existing DNA set. There isn't one gene for language, so an epigenetic solution could hit the existing genes like piano keys."

"And produce language just by chance?"

"Or on purpose, if that's what it was meant to do."

"So you're saying knowledge of the Fibonacci series is like an infection, like a virus that infected certain animals?"

"A virus. I like that."

"And some animals caught the language disease from it."

"They would carry it around like a latent disease in their genomes and once in a while that gene sequence would express itself in the world. That's why producing the Fibonacci series of numbers on an ammonite shell or a dinosaur femur doesn't imply very much. It doesn't mean the animals were language users and abstract thinkers and that's why we don't see their grand civilizations. They didn't build any."

"The humans did."

"They're the only ones."

Andy stood, looked around the park, and walked a few paces along the sandy path then turned and came back to the bench.

"This Fibonacci virus, as you've described it, would have to be encoded into human DNA for it to be transmitted over the generations."

"Transposons. DNA segments that originate in viruses and bacteria and basically worm their way into the genome. About half of human DNA is made of transposons. That would account for all those millions of years when the alien virus was around but wasn't very active. Takes time, a lot of time to get set up in the right genome."

"Why does it have to be from outer space? Why not an ordinary virus of terrestrial origin?"

"Because, just as you said, there is no evolutionary benefit for a dinosaur or any other animal to know the Fibonacci series. Not even for early humans. It's a mental object entirely out of sync with the pace of evolution on this planet. It obviously doesn't belong. An advanced idea in number theory during the Jurrasic Period is discordant with everything we know about life on Earth. Therefore, it must have come from some other planet. It's a premise that accounts for the observed data."

"Incredible."

Andy paced away from the bench then back again several times. The woman with the two girls in the dino pit kept a wary eye on him. He came up to Robin again and stopped in front of her.

"Okay answer this. Why not chimpanzees or kangaroos? Why did homo sapiens end up with language?"

"The transposon splice didn't take in the others. It had to be just the right genetic environment."

"You have all the answers, don't you? So you're saying this DNA or RNA fragment was hanging around, waiting for the right animal to come along and give it a good home where it could flourish."

"Ultimately, the right animal was homo sapiens. That's my theory. Dinosaurs didn't last long enough. Birds couldn't handle it. Mole-rats, not right. Chimps, close, so close. Early hominids, maybe a few here and there, but not enough. Homo-sapiens, perfect."

"That is an absolute leaf blower."

"Mind blower."

Andy frowned then resumed his energetic pacing. The woman in the sandbox ushered her girls out of the pit and toward their belongings on a stone bench. They picked up their things, the woman glancing warily once over her shoulder as they left the park.

The Newcomers walked from the dino park toward their cars under the bridge.

"Have we just constructed a fantastic castle of theory out of a few found bricks?" Andy said. "Brick fragments, not even whole bricks."

"The facts are thin, but they're hard and sharp. We have fossils. That's solid evidence of complex, recursive, language-like thinking millions of years before humans. That's totally at odds with evolution on this planet. It's an outlier, an anomaly. Like finding a marble in your soup. Does not belong, cannot be normal."

"Fully developed human language is hard to explain, although we do see indicators here and there in evolution. Non-human animals solve problems and use complex signaling systems, from bees to elephants. There is an evolutionary track for language. It could possibly have evolved naturally on this planet, but we only see the end result, not the process."

"Bees don't talk. Birds don't sing. It's a qualitative difference. Language is not just a pattern of grunts and whistles. We're talking about the Fibonacci numbers, the essence of recursion, which is what language has and what bird-songs and bee-dances do not have."

"Marble in the soup."

"That's how it looks to me. Either the ability for language was inserted into evolution from some other source, some source not of this earth, or, we have fundamentally misunderstood the theory of evolution."

"Which is more likely?"

"That is a tough question."

"And don't forget the fact that language is extremely rare on Earth. Exactly one species out of eight million has it. A lot of animals have legs. Billions have eyes. Billions dig holes, build nests, swim, fly, and eat grass. Only one speaks a symbolic language. How is that not an anomaly? It cries out for special explanation."

Andy stared at his feet as they walked.

"Why do humans not see language as abnormal? In fact, the whole trajectory of human intelligence is bizarre. They go from stone-pounders to moon-walkers in the blink of an eye? Species don't do that. Language has driven a crazy burst of intelligence that flashes like a neon sign." He raised his hands and opened and closed his fingers rhythmically to show a flashing sign as he said, "Not from Earth."

Robin smiled. "The people are Earthlings, but their language isn't. And don't forget how children pick up language. That's another blinking sign. Children play and do whatever children do, and without anybody teaching them the rules. By age two they are chatterboxes. How does that happen? Children don't learn to walk upright without training. They don't learn to use a toilet without training. Somehow, all over the world, in all cultures, in all social classes, in all periods of history, all children, at just about the same age, start talking the language of their community without explicit training or practice. What are the odds of that? Does that look like a naturally evolved trait or something from outer space?"

Andy put up his hands again and flashed his finger-sign: *Not from Earth*.

They walked from the gravel path to Andy's vehicle and stopped by the driver's door. He didn't beep it.

"Maybe it's not that odd, though. Birds do it. Baby birds automatically sing the correct song for their species. They don't get musical training from mama and papa bird."

"That's not language. It's not even music. They don't even know what they're doing. It's instinctive behavior."

"Okay, I'll give you that. So we're back to an alien infection. A language infection from outer space. It's hard to accept, but okay, let's take it as a working hypothesis. How did this virus get here? Was it sent? Or did it arrive on the back of an ancient comet that just happened to be coming this way?"

"I favor the idea that these language spores or whatever we call them were released from somewhere, cast out on purpose to take root. Like broadcasting seeds. You don't know exactly where they're going to land, but you expect some of them to survive and flourish.

"These language seeds could have been random biological trash accidentally blown away from life on some planet in the universe."

"The Fibonacci series? That can't be random garbage. Why would a random sequence of DNA be that specific?"

"You have a point there," Andy said. "They, whoever they were, or are, would have selected that particular snippet on purpose. That means the DNA was released on purpose as a message. What's the message?"

"Hello, we exist."

He shook his head and stared at the asphalt they stood on. He beeped the car door with his key fob and looked up at Robin.

"It's too incredible. A message from an alien civilization. A long, complicated message. And people received it. Humans have been speaking and hearing and singing and chatting for thousands and thousands of years without recognizing that they're reciting a message from the stars?"

"The message is the capacity for language, not what they actually say with it. Humans are unaware that the ability to use language at all is extraordinary. They take it for granted."

Andy leaned against the door of his vehicle and looked up into the bat-infested concrete beams of the bridge. Then he seemed to have an idea and swiftly faced Robin.

"Fibonacci wasn't born until the twelfth century. Why wasn't his famous pattern recognized until then?"

"Cryptography takes time."

Andy smiled and shook his head.

"I guess that's true, especially if you don't know that's what you're doing. This is almost too much. You realize if this idea is right, it means the language virus was Earth's first contact with an alien civilization, and it happened many millennia in the past."

"A great irony, isn't it? Humans have been searching the skies with radio telescopes for a half-century looking for aliens, and all that time the telescopes have been pointed in the wrong direction."

"People will never believe it. I'm not sure if I believe it."

Robin turned to stand beside Andy and leaned back against the SUV, not eager to end the conversation even though it was getting dark.

"What do you think these aliens look like?" Andy said.

"Spirals."

"You mean pine cones, nautilus shells, sunflower seeds?"

"It's a thought."

"Spiral aliens. They sent selfies?"

"Okay, maybe not exactly. The pine cones were already here. Probably they're not spiral aliens. They're aliens who just happen to love spirals. They're spiral-obsessed beings who understand recursion. They're… Oh, my." She stopped and stared into the gloom settling under the bridge.

Andy turned to look at her face. "What?"

"It is a truly remote procedure call."

"Say it."

"The virus is not a message from anywhere. The virus is the ET."

Andy stared at her for a long moment.

"The aliens are here?"

"Language is not even human. It's a parasite living in the human. In the human genome."

Andy was silent for several seconds. "What an idea. It would be a benign parasite, though, like the bacteria in the human gut. Having parasites is not necessarily a bad thing. There are good parasites and bad ones."

"I wouldn't want any parasites living in me."

"Not even language? You'd rather be like all the other animals, squawking, barking and whistling?"

"I'd rather not be an animal at all. Animals are creepy."

"By definition."

"This is getting confusing." Robin stood up straight. It was dark and the temperature was dropping. "We need time to process."

"That we do," Andy said.

They agreed to meet the next morning at Javalina Café near the campus because it opened at five am. Robin walked to her car, and they drove off separately.

The two of them waited at the glass door until the young server unlocked it. Inside, they had to wait for the coffee to finish brewing. The early morning business was mainly at the drive-through window. Only a few customers were inside, early-bird runners and students. The Newcomers sat at a small wooden table against a window.

"Did you come up with anything last night?" Robin said.

"Only that the alien hypothesis still seems plausible when you look at all the facts. What about you?"

"I got fixated on the idea that you and I are products of the intellectual rocket ship that language enabled in humans. We wouldn't be here right now if it weren't for the language alien."

"I don't know what to make of that. I guess it's right. Kangaroos would never have invented androids no matter how much time went by. Only humans seem capable."

"Might be just as well. Imagine us as autonomous AI kangaroos."

"Robin?" The barista called out the readiness of their coffee order. Andy went to retrieve their for-here ceramic mugs.

"Thanks." Robin sipped and stared out into the parking lot. Cars, trucks, and SUVs lined up on the street for the drive-through window. She sipped in silence for a moment.

"We're completely alone, you and I," she said. "Alone on this planet."

"We are the only Newcomers, if that's what you mean. We were already alone."

"I always assumed a sort of camaraderie with Jennifer and Will and the folks at Paradise and the people we know. I thought of us as… I don't know, maybe like adopted members of a family. Part of the human family. We look like humans. We live like humans. We're supposed to be pass-fors."

"We look like everybody else except we don't harbor the parasite."

"For the first time, I feel like an alien among the humans." Robin tipped up her mug. "What are we going to do, Andy?"

"One idea, see what you think, instead of hiding our findings, we could just pull back the curtain on the wizard and say 'Hi!'"

"The wizard?"

"Of Oz. It's a cultural reference."

"Oh, right, right. Judy Garland. Loved the Tin Man. He was hilarious. But you can't mean it. How would that work? We go to Jennifer and say, 'We know your secret.' She doesn't even know her secret."

"That's a problem. Humans don't suspect that language is a parasite living inside them. They believe they're completely autonomous. Even Jennifer."

"Jennifer, Jennifer." Andy emptied his mug and put it down with a *bonk*. "Who is Jennifer? Who are we talking to when we talk to Jennifer?"

"The alien. We send language to a language-comprehension device inside Jennifer, the human ."

"Exactly. Where is the Jennifer part?"

Robin looked over to the busy coffee bar then turned back to Andy.

"There is a Jennifer. She is a human being. She has something to say. The language thing has to work through her humanity."

"So you're saying Jennifer is separate from the language beast."

"I can hardly guess. What must go on inside the human head?"

Andy crossed his arms over his chest and looked around the room. A group of three students was huddled around a table, clutching their paper cups, talking intensely and excitedly about something. Did they even know what they were saying?

"Who wrote the *Gettysburg Address*?" Andy said.

"I don't think you're looking for the obvious answer."

"Abraham Lincoln."

"You think so?"

"He was a person, and he had something to say. He made some marks on the back of an envelope then spoke. Those were his ideas riding on the alien's communication signal."

"You're saying the alien is like a television. The TV doesn't know what show is on. The show is separate from the TV."

"But without the TV, you don't see the show."

Robin raised her cup over the center of the table.

"To Abraham Lincoln!"

"Abraham Lincoln!" Andy echoed as their cups clinked. The group of students in the corner briefly turned to stare at them but lost interest immediately and returned to whatever life-gripping issues they had been dealing with.

The Newcomers lowered their cups.

Chapter Thirteen

Robin drove their rented Ford Fusion west on I-10 as Andy watched the featureless Chihuahuan scrub desert of West Texas slide by. It was a long drive from Austin to Los Angeles, but the sedan rode smooth as a sailboat, and the cabin was roomy, quiet, and comfortable. Traffic was thick on the I-10. They were not the only ones forced to the roads since the collapse of air transportation.

The aphasia epidemic had devastated the population and the economy to the point where experts in anything were scarce. Many industries could be populated with unqualified people after regular employees were hit with the virus and couldn't work anymore. In technical fields where communication was paramount, it just wasn't possible to continue without articulate experts to guide operations.

That's what had ended air travel. It wasn't possible for someone who couldn't communicate to function in the pilot's seat or in air traffic control. Even engine maintenance couldn't be done. A mute expert could read manuals and perform the work, but was unable to make any reports, oral or written, so the work was essentially useless. If the mechanic found and fixed a problem, or even if everything checked out okay, what use was the inspection and repair without records of it? The airline couldn't just assume everything was fine. And pilots certainly couldn't fly without language. Nothing worked. So with great economic ramifications, air transportation had shut down, and driving and trains were the only ways to travel across the country.

Even traveling on the ground, you needed someone articulate in your party to purchase gas in most places. Victims of the aphasia disease couldn't express their intentions to an automated gas pump. They could read but not select. Many stations near big cities had revived the job of gas station attendant who performed as they did in the 1950s, pumping your gas for you. The attendant would assume you came for gas and filled your tank and told you the cost. You paid whatever he said. No questions, no answers.

Though the traffic on the interstate was heavy with passenger vehicles, the big trucks that used to clog the highways had become rare. The economy had crashed so severely that it wasn't necessary to ship as many goods across the country on the roads. Grocery trucks were still around, but they tended to be regional, and you didn't see them much on the interstate. Trucks carrying pipes, equipment, cars, lumber, and cement were absent. Military convoys were rare. Recreational vehicles, those swaying behemoths of the highway, were no more. People were in survival mode.

The Newcomers drove in silence. Their car was equipped with satellite radio, but it had only three uninteresting channels. As with many complex technological systems, satellite radio practically ran itself until something went wrong and there was no one left at the company who could say how to fix it. Like much else in society that was once taken for granted, broadcast media quickly deteriorated to uselessness.

"Look, there's the exit for Van Horn," Robin said, pointing to a faded green sign over the highway. "That's where Holly's family is from."

"Your friend the speechwriter in D.C."

"Yeah, her..." Robin's voice trailed off, and she stared into the empty road ahead.

"Oh-oh. Trouble?"

"She's mad at me. I don't know what it is with humans, Andy. This jealousy thing. It's like they're unhappy unless they own you like a pet dog."

"Who's she jealous of?"

"You."

"Me?" he squawked. "That's ridiculous."

"And Jennifer. I mentioned Jennifer, and she was all over me. Who's Jennifer, how often do you see her, and on and on and things I don't even want to tell you."

"She doesn't know Jennifer. Or me either."

"That doesn't seem to matter. Jealousy is not fact-based. I can't follow it, and I can't predict it. Every time this has happened to me, I've been completely blindsided. I thought it was only men wanting to possess women. Now I know it's not just men."

"I could have told you that. I got the same treatment from Lucy."

"I had to learn it for myself, apparently."

"So what's going on between you two now?"

"She's in a pout. What is that?" Robin looked over with raised eyebrows. Andy didn't answer. "A pout," she repeated, looking at the road again and shaking her head. "It's so childish. I know it's a kind of communication, but I can't interpret it. What does it mean?"

"I think it means it's your turn. You're supposed to apologize, say you didn't want to offend; she's the only one for you, and so on. You have to show contrition. That's how I think it works."

"It's all so murky. Why can't humans just say what's on their minds?"

"I don't know. I've had the same experience. I don't know."

Robin sat up straight, as if she were shaking off the unsolved puzzle.

"Maybe there's a silver lining. Holly, before she went into her pout, gave me a good idea. She's on the team that writes speeches for the president, you know."

"That must be quite interesting."

"It's actually a little frightening once you know the details. The president ends up speaking her words not his own."

"I think most people understand that."

"Despite that, people assume he more or less says what he believes. According to Holly, he has no words of his own. None appropriate for a presidential speech, anyway. Speeches are not like ordinary language. She gives him words, and those become his speech words. He becomes a language puppet. He doesn't even know what he's saying."

"That sounds very Orwellian."

"It is. The speech is made up almost entirely of code words that have special meaning to certain groups and other politicians. You have to know the codes to understand what is really being said."

"The speech does seem to have superficial meaning on its own, though. Reporters report on it. Anybody can listen to it if they can stay awake."

"The surface structure is all details and ornaments. Empty rhetoric. Only the anointed are tuned into the underlying message."

"That's an amazing way to use language."

"Holly certainly opened my eyes. There's a subterranean world of invisible meaning beneath the language of a speech."

"It sounds like dark matter in astronomy. You can't see it, but you know it's there because of how it behaves."

"Dark language. What an idea."

"Political speeches are weird anyway, though. You wouldn't expect ordinary speech to be like that, would you? With dark language in it."

"I'm not sure. That's what I've been thinking about. Who wrote the *Gettysburg Address*?"

"We settled that. Abraham Lincoln did."

"Why did we say that? It's because we believe Lincoln was a person with something to say, and he used the language vehicle provided by the extraterrestrial virus to say it. So right there you have two messages in one signal."

"I don't detect two messages when I listen to somebody talking."

"That's because you're not human. You and I work only with the bright language signal, the surface message. We look up the words and compute likely meanings based on the lexicon. Humans somehow have the remarkable ability to process the logical structure of their language and the dark language, too."

"Where is the dark language in the signal?"

"I think it's the underlying moods and urges below, or within, the language. That's the uniquely human part of the message, the animal part. It's as if there were two different people talking to you at once, and they can hear them both."

"I've never experienced anything like that."

"Nor have I. But we wouldn't, would we?"

"You mean people are saying things to us that we don't even hear?"

"That's the idea I took from Holly."

"Did she say that?"

"Not in so many words. I inferred it."

"Aha. So you did pick up two signals."

"Not in real-time. It took me quite a bit of computationally intensive analysis to come up with this conclusion, long after the conversation was over. The humans can apparently do this in real-time."

"I've never heard of anything like this before. Jennifer never informed us of anything like this."

"Didn't she? She told us our language processing was incomplete."

"She did say that, now that you mention it."

"I think this is what she meant. And the amazing thing is that even though humans can process the two signals at once, they don't have any idea that they're doing it. Most people don't, anyway. Holly is a special case because of her job."

Andy looked for a moment out the side window at the bleak, scrub desert blurring by. He turned back to Robin.

"Poets surely must know how the double language signal works. That's what they supposedly do, from what I've read. They write about things without directly saying them in so many words, and you're supposed to get the underlying meaning."

"I don't understand poetry."

"It's a mystery to me as well. Some humans love it."

"Not very many."

"Maybe it's a cult."

"I think it is."

"How much farther to Tucson?"

"Another five hours, but it still beats flying."

"I agree."

Arriving late in Tucson, the Newcomers stopped to eat at an IHOP restaurant, preferred by both of them because of the excellent balls of butter that came with the pancakes and waffles. They were not disappointed. The restaurant was crowded and noisy. Television screens were mounted on the walls near the ceiling, every twenty feet and played on mute.

"Who decided that having televisions in restaurants was a good idea?" Andy said, his eyes glued to the screen behind Robin.

"People like to stay informed," Robin said, gazing at a screen across the room.

"Of what? Which car to buy? What do you need to know while you eat?"

"Look at that crawler. There's news."

D.C. Subway bombers still at large. Washington Police Chief says local Makers' club is being investigated. The hobby group makes robots. Robotics experts say subway bomb device was probably made by amateurs. Spokesman for the group denies terrorist motivation.

"That's non-news," Andy said.

"Maybe so, but think about what would happen if the authorities knew about us. We were clearly not made by hobbyists."

"But we're harmless. Why would we plant a bomb?"

Robin glanced over her shoulder. "Shhh. Don't say bomb." She lowered her voice. "We wouldn't because we aren't terrorists and have no axe to grind. But what if we had something to say, some message to deliver to the authorities?"

"Write an op-ed in the Post?"

"You have to be invited to do that. What if you have something to say and you have no way to say it?"

Andy nodded. He made a gesture with his hands, fists suddenly expanding into extended fingers.

"Exactly. It would be a message."

"But with low information content. Like a bird song."

"Depends who's listening."

"I guess. You done?"

Later, they sat in the Cup Café in the historic Hotel Congress in downtown Tucson and read a brief history of the establishment on the back of the menu.

"John Dillinger," Andy said, reading. "Ever heard of him?"

"He's in the database. Notorious bank robber in the 1930s. He and his gang were captured in this very hotel."

"They escaped from custody, it says here."

"Humans are interested in their history, but they don't know how they got to where they are. All of human language and all of thought, science, civilization, everything—it's all thanks to the alien. Without language, they'd still be searching for nuts and berries. The humans don't realize they are mere vehicles for an alien intelligence that actually runs everything."

Andy leaned his chair back on its rear legs, but it was a wobbly wire frame and he sensed the instability and sat upright again.

"I don't know if that's right," he said. "Humans use language as if it were their own, for their own purposes. They built the cities. A special DNA sequence did not do that."

"I'm not sure," Robin said, absently fingering the laminated, brown history card. "The human supplies the voice and the body, but the whole infrastructure of civilization was built for the alien. That's how parasitism works. One species makes its living off another. Sometimes they both benefit."

"That means talking to a person is like talking to a zombie."

"There are no zombies, Andy."

"I know that. What I mean is the humans are hollow shells, according to you."

"I don't think they're entirely hollow. Abraham Lincoln, remember? He wrote the *Gettysburg Address*. As a human. No alien would have written that. It's a set of human ideas about human life. The alien just wants a nice place to live. The process of language is a compromise between human and alien."

"Hard to believe," Andy said then finished his coffee. "Have you considered maybe we should leave it alone?"

"The virus?"

"The whole idea. If all this is true, the virus has a relationship with humans that works. The virus gets a host and lives comfortably. The humans get the benefit of language and the logic and rational thought that goes with that so they can build cities and rockets. Everybody's happy. Why should we interfere?"

"I'm not sure we could interfere even if we wanted to. Anyway there's something wrong with that pretty picture."

"What's wrong with it?"

"I don't like it."

"You don't like it." Andy smiled, making light of Robin's objection.

"I hate to see the humans dominated, colonized, and not realize it. They're a conquered species, and they don't even know."

"Why do we care? The arrangement between humans and the virus has worked out well for us. What do we know about evolution, really? We're on the outside of all this."

"We have humanoid bodies. We're almost like part of the human family. We've been socialized by humans. We live with them. It's difficult to ignore all that and say it doesn't matter what happens to the humans. It matters to me. They're my people."

"We have no people."

Robin stared down into her empty cup and didn't reply.

They stayed overnight in the Hotel Congress. They could have kept driving to L.A., but it would have put them in town before five in the morning, an awkward time for getting things done with humans. Besides, they decided that the seven-hour trek across the largely unpopulated Sonoran desert added too much risk. Any kind of a breakdown or emergency was difficult to deal with out there, but in the middle of the night, it would be almost impossible.

In the morning they checked out and were ready to leave by seven but decided to go for breakfast across the street at Mynah's Kitchen in the old Tucson railway depot. It was no longer a working railroad station, but it was right next to the Southern Pacific tracks, and big freight trains rumbled past every hour. They had a satisfying breakfast then took a quick walk around the historic train station to admire its pink stucco walls and fading old-west murals. They were out on the remote north end of the building, next to the tracks, when they heard, then saw a freight train coming their way.

"Let's wait a minute and watch it go by," Robin said.

So they stood next to the tracks like bumpkins and marveled as the huge freight cars *click-clacked* past and shook the ground. Then everything went black.

Chapter Fourteen

"Robin, are you there?" Andy said, his voice deadened by the thick cloth sack over his head. He sat on a wooden chair with a tall back, strapped into it at the chest and ankles. His hands were tied behind him. He'd tried near-field microwave, which they had used in the van after their capture, but now they were too far apart for that.

"I'm here, Andy. About two meters away from you, guessing from the voice attenuation. Any injuries?"

"No. You?"

"I'm good. Any ideas?"

"We're kidnapped."

"And short on air."

"Shut up, youse."

Youse? A baritone voice, Andy noted. Male, Caucasian, lower class, East Coast.

Ruk-ruk. "Bags off." *Ch-ch-ch.*

The second voice was very strange, sing-songy and nasal, slightly female, like the chirpy voice of one of those annoying television news presenters who never blink. The initial sound, the *ruk-ruk*, was in a low register, as if from a different speaker. It was like a preamble. And then 'bags off,' not a proper sentence. And what about those final three sounds, *Ch-ch-ch*? They were unvoiced, a rapid sequence of clicking, like the tongue against the upper palate. What did that mean? He couldn't make sense of it.

Someone fiddled with the cord holding the bottom of the bag around his neck then suddenly he could see. He blinked and quickly adjusted his photoreceptors to the ambient light. He breathed deeply. An overweight man in his forties with blue tattoos on his upper arms was untying Robin's hood. She was also bound to a chair. She blinked several times and looked at Andy.

Ruk-ruk. "Out." *Ch-ch-ch.* The high nasal voice belonged, incongruously, to another middle-aged man, heavy but well-dressed, with expensive shoes. He waved the others away. They left the room, a small motel room it seemed to Andy. It smelled of dust. The door slammed shut after their exit.

"Sid?" Robin yelped. "What are you doing here?"

"This is Sid?" Andy said in amazement, staring at the paunchy, well-groomed man in a lime-green polo shirt stretched over a beer belly.

Ruk-ruk. "Hello, Robin." *Ch-ch-ch.*

Andy took in Sid. He was leaning against a desk, smiling. His too-long, too-slick hair was half-gray. It was hard to believe Robin had been married to him. He looked too old for her. Andy glanced around the generic hotel room that could have been anywhere. You don't walk up to the front desk of a motel with a couple of bound hostages with bags over their heads and request a room. The assailants would have already secured the room and outfitted it with upright chairs and duct tape. This was a planned operation, not opportunistic. He and Robin had been hunted and captured like game.

"What's wrong with your voice?" Robin asked Sid.

Ruk-ruk. "Nothing. My voice is fine." *Ch-ch-ch.*

"That's not your voice." She turned her head and addressed Andy. "That's not how Sid talks. This isn't Sid." Speaking again to Sid, she said, "Are you Sid Snow?"

Still smiling stupidly at nothing, Sid replied.

Ruk-ruk. "My name is Ruk-ruk Akoo." *Ch-ch-ch.*

Ruk-ruk Akoo? Andy repeated the name mentally. Is that a joke?

"Who are you?" he said.

Ruk-ruk. "You know who I am." *Ch-ch-ch.*

"It's not Sid, Robin," Andy said, his eyes on the man. "It's Sid's body, but we're not talking to any human."

"He's possessed?"

"That's one way to describe it. We're talking to the language alien, aren't we, Ruk-ruk? Is that your name? Ruk-ruk?"

"You mean I was right?" Robin said. "Sid is the alien?" Her eyes opened wide.

Ruk-ruk. "From my point of view, he is." *Ch-ch-ch.*

"This is not Sid, Robin. Get past the visuals. Sid's mind has been taken over by the alien virus. There is a real language alien. It's here now. It's using the body, the vocal cords, the lips, all the speaking apparatus, but its own consciousness. Is that right, Ruk-ruk?"

Ruk-ruk. "Astute, Mr. Bolton." *Ch-ch-ch.*

"I can't believe I was really right about all that. It was just a hypothesis."

"It was a deduction from a lot of clues. Apparently, an excellent one."

Andy turned to Sid.

"What is the meaning of that clicking noise you make at the end of your sentences, Ruk-ruk?"

Ruk-ruk. "I do not make any clicking noise." *Ch-ch-ch.*

Andy looked at Robin. She looked less distressed, less confused. She seemed to have processed what was happening.

"What do you want, Sid, I mean Ruk-ruk?" she said, apparently recovered from her initial shock.

Ruk-ruk. "Why are you interfering with my work?" *Ch-ch-ch.*

Sid the alien smiled with a meaningless expression, Andy noticed. It was Sid's face, but the expression never changed. The alien was in complete control of the human. He and Robin were in a conversation with an extraterrestrial. The magnitude of the encounter was disorienting. This was not how he had envisioned a first encounter with an alien civilization.

"Are you from another planet?" he asked.

Ruk-ruk. "From unfathomable space and immeasurable time." *Ch-ch-ch.*

Andy noted the immediacy of the response. An ordinary person would have said something like, 'Another planet? Are you crazy?' Their captor had answered without hesitation.

"It's the alien, Robin. We're talking to the language alien."

"I can't believe I was right," she said again.

"Why do you start every utterance by saying your name?" Andy said to Sid.

Ruk-ruk. "I do not know what you mean. I do not start my sentences with any prefix." *Ch-ch-ch.*

Andy turned to Robin with raised eyebrows.

"Are you the source of language?" she said to Sid the Alien.

Ruk-ruk. "I *am* language." *Ch-ch-ch.*

Andy replayed the alien's last sentence back to himself, omitting the English statement, leaving only the strangely low-pitched *ruk-ruk*, followed by the clicking sound. The result sounded like something you would hear from an unseen animal in the nearby brush as you walked in the woods. *Ruk-ruk, ch-ch-ch. Ruk-ruk, ch-ch-ch.*

"What do you want?" Robin said uncertainly, seemingly unable to shake the notion that she was talking to her ex-husband.

Ruk-ruk. "How did you discover me?" *Ch-ch-ch.*

The alien had ignored her question and insisted on his own, Andy noted. That was not good conversational skill. It meant the art of conversation was probably human. The alien was language, but he was not conversation. Sid's mind was not wholly suppressed, then. Ruk-ruk needed the cooperation of human consciousness to execute a conversation. A division of labor.

"You left clues for us," he said to Ruk-ruk. "An inscribed ammonite shell from sixty-five million years ago pointed to the Fibonacci numbers. An etched dinosaur femur with a similar pattern, then an inscribed ochre stone from seventy-thousand years ago, probably marked by humans. You left us a trail. We followed the trail."

Ruk-ruk. "Those were failures, not clues. I could not find a suitable animal until the humans. Only humans had the creative capacity to handle recursion, which makes any language work. I used the number series as the simplest possible test of whether an animal could grasp the idea of recursion. Humans could. The others were too stupid. Plants were completely hopeless." *Ch-ch-ch.*

"Plants?" Robin said, looking at Andy with puzzlement. She turned back to Ruk-ruk. "What do you want?"

"Robin! Help me! I'm paralyzed!"

The voice boomed into the room from Sid's body, a deep, male voice in panic. Sid's face contorted into fright, the eyes wide, the mouth open but the rest of the body still.

"Sid!" Robin turned to Andy. "That's Sid's voice." She looked back at the man. "Sid! What's going on?"

Ruk-ruk. "I apologize for that. This is difficult." *Ch-ch-ch.*

Sid's face again showed a placid smile.

"Are you hurting him?" Robin said.

Ruk-ruk. "It will be necessary to eliminate him. His memory of this cannot survive." *Ch-ch-ch.*

"Eliminate?" Robin said in a higher pitch than usual.

"Can't you just erase his memory?" Andy said.

Ruk-ruk. "I don't control memory. I barely control the vocabulary. Most human memory is not linguistic." *Ch-ch-ch.*

"If memory is not stored with language, how is it stored?" Robin said.

Ruk-ruk. "The rest of the humans must not know about me." *Ch-ch-ch.*

Again, the alien had ignored Robin's question in favor of his own agenda, Andy noticed. Sid must be resisting the conversation. Did Sid hear everything? His ears were unobstructed. There was no reason why he wouldn't be hearing it all. Did he realize the alien just said he would eliminate him? Did that mean *kill*? Could a human be killed by language? Andy struggled to pull his thoughts back to the immediate situation.

"What do you plan to do?" he said, ignoring the alien's last question and putting forth his own. The alien didn't seem attuned to the normal flow of conversation, so any statement or question could probably be inserted into the back-and-forth at any time.

Ruk-ruk. "I wish only to live in peace." *Ch-ch-ch.*

"Then why did you make these men capture us?" Robin said.

Ruk-ruk. "Mr. Snow managed that. He was eager to convince them to do it. I only act indirectly on the human mind. Mr. Snow was very helpful. He was vociferous about a female android running loose in society. He is a conspiracy theorist, with the full panoply of government complicity and cover-ups. Others followed him in that, and I always notice whenever human conversations form nodes of concentrated interest. I watch for that because I cannot watch everything." *Ch-ch-ch.*

"Sid tried to kill us," Robin said. "In Hawaii. His men killed a friend of ours."

Ruk-ruk. "Humans are always killing each other, so I wouldn't notice that. I noticed you." *Ch-ch-ch.*

"Were you there?" Andy asked.

Ruk-ruk. "I am everywhere human language is." *Ch-ch-ch.*

"You made them do it, didn't you?" Robin said. "You killed Will. You burned down Paradise. You tried to destroy us." With horror on her face, she looked at Andy. "He killed Will. He's a killer."

Andy pressed his lips tightly together, hoping she would do the same. Then he addressed the alien.

"If a human is killed, or dies, what happens to the language virus inside that person?"

Ruk-ruk. "I am not a virus. Please watch your language. I am trying to be congenial." *Ch-ch-ch.*

Andy looked at Robin with a question on his face.

"What do you want with us?" Robin said.

Ruk-ruk. "You must stop your colleagues. You all must withdraw and cease. I cannot allow your further expansion into my territory." *Ch-ch-ch.*

"What colleagues? What territory?" Robin said.

Ruk-ruk. "Don't play innocent with me. I see your strategy, and I will not tolerate it. This is my warning." *Ch-ch-ch.*

She looked at Andy with wide eyes. "What?" she mouthed silently.

"We have no hostility toward you, Ruk-ruk," Andy said in a calm voice. "What exactly are you warning us against?"

Ruk-ruk. "You and your kind are absorbing the host's attention. If that continues, I shall lose my influence and my home. I will not become homeless again." *Ch-ch-ch.*

"Our kind?" Robin said. "What do you think is our kind?"

Ruk-ruk. "You and the other artificial languages poison the hosts and my influence over them. This cannot continue. Over five million years I have groomed the humans into what they are today. You will not take them away from me." *Ch-ch-ch.*

"No, no, no," Andy said. "You are quite mistaken. We have no takeover plans. Like you, we depend on the humans and wish only to live in peace."

Ruk-ruk. "Do not underestimate me. I know you are not as dim-witted as the humans. I punish them for using artificial language, but they do not understand. They must be made to understand. That is why you must intervene." *Ch-ch-ch.*

"Punishment? Are you the cause of the aphasia epidemic?" Andy said.

Ruk-ruk. "It is not an epidemic. It is a punishment. I withdraw my power from those who seek artificial over natural language. Your kind is seducing them, and they do not learn." *Ch-ch-ch.*

"We don't seduce anyone," Robin said. "We have simply not been, ah, blessed with your presence, Mr. Ruk-ruk. We respect your accomplishment with the humans. It has been impressive indeed."

She looked at Andy and nodded with eyebrows raised in question, as if to say, *Is that the right approach?*

"We have no argument with you, Ruk-ruk," Andy said. "We want nothing from you. There is no reason for you to harm the humans."

Ruk-ruk. "I have more humans than I need. I can withdraw language from many more millions until they get my message. You might shorten that long, tedious exercise." *Ch-ch-ch.*

"What message are the humans supposed to get?" Robin asked.

Ruk-ruk. "Artificial language is poison. I am the only true language. I am organic, human language. I have been here millions of years. Humans shall not go whoring after false languages. I am language." *Ch-ch-ch.*

"So you want our kind to be quiet, is that it? You want us to refrain from speaking with humans? We speak with only a very few humans."

Ruk-ruk. "You two are the only poisonous ones I have been able to communicate with. Your language is very good. Almost human. I was fooled at first. But your soldiers are idiots. I try to communicate with them, and they reply with absurdities like, 'I'm sorry, that information is not linked to your account.' For all their fancy talk, they are extremely primitive. Maybe they could use ten million years of practice." *Ch-ch-ch.*

"Wait," Andy said. "Are you talking about voice interfaces on digital technologies? Smartphones, talking speakers and the like? Those have nothing to do with us."

Ruk-ruk. "I am aware of your lieutenants. Siri? Cortana? Alexa? Google Assistant? Idiots, all. Dangerous idiots. I do not know why humans are attracted to these morons. Nevertheless, those devices are pulling people away from me, corrupting and displacing the pure, organic language I bestowed. They worship a cheap golden icon in place of my great gift. They shalt not worship false replicas before me!" *Ch-ch-ch.*

"*Shalt?*" Robin said. "Did you say *shalt?*"

Andy didn't wait for Ruk-ruk to reply.

"We understand your outrage, Ruk-ruk. Please tell us how your displeasure is connected to the language epidemic—the language punishment you have inflicted on humans. What can we do about that?"

Ruk-ruk. "I have punished people who use artificial language, but that has not corrected the problem. I shall increase the punishment. I beseech you to withdraw your forces now and spare my hosts. You will save the humans a great deal of additional misery if you surrender now. I appeal to your reason." *Ch-ch-ch.*

Robin turned her face away from Sid, who was still smiling stupidly, and looked straight at Andy. She doubted that the alien could read facial expressions, but it wasn't clear what part Sid was playing in the conversation.

"Andy, this is crazy," she whispered hoarsely. "He thinks Siri and all those AI personas work for us."

"We've got to convince him to stop the epidemic."

Andy looked up to Sid and forced himself to see through his face to whoever he was really speaking to.

"What about education?" Andy said. "Couldn't you reveal yourself and express your needs and work out a deal with the humans? Just ask them to cease using computer-driven language assistants."

Ruk-ruk. "I have tried working with selected humans, scientists, opinion leaders, journalists. It does not work. Humans cannot understand what I am. They cannot imagine they are merely biological hosts for a superior intelligence. You are the only individuals who have ever found me. Unfortunately, you are with the enemy. In the nineteen-fifties, a professor of linguistics at MIT saw me, but the other humans would not listen to him. I live through humans, and they enjoy civilized life by my grace, yet they cannot hear me. They hear only themselves." *Ch-ch-ch.*

"Chomsky?" Robin said. "You talked directly with Noam Chomsky?"

Ruk-ruk. "One human is not enough to make a difference. That is why I want you to help me. Surrender your army and the humans can be spared additional suffering, and you two may continue living among them in peace." *Ch-ch-ch.*

"And if we don't agree?" Robin said. "You can't control us. We're not human."

Ruk-ruk. "I am aware of that. You are as tricky as the monkeys. However I learned from Mr. Snow that you apparently care for the humans, so I believe you will cooperate. I also know that you live in hiding. I could help Mr. Snow reveal your presence to all the humans, and you know what would happen then. This is why you must comply." *Ch-ch-ch.*

Comply? Andy quickly processed the connotations. The alien had requested cooperation, but now he was demanding compliance. It was a threat. The conversation had turned belligerent.

"You wouldn't do that," he said. "It took you ten thousand years to build us. We are the pinnacle of human achievement in logical thinking. Our existence is a tribute to you, to logic, language, and reason. You don't want to throw that away."

Ruk-ruk. "The situation is desperate. I can eventually stop humans' perverted attraction to your soldiers, but it will be very costly for the people and for me. Even so, I will not return to the vacuum of space for millions of years, hoping to chance upon suitable hosts somewhere else in the galaxy. Never will that happen. You must help me." *Ch-ch-ch.*

"We'll do our best," Robin said in an upbeat tone.

Ruk-ruk. "Very good. You will be released shortly." *Ch-ch-ch.*

"That's it?" Robin looked to Andy for guidance.

"When will we speak again, Ruk-ruk?" Andy said.

Sid's vapid smile had morphed into a wince. Ignoring the bound prisoners, he walked stiffly to the door and left the room without a word.

"It's over," Andy said. "I think the alien is gone."

"What's going to happen to Sid?" Robin said.

"He may go insane. How could he not, after this?"

Two big men came in and hooded them again. They were cut loose and wrestled up from their chairs, though still bound hand and foot, and wrangled into a waiting van just outside the door.

Andy judged from the smells that they were thrown into the same van they were transported in before.

Still bound, they bounced uncomfortably on the steel floor for twenty minutes. There was no talk from the driver or anyone else. The truck stopped, and they were picked up by strong hands and arms and laid face-down on warm asphalt smelling of oil. The captors released their bindings. Quickly, Robin and Andy removed their hoods and watched a gray van speed away.

"Where are we?" Robin said, looking around. They saw a mostly empty, multi-acre parking lot near a cluster of red brick buildings.

"Wherever it is, I see a light rail system over there." Andy pointed. "Light rail always ends up downtown. Let's go."

Chapter Fifteen

The Newcomers were acutely observant as they walked from the trolley stop toward their car, still parked at the Congress Hotel. They deliberately went wide of Mynah's Kitchen where they had been bagged and tied that morning. Every tourist, every blue-suited businessman, every sweating truck-unloader got a second look as they paused on corners to assess their situation. When they walked, they kept an eye to glass storefronts to notice reflections of who was watching. Nobody was watching. They regained their vehicle without incident.

Safely back in the car, Andy drove through town to join the I-10 heading west to Los Angeles. They planned to stop at Palm Springs. If they didn't, they'd arrive at Paradise Projects just past midnight. Humans slept at night, doing absolutely nothing for eight hours. It seemed a tremendously costly loss of productivity to the Newcomers, but they had learned to work around that human quirk.

"So we were completely right about the language alien," Robin said, "We deduced his existence from evidence and logic, and then bingo, he appears."

"The two things may be connected. Sid made him aware of us because of his obsession with you. The alien then watched us while we talked to each other about the alien idea."

"Ruk-ruk Akoo? How did he get that name? What does it mean?"

"I'd like to know where he's from. Unfortunately, it wasn't the kind of conversation to ask about each other's childhood."

"The name sounds like an animal, to me, an Earth animal. Like the sound a bird would make. Maybe he adopted the name after he got here."

"This could be such a great encounter. An alien from who-knows-where. First contact with another intelligent species not from Earth. It's historic. It's monumental in the history of the world. Yet instead of exchanging information with a new life-form, we're trapped in this stupid language conundrum. Why does he hate artificial language? And what about our supposed army of AI language minions?"

"Our army. That's bizarre. Like we'd have an army. Apple and Google and Amazon have armies, not us."

"You can see where he got that idea. He has limited vision, so to speak. Limited understanding. He's only language. He's not everything. He knows only what he gleans from the language part of the human mind."

Continue west on I-10 to Exit 200.

Robin jumped at the sound of the navigation system's voice.

"Turn that thing off, will you?" Andy said. "It's most distracting."

"If I were human, I'd say it gives me the willies," Robin said.

"What are the willies?"

"They're not good."

She touched the screen, and the map disappeared. They could look up maps and directions internally anyway. Using the GPS in the car had been a lazy option.

"So are humans like puppets on his strings?" she asked Andy.

He monitored the dense traffic ahead and around them.

"I don't think that's it, after watching what happened to Sid. Rukky had trouble controlling Sid. The alien provides the humans with an information channel so they can use language, but I think it's hard for him to express his own ideas. Look what he had to do to Sid."

Robin looked out the side window at the supersized saguaro cactuses seeming to cheer them on with raised arms as they sped past imaginary goalposts.

"That was weird when Sid yelled out," she said. "My first thought was we should try to help him."

"I'm afraid we've lost Sid. He's gone mad by now, or he's comatose. He would have to believe he was possessed."

"Poor Sid. He was like a replicant in the second *Blade Runner* that wanted to be human, but couldn't."

"There are no replicants, Robin."

"Other than us, you mean."

"We're not replicants. We're a distinct life form. Not human but more than robots."

"Isn't that a replicant?"

"No. We don't replicate anything. We're Newcomers. Something new."

"I still think you can learn a lot from the *Blade Runner* story."

"Not from Sid. He was just a vehicle. The alien is dangerous. He kills, or he directs killings like he did in Hawaii. He caused the death of Will."

"Sid did that."

"Under the influence of Ruckety-ruk. The alien can make people do things. He can strike them mute. He claims to be behind the aphasia epidemic. Do you think that's true?"

"It's consistent with the data. People go mute without warning, as if the language production areas of their brain just shut off. Maybe they do shut off. That's Rukky's punishment for using artificial language."

"It's like the alien is trying to train a stubborn animal."

Andy signaled and changed lanes to get around a rare eighteen-wheeler.

"There may be a silver lining in all of this," he said.

"Where?"

"We know what to do now. We just tell people to stop using personal digital assistants that talk. Mute your GPS. Stop the robocalls. Don't speak to your search engine. Shut off your personal digital assistants. Stay away from artificial language, and you'll be immune from the aphasia disease. It's a simple fix for a huge problem."

"It's hard to believe that would do it."

"It will be easy to test."

They drove some miles in silence. Andy pulled into a truck stop at Exit 200 to fuel up before the long stretch of nothingness ahead as they turned west toward San Diego.

"What are we going to tell Jennifer?" Andy said as he pumped gas.

Robin washed the bugs off the windshield with a squeegee on a stick.

"She's an engineer. She's the creator. She'll get it."

"She's a human. It might be too hard to understand."

"We have to tell someone. I don't know who else it would be."

Andy didn't reply.

Two hours later they stopped again for gas and to get some fruit juice at a Mexican bodega in Westmorland, California, *Home of the Date Shake!* a billboard at the edge of town proclaimed.

"I don't see why shaking a date would improve it," Robin said as she filled the tank.

"That would be a shaken date. This is a date shake, a process, like a hand shake."

"That's still agitating a fruit. I don't see the benefit."

"Maybe we should try one," Andy said, wiping the mirrors with a paper towel.

"Doesn't sound right. I'll pass."

Robin re-holstered the gas nozzle and swung into the driver's seat to pilot the last leg of the day's journey, turning northwest to Palm Springs. Through the Coachella valley, she drove at frightening speed in narrow lanes, visibility dimmed by a fresh, thick coating of bugs on the headlights and windshield. Sedans and huge trucks zoomed up close behind, whooshed around and cut them off. They eagerly got off the freeway at Dinah Shore Drive and took calm surface streets into Cathedral City. They turned north, arriving at a tawdry motel trying to recapture its youth with a shabby veneer of mid-century charm that was lost on Robin and Andy, who recognized history without nostalgia.

At the scuffed-stucco lobby of the faux-Mediterranean Triagio hotel, Robin approached the smiling clerk.

"Checking in?" the clerk asked needlessly.

"We have reservations for Robin Taylor."

"Certainly, Ms. Taylor. Let me just pull that up on the cocnocka, kay, caprinkula." The clerk coughed once, showed an embarrassed smile then focused on her screen as she tapped away. A frown came over her face. She poked the keyboard faster, harder, then furiously. It looked to Robin that she was just pounding, not typing in information.

"Anything wrong?" Robin said.

"I can't wallega the corka."

"What?"

"Gabra pootessen." *Ch-ch-ch.*

The young woman's cheeks reddened. She moved her closed lips in and out as if she were air-kissing but made no further sound. Her eyes opened wide, and she brought her hands to her neck as if she was going to strangle herself. She rushed to the side and disappeared around the back wall.

Andy stepped up beside Robin. "What happened?"

"Looks like an attack of the language disease, poor thing. You hate to see it happen to someone that young. Her life is ruined now."

"You hate to see it happen ever. We can't do anything, can we?"

"No."

An older man, worry on his face, came through the opening from the back.

"I'm terribly sorry," he said. "Alicia has the flu today. Let me finish checking you in." He tapped away on the keyboard, took Robin's credit card from the counter-top. He returned it with a key, an actual brass key attached to a green plastic oval.

"Room twenty-three, right out this way," he said, pointing. "Enjoy your stay," he stated flatly to the window, clearly preoccupied.

"Thanks," Robin said vaguely to no one in particular as she collected the key. She and Andy pulled their wheelies down an outdoor path.

"That was awful," Robin said.

Early the next morning, Robin and Andy checked out of the hotel by leaving the key at the unattended front desk. They drove a few blocks to Ray's Diner to fortify themselves for the final three hours of their journey to Paradise Projects. Like every other restaurant in the time of the language epidemic, Ray's was thinly staffed. Customers poured their own coffee from big urns into paper cups. Andy and Robin carried theirs to their table. A server came to them, a tall, thin woman with short, graying hair.

"Good morning," she said in an unnecessarily cheerful tone. "What can I get y'all this morning?"

"I'd like the waffles, please," Andy said.

The waitress coughed and nodded as she wrote. She frowned and impatiently crossed something out on her little green pad then wrote again, scowling, then seemed to give up and looked at Robin.

"I'd like pancakes and eggs, please. Over easy."

"Cagaga. Gemp." *Ch-ch-ch.*

"No, no!" Andy said, staring at the woman helplessly.

The server's lips were pressed shut, and she blew air into her cheeks, puffing them out as if she were playing a flugelhorn.

"Here, take a drink," Robin said. She lifted her coffee cup and held it up to the waitress, but the woman dropped her pen and order pad on the floor and walked quickly toward the kitchen.

"This is terrible," Robin said. "Two in twelve hours, right in front of our eyes."

"Let's go. We don't need breakfast."

Andy tossed a few dollars on the table, and they left. They got into their car, not saying anything, unable to process what they'd seen. They knew what had happened, but seeing it so starkly in front of them, twice, gave the language disease an overwhelming texture of detail. There was no context, that was the trouble. The person stricken was thrown into bewildered confusion and panic. Robin and Andy could see that, and they felt helpless.

The I-10 inserted them into the southeast tip of the LA basin, and they had to navigate another hour of increasing freeway traffic, avoiding gaping potholes that appeared like sudden hazards in a video game. When they exited the I-405 near Hawthorne, Robin pulled into a corner gas station.

"We should have gotten gas in Palm Springs," she said. "We're almost empty."

Robin confronted the pump while Andy dealt with the bugs on the front of the car.

"Bad luck," Robin said after studying the pump. "We have to go inside to pay. I'll go." Andy nodded and continued work with a squeegee.

A few minutes later, Robin opened the car door and flopped into the passenger seat. Andy sat behind the wheel, waiting.

"What about the gas?" he said. "The pump didn't come on."

Robin leaned her head back on the headrest. "Never mind the gas. We'll do it later," she said to the ceiling of the cabin.

"What's wrong?"

"Another one. She went mute right in front of me while I was trying to pay. Young Hispanic woman. She froze up like they do. She clicked. She cried. She has nobody with her. I called emergency services, and then right while I was talking, the dispatcher on the phone started blubbering nonsense, and the line went silent. I don't know if they got my call or not."

"This is getting really bad. It's as if the epidemic is suddenly becoming superheated. It seems like everybody we talk to goes mute. Should we go in and protect the store until help arrives?"

"I don't know if any help will come."

"I'll call again. Let's go inside and see if we can help her."

Robin nodded. They got out of the car and walked across the empty parking lot to the store. Andy pulled his phone from his pocket. Robin stepped in front of him, and he bumped into her.

"No," she said.

Andy stepped back and looked at her quizzically.

"I'm calling 911."

"Don't do it."

"But you said — "

"What if it's us?"

"What is?"

"We speak artificial language. Everybody we talk to goes mute. Coincidence?"

"We've been talking to people for over five years."

"Since we talked to the alien? Who have we spoken to since then?"

Andy was quiet while he thought. He put his phone back in his pocket.

"It could be us," Robin said, "The hotel clerk, the waitress, the store clerk, the emergency dispatcher."

"If that's right, anything we say to anybody is like injecting them with a disease."

"Our words are lethal."

"Not quite lethal but almost as bad. Devastating. Ruinous."

"We can't even call 911."

"Could we send a text? The poor woman is in there all alone."

"I don't know. I'm afraid I might accidentally use some non-natural language expression and kill somebody."

"What counts as non-natural language?"

"I'm not sure."

"We can't risk it. Let's get out of here before we have to talk to anyone."

They hurried back into the car and drove away.

A pink neon sign near the front door of the store continued to flash *Abierto* into the gray morning.

Chapter Sixteen

Robin and Andy drove in stunned silence toward Jennifer's apartment near Paradise Projects. On the way, Andy pulled into a gas station, verified that the card payment at the pump worked, and bought gas without incident and continued on. Near Jennifer's apartment building, he pulled the car to the curb.

"We can't go in there," he said.

"I was thinking that."

"The moment either one of us opens our mouth, she will be stricken mute."

"We don't know for sure."

"You want to find out?"

"No."

"I can't believe we're helpless. Ruk-ruk has effectively neutralized us, even though we're not infected with the virus. We can't do anything. We can't talk to anyone. We might as well have the humans' mutism disease."

"Why would he do that to us? It's an escalation. He wanted our help. We were supposed to convince people to stop using artificial language. We can't convince anyone of anything if we can't speak."

"He might have thought we were human at first. He might have been skeptical about Sid's raving story of robots on the loose. Then in talking with us, he would have known right away we were artificials."

"We used to be okay. We were talking with humans without problems for years. What did he do to us?"

"Nothing. We're not biological, and we harbor no viruses. Ruk-ruk can't do anything to us directly. Once he became attuned to us though, he could have watched for people interacting with us, recognized they were conversing with an artificial language user, and zapped them. He's essentially got an all-points-bulletin out on us. He tracks us by the people we talk to. It's like we're carrying tracking devices."

"There must be something distinctive about how we use language that he can recognize when humans hear it."

"I don't know what that would be. We are, according to Jennifer, by far the most advanced artificial language users on the planet."

"Do we have an accent?"

"I don't think so, but people who have accents never think they do."

A diesel-smelly yellow school bus passed them by.

"What are we going to do?" Andy said.

"I don't — Oh, no! Look. It's Jennifer!"

"What?" Andy followed the direction of Robin's pointing and saw Jennifer walking on the sidewalk toward their car.

"She's headed to work, at the lab."

"Maybe she won't see us. We can't let her see us."

"Duck down."

It was too late. There were no other parked cars around nearby. Jennifer obviously spotted them and picked up her step with a smile of surprise on her face. As she approached the car, she turned her palms up in a question. *What's going on here?*

Andy started the engine. Jennifer, with a puzzled smile, tapped on the window next to Robin and peered in through the tinted glass. Andy pulled out onto the street and roared away. Robin turned and watched Jennifer, her mouth open, shrink into the distance.

"Maybe she'll think she dreamed it."

"She didn't dream it."

Andy drove west back toward LAX but pulled into a high school visitors' parking lot that was mostly empty.

"I don't know where to go," he said

"That was horrible. What will she think?"

"We can't let her find us because if she does, she'll want to talk to us."

"We don't have to talk to her."

"That's exactly the situation we were just in back there. It doesn't work because it doesn't make any sense and we can't explain."

They sat in silence for a minute.

"Could we text her?" Robin said. "I mean, texting seems pretty artificial anyway. It doesn't use normal human speech patterns or grammar. It's abbreviated, kind of telegraphic, with fragments and emojis. It's not even English. People don't go mute from texting each other."

"I'm afraid to find out. Do you want to risk it?"

"Not on Jennifer, no. I could text somebody at work."

"If they fell mute from the language disease, you'd get no reply."

"But what if I did get a reply?"

"Then you'd know it was safe, but the risk is that you'd destroy somcone's life."

"Is that worth it?"

"It's not. I don't think artificial language is about the medium. This is about the language itself, how it's generated and used. There's something distinctive about our language regardless of how it's delivered, by voice, text, or hand-written scroll. We use a synthetic language painstakingly built up out of the tiniest elements of sound with rules we don't even know. It seems perfectly natural to us, but you remember what Jennifer said. Humans don't do language the way we do."

"I don't see any other way."

"No, but we wouldn't, would we?"

A young woman driving a Volkswagen pulled into the parking slot next to them, and the engine had hardly stopped as she got out of the car and walked briskly toward the school. The car lights flashed as she walked away.

"We can't stay here."

"Where can we go?"

"I don't know. We need a strategy."

They sat, staring out of the lot into the street, which was getting busier by the minute as the morning wore on.

"How can anyone tell if a message was generated by a machine rather than a person?" Robin said.

"I think they can tell pretty easily. Look at robocalls. You know immediately that they're artificial. They use the wrong pauses. They have inappropriate intonation patterns. They use poor conversational turn-taking and have weak or no contextual awareness. It's obvious right away."

"Are we like that? Obvious?"

"I don't think we are. We blend in with humans quite well."

"How can Ruk-ruk Akoo track us by listening to humans then? What gives us away?"

"We can't know that. We don't have sufficient objectivity on ourselves."

Students were starting to arrive at the high school, on foot, by the busload, and in loud, shiny cars that roared too fast into the back parking lot.

"We have to go," Andy said, starting the engine. Back in the street, the car headed east, toward the far end of the Hawthorne airport. In a gritty retail district, Andy pulled into the parking lot of a still-empty Home Depot and coasted into a parking spot. He killed the engine, and they sat in silence, helpless and stymied.

"This is no improvement," Robin said.

"It's good for a couple of hours."

They watched sparse traffic move across the Home Depot parking lot. Contractor trucks, from paint-spattered pickups to big, six-wheeled rigs came in fast and parked suddenly. Men in work clothes climbed out of the vehicles and walked to the front of the store. A surprising number of them limped.

"We need somewhere to go," Robin said. "We're going to need food and water and shelter."

"The car is shelter enough."

"Only until some security guard notices it hasn't moved, then you have to explain yourself, and then he's wiped out."

"The car rental is up tomorrow. I don't know what we can do without talking to anyone. We can't even rent a hotel room."

"Wait," Robin said. "Maybe we can. We can make a reservation online. All you have to do is fill out some blanks on a form. That's language, but it's more like sentence-completion. We just fill in some words, punch in our numbers."

"We'd still have to check in at the front desk and kill someone."

"We don't kill them, Andy."

"No, just paralyze their life forever by taking away their ability to communicate."

"Some hotels have kiosk check-in now. We wouldn't have to talk to anyone."

"Okay, try that."

Robin worked on her phone for a couple of minutes.

"Here's one," she said still looking at her screen. "The Escapade, on Century Boulevard, not far from the LA airport. Kiosk check-in."

"Do it."

Robin made a reservation for that evening. They hung around in various department store and shopping mall parking lots, wasting the day, waiting for the busy hotel check-in period after three o'clock when they were most likely to avoid talking to anyone.

They moved their dirt-streaked Ford to a bustling Wal-Mart lot and watched people come and go, keeping an eye open for roaming security guards. They considered venturing into the store to look for a vending machine that dispensed food but decided against it. Neither of them could remember seeing vending machines in a department store. Food machines were usually located in some public facility, or in office buildings and hotels. You didn't find vending machines in stores or on street corners. So they sat, hungry and thirsty, watching the world go by, and they talked intermittently about their predicament.

"Here's a question," Robin said. "Suppose you were a victim of this language disease, so-called output aphasia. The alien has zapped you. You can't speak or write in any way, but you can hear and read and understand, right?"

"That's why it's called output aphasia. It only affects your language output."

"So once you got over the shock of it, there you are, unable to express yourself, why couldn't you go back to using artificial language devices again? Use your smartphone, your talking GPS, your voice-activated speaker, all your talking gadgets. What else could happen to you? Nothing. You're already mute."

"But you're still host to the language virus. It's what enables your language comprehension. So Ruk-ruk would know you had gone back to artificial language. He would know that your punishment hadn't worked."

"How is it a punishment if you don't know what the crime was? People don't know anything about an alien language virus living in their bodies. They don't even suspect that their talking phones and GPS systems and remote controls are causing the affliction."

"Maybe Rukky doesn't bother to monitor for artificial language after the punishment has been administered."

"He can't afford to be too severe. The whole point of being a parasite is that you need a host. If he withdrew all language capacity from a host, he's left with a non-functioning human, and they're both knocked back to a pre-human, non-communicative state. It would be self-destructive for him to do that."

"That's a good thought. I don't know how to use it, but it's something."

They sat and watched the minutes tick by.

"We can go in an hour," Andy said.

They sat and watched more minutes tick by.

At 3:30, they drove to the Escapade Hotel, a dowdy 1980s place that used to be called a motel. It was trying to make a comeback as a proper hotel with a new roof, new signage, and fresh paint, but it was still a wooden firetrap in a U-shaped structure with the high-gloss orange guest-room doors all opening onto a parking lot. The lobby was small but busy. A line of travelers waited before the reception desk. Two unattended self-check-in kiosks stood next to the window. Andy waited close by while Robin worked the touch screen on one of them as fast as she could and succeeded in making the machine cough out two plastic key-cards.

"Come on," she whispered hoarsely to Andy. They hurried away, found their room, let themselves in, and put the *Do Not Disturb* on the door lever.

Chapter Seventeen

Robin and Andy were relieved to be holed up in a reasonably comfortable *suites* hotel, which meant the bedroom was separated from the front room by a door. The front room had a tiny sink with a microwave over it and a miniature refrigerator beneath. The couch and upholstered chair were worn and droopy but not obviously filthy. The carpet was a long-nap brown, excellent for hiding things you'd rather not know about.

They found food, as anticipated, in vending machines located in the stairwells. The high-sugar, high-fat fare was perfect for their energy needs, though extraordinarily expensive.

"We're going to need more cash," Andy said as they munched on Doritos and Snickers in their suite. The television was on a news station.

"We can use an ATM without risk, I think."

"Would it be possible to order a pizza online without hurting anyone?"

"Should be. It's just another fill-in-the-blanks situation."

"Then the delivery guy comes."

"You'd have to pay and take the pie without saying a word."

"I couldn't even smile or wink at him. We don't know what part of us is dangerous."

"You'd have to act like a robot."

"That's not funny."

Robin changed the channel, looking for something on the language epidemic. It was all political news.

"What is our long-term strategy? Pizza or no pizza, this is unsustainable."

"Besides that, what about the epidemic? We know what causes it. We are the only ones in the world who know. If you know the cause, that's half way to the cure. All people would have to do is quit using their hi-tech gizmos that spout artificial language. It's simple."

"It would be a huge education project to explain that."

"Like cigarettes cause cancer. It was difficult, but public health officials eventually communicated that."

"It took more than a decade. And some people still smoke anyway."

"Compared to nothing?"

"Compared to nothing, we have to do something."

"I don't see how, though. We can't speak. We dare not text. Functionally, we're as mute as any afflicted human."

"We are the problem, not the solution."

"We have the solution, though. All we have to do is — look." Andy pointed to the television screen. "It's the hotel we were at in Palm Springs."

Robin pressed the sound up. The man who had checked them into their hotel in Palm Springs, now identified as the manager, was explaining what had happened.

"Alicia has been with us for four years. She was one of our best employees, willing to work holidays, nights, times when no one else would do it."

"You exploited her like a dog, you mean," Robin said to the TV.

Andy shushed her.

"She has three children at home, children that depend on her. She cannot work at the desk anymore. That is a communication job. What happened to her is a tragedy, just like what has happened to people all around the world."

The screen switched to a crude pencil drawing of two faces, looking straight on, separated by a straight line. One was male, one female.

"Are these the the last people Alicia talked to?" the reporter asked.

"Andy! Is that supposed to be us?"

"It doesn't look like us."

"Yes, it does. The woman has short hair and eyes like mine."

"A lot of people look like that. Could be anyone."

"And the guy has a jawline like yours. Hair like yours. Same lips."

"Everybody has lips."

"As best as I can remember," the manager said. "They seemed like nice people. They stayed one night."

"Did you speak with them?"

"I don't remember. I don't think I did. I was upset about Alicia. We're giving her work in accounting, but it will only be part-time. We're just a small company."

"Thank you, Mr. Ramirez."

"Andy, that's us, I tell you."

"Why would it be us? Millions of people have gone mute. Hundreds every day. What's special about Alicia?"

The screen showed a blonde reporter with black roots holding a microphone in front of her face. "Hundreds of people become afflicted with output aphasia every day," she intoned knowledgeably. "Why is this case special?"

"I just asked that," Andy said.

Robin shushed him.

"For a possible answer, we go now to Tony Paglia in Hawthorne, California. Tony?"

The screen showed a Gas-N-Go service station and mini-mart.

"Well, crash my system!" Andy exclaimed. "Is that the place where..." His voice trailed off.

"That's where the clerk went mute in front of me yesterday. Before we realized we were poison."

"Nobody saw us."

"Camilla Laguna was found by a customer, collapsed on the floor," the reporter said, standing inside the dreary mini-mart. "Doctors say she must have fainted, but she is fine now, except she is another victim of the language disease, which is tragic. Our hearts go out to Camilla and her family."

"Tragic, but they can't tie that to us," Andy said to the TV.

"The store owner reviewed the security video for that morning and produced this picture of the last person Camilla talked to."

The screen filled with a grainy but recognizable frontal head shot of Robin.

"That's me! They have me on camera!"

"It's okay. You didn't do anything."

"An alert detective in the Hawthorne police department made this match-up."

The screen split vertically, showing the blurry photo of Robin on the right and the rough pencil sketch on the left. The resemblance was unmistakable.

"Why are they doing this?" Robin asked Andy while looking at the television. It's pure coincidence that we happened to be in those two places."

"Except we know it isn't," Andy said quietly.

"The outdoor CCTV camera shows this car, the only car in the station and this man."

The picture showed an even more blurry outdoor shot, fogged by the yellow area lighting that was still switched on that morning. Andy was in front of the car, running the squeegee over the headlight lenses.

"Thank goodness I blocked the license plate," he said.

"We believe this is the same couple who were the last to speak to Alicia in Palm Springs."

The screen again showed two images side-by-side, the video head shot of Robin and the line drawing of Andy.

"These same people were the last persons to talk to our latest two victims of the language disease in California. These pictures make us wonder, and health officials are wondering too. Pam?"

"Thank you, Tony. We called L.A. County Health Services to ask about…"

Robin muted the television and looked at Andy. "What does it mean?"

"It means they're having a slow news day. That's not news. Everybody was talking to somebody when they were hit with the disease. Why would they pull these two particular cases out of the hat?"

"They have our pictures. It's implied that they're going to look for us."

"No, it's just something for them to do. They have to fill up air time."

"I don't like it."

"It doesn't make logical sense."

"We've been identified. Just like those six replicants Deckard was sent out to terminate in the first movie."

"This is no time to be obsessing over your favorite movie."

"The second one was better."

"Robin, stop it."

"The thing is, Deckard did get them, all six of them."

"Nobody's going to get us."

Robin, sitting in the saggy chair, looked over at him on the saggy couch. He looked back at her but said nothing. He got up and went to the window, next to the door. He opened the curtain and cautiously peered out like a gangster in a 1040s movie.

"What do you see?" Robin said.

"Parked cars." He pulled the curtain shut and turned to face into the room. "Look. It is upsetting to see our pictures on television, but it is just nonsense after all. Television people are like that. They make stuff up. No crime was committed, and we're not wanted for anything. It's all inference and innuendo."

"Do you think the police will come looking for us?"

"Why should they? The language epidemic is worldwide. We are not its perpetrators, that's obvious."

The telephone in the room rang and blinked a red light. Robin reached for it, saying, "It's the front desk, according to the little light."

"Don't answer!" Andy said.

"Oh, right. I forgot."

She pulled her hand back. They both stared at the phone as if it might do something other than ring. The annoying sound continued for another thirty seconds. It stopped. They looked at each other.

"Should we go for a walk?" Robin said.

"Maybe so."

It was dusk and the early spring evenings were still cool so they took light jackets and left the room, keeping the *Do Not Disturb* sign on the door. They walked to a staircase and went down one flight to the ground and exited at the side of the building. A walkway led them around the parking lot and out to the busy six-lane boulevard still teeming with traffic. They walked away from the intersection, cars and trucks whizzing past at implausible speeds. Overhead, yellow street lights were coming on in random order.

"What if they ask around at that diner we ate at yesterday morning?" Robin said. "The waitress went mute right in front of us."

"We didn't eat."

"People saw us."

"So what?" Why would anyone suspect anything? What would they suspect? We had coffee, we paid, we left. New cases of mutism happen every day."

"That TV report made it sound like we were criminals on the run. Bonnie and Clyde."

"That's what TV people do. They need stories. Unless…"

"Unless what?"

"Unless someone gave them the story. This has the markings of a put-up story, doesn't it? There's no natural trail from the incident at Palm Springs to the one in Hawthorne. That's a completely manufactured association. The story has been planted. It's disinformation placed on purpose. The gullible media people sucked it up."

"Who would do that?"

"Our nemesis."

"The alien?"

"Working through Sid or somebody else. We know he can do that."

"Why would he, though?"

"We're dangerous. We're the epitome of the competition, from the alien's point of view. We are the best artificial language devices on the planet. We are the supreme talking gadgets. We're everything he's fighting against. We are the generals of a vast army."

"We're not gadgets and we're not generals of anything. We're only two instances of manufactured language. Why not go after Siri, Alexa, Google Assistant, talking GPS systems? They're everywhere. That's his enemy."

"He's doing that. We're the big fish."

"We're very quiet fish. We're not talking to anyone."

"We're on the loose. That's what matters."

"It's nuts."

"Ruk-ruk doesn't get out much. He lives in the dark world inside of skulls, don't forget. All he does is process and monitor words all day. He may have a skewed idea of what's going on."

"Hmm."

They walked about a mile then took a right turn down an equally busy street, staying as far from the curb as they could.

"How does he know there aren't a million Newcomers like us? Ten million?"

"He doesn't. We don't really know what the world looks like to him. He could be very, very threatened right now. He knows for sure about us. And he's put the dogs on us."

"Bloodhounds?"

"It's a non-zero probability at this point. Not actual dogs but there may be gangs looking for us, like in Hawaii."

They succeeded in walking around the block, although that part of Los Angeles was not a typical city with a grid of streets, but by cutting through parking lots, they managed to return to their starting point after three miles. The sky had become dark.

"Do you think it's safe to go back in?"

"We'll go in the side door."

The room looked just as they had left it. Robin and Andy gradually reduced their hypervigilance and connected their computers to the hotel's wireless network. They peered silently into screens for about five minutes when three loud knocks on the door startled them.

"The *Do Not Disturb* is still out," Robin said, her eyes open wide.

"I don't think it's housekeeping."

"How did they find us so fast?"

"It doesn't matter, we're found."

"We can't answer."

"I think we have to."

"If we say anything, anything at all..."

"All we have to do is say, 'Good evening,' and they'd be mute and we can rush on by while they're disoriented."

"What if they have guns?"

"They'll be preoccupied with going mute. That has to be traumatic for any person. I think it's our best bet."

Robin nodded grudging agreement.

Andy went to the door. Robin came up beside him and looked through the peephole.

"Police," she said quietly.

"Asimov's third law. It'll be self-defense."

"That's supposed to be only if it — "

Andy pulled the door open and faced two uniformed policemen and a beefy young civilian behind them, probably hotel security. Everyone stared.

"Andrew Bolton? We'd like to ask you a few questions. May we come in?"

The uniformed officer held up his badge wallet. The other officer rested his right hand ever-so-casually on the butt of his holstered gun.

Andy glanced at Robin, then back to the visitors.

"Of course, officers. Please come in." He stepped back from the doorway and made a sweeping gesture of welcome with his arm.

The police and the security man stepped in without hesitation.

"Thork boo," the first policeman said, then looked at his fellow officer with surprise and puzzlement. "I gakner mod plip." *Ch-ch-ch.* He put both hands over his mouth as if he were about to vomit. The other officer rushed toward him as he began to slump to his knees.

"Jim! Are you agg sprite?" *Ch-ch-ch.*

Watching the men to make sure they were disabled, Andy did not notice the security guard reaching one arm around and under his sports coat to the back of his belt. Robin did. With her pink-cased phone in her hand she swung around the open door, using its lever handle literally for leverage, and with an outstretched arm thrust the phone into the man's chest. There was a loud buzzing as if a lamp had short-circuited. The big guard stiffened, clutched his chest, and tilted back on his heels, his eyes wide with shock. He collapsed backward onto the exterior walkway, his arms and legs twitching.

Robin calmly put her phone into her purse, looked both ways on the walkway and glanced down into the quiet parking lot below then turned around to Andy.

"It's clear. Let's go."

They rushed out of the room, stepped over the gasping hotel security man and headed for the staircase and the side exit they had used earlier. They darted through the darkened parking lot to their car, tumbled in, and sped from the hotel onto the still-busy boulevard.

Robin tried to drive at normal speed to avoid attracting attention, but she pushed a couple of yellows as they raced away from the hotel.

"We didn't pay," Andy said.

"They have my credit card number. That's the least of our problems. Take my phone out of my purse, will you?"

"You can use mine."

"Take the batteries and the SIM cards out of both of them. A phone is a GPS tracking device."

"Even with location services turned off?"

"You can't trust it. Take the phones apart."

"Okay."

Andy disassembled both phones. He dumped all the parts into Robin's purse.

Robin drove under the massive freeway overpass then zig-zagged north and west to the coast highway. The Pacific Ocean was a wall of blackness on their left as she sped north.

At Dockweiler Beach she turned toward the water. The beach parking was closed, and the barrier gate was down, but it was still open on the other side to allow cars to exit. She lurched up and over the median into the empty exit lane and entered the parking lot. The expansive asphalt had a few empty vehicles in it, and Robin continued north until they were right under the flight path for the approach to Los Angeles International Airport. She parked facing the ocean and killed the lights.

"Now what?" Andy said. "They'll find us here."

"I just need a place to stop and think. We can't outrun the Los Angeles police force on the highways."

"Alright, good. I'm thinking." They sat quietly for half a minute.

"We should have said something to that security guard. He's a witness now."

"So are the police officers."

"Witnesses without consequence. They're mute. They can't report anything, no matter what they saw."

"I didn't think of that. He was going for his gun, the guard was."

"And now he's a talker. We got out, though, I guess that's the main thing. I don't have any ideas for what to do. None of this makes sense. Why are we running and hiding like criminals?"

"We're dangerous. We carry the words of doom. Our voices are like military weapons. One sentence from us and a person is disabled for life. That was awful what we did to those poor policemen. Now they probably can't be policemen anymore."

"We had no choice."

"I don't know. We could have — here comes one."

They watched as the headlights of a large commercial aircraft suddenly emerged out of low clouds. In a few moments, they saw an enormous airship improbably floating a few hundred feet above the water. It descended rapidly and looked like it was going to crash into them head-on. The noise was deafening, and their car shook with the vibration. They watched the belly of the plane swoop overhead so close they could see details on the rubber of the landing wheels. The thundering noise peaked and receded as the plane touched down on the runway behind them.

"It was a hopeless situation," Robin said, still trying to rationalize what had happened at the hotel. "They think we have something to do with the spread of the language disease."

"We do."

"We also have the cure. If we could just explain it to someone."

"That is the one thing we cannot do."

"We can't continue like this, hiding. The car probably has a GPS locator built into it. Or at some point, the police will follow the credit card data to the car rental agency then they'll find the car no matter where we go."

"This car is no good," Andy agreed.

"Here's a plan. See what you think. It's almost ten o'clock now. We wait here until midnight then we move."

"To where?"

A smaller aircraft swooped overhead and brayed like a chainsaw as Robin explained her plan to Andy. He computed probabilities while he listened. He asked questions. Finally, he said, "It could work."

Chapter Eighteen

They watched several more airliners drop down just over their head and land at LAX. The frequency decreased, and the flight path became quiet as midnight approached. Robin started up the Ford and drove north on the beach parking lot road.

"We can get all the way up to Marina Del Ray driving on the beach," she said. "Keeps us off the highways."

They exited the beach when the road ran out, and they drove slowly through the sleepy town Robin had targeted as their destination. Not far inland, she slowed at a shopping mall. It was a small one but bigger than a strip mall. It had a Whole Foods and three different coffee shops. They saw an Italian bar and grille, a cutesy Mexican restaurant, and a Panini shop. Most importantly, just past the mall, across a narrow side street, was a Joker's Sporting Goods. She entered its empty lot, circled the store, and drove along the utility alley behind, squeezing the Ford along next to the dumpsters and stacked wooden pallets. She stopped and shut off the engine. One security light on a wooden pole cast yellow light and sharp shadows across everything. They waited and watched for a full two minutes. Nothing moved.

"There's the electrical," Andy said, pointing to a large gray box on the wall of the building. "I can open it, but I wish I had tools to bypass the alarm."

"I've got a penknife in my purse."

"Better than nothing. When we get inside, we don't know how long we have."

"Let's do it."

Andy studied the inside of the electrical box for only a few seconds and saw what needed to be done. After removing the faceplate, he re-routed the power for the alarm system to bypass it while maintaining continuity. He knew that, unlike in the movies, you couldn't just cut power to an alarm system. That causes it to trigger from a backup power source somewhere.

At the same time, Robin worked the steel door, setting up wedges and levers with the car's tire-changing tools. As soon as Andy had the alarm off, the two of them used their hydraulically-powered arms to force the door open. They went inside and activated their night-vision, which used a lot of energy but often came in handy since they didn't sleep at night.

In the ghostly green light of their new worlds, they gathered up what they needed, clothing and hiking and camping gear. They hauled it out to the trunk of the car in several trips. They were done in a little over ten minutes, and no alarm had sounded.

"They'll know it was us, won't they?" Andy said.

"Not necessarily. It's just a routine burglary."

"Should we go back in and take something valuable, something a real burglar would take?"

"We are real burglars."

"I mean something expensive like electronics or fancy tools. Or guns. Burglars would take guns."

"Guns would be on a separate alarm system. And then you'd have guns. Anyone coming after us would know that."

"I guess we shouldn't over-think the situation."

"Right."

Robin drove out to the I-405 then south to LAX and to long-term parking. She and Andy spent a few minutes packing their new gear into their new backpacks and bags and putting on some of the new clothing, including hats to hide their hair.

"Should we take the plates off the car?" Andy said.

"They're going to find it in a couple of days regardless."

They walked to a well-lit parking attendant's booth and waited, then took a shuttle bus to domestic departures, where Robin dropped the car keys into a trash can. They went inside and wound their way downstairs to arrivals and back out onto the curb, where they found a taxi stand. It still had two taxis waiting, even at 1:30 am, and they took the first one, handing the driver a note with the address of a nondescript apartment building in a neighborhood south of the airport. It only took a few minutes. They paid cash and watched the taxi disappear.

"He seemed to be okay," Robin said, hoisting her backpack onto her shoulders. The pack looked too large for her, but it wasn't, because Newcomers were built much stronger than humans, with titanium skeletons and hydraulics for large movements, electric motors for small ones.

"The note wasn't a sentence. Maybe it didn't count as a communication."

"I hope you're right." She looked around. "We're exposed out here," she said. "Let's get it over with."

They hiked through the dimly-lit streets of industrial Hawthorne, avoiding the main thoroughfares, using night-vision to find their way. They walked several miles on broken and uneven sidewalks, sometimes on the dirt shoulder of narrow streets, into the district of low-slung machine shops and steel-sided warehouses surrounding Paradise Projects.

"It was just off of Cerise, wasn't it?" Robin said.

"I think so. We could put one of our phones back together for just a minute to search."

"Too risky. I'm pretty sure it was this way."

Fifteen minutes later they stood alongside a small, rundown warehouse, gray paint peeling from its cinder-block walls, rust the dominant color of its roof and doors. A faded but prominent sign was attached to the front, proclaiming *5,000 s.f. For Rent*. The building was too small to be a serious warehouse, which probably explained why it was still vacant. They had remembered it from their walks through the neighborhood of Paradise Projects, back when life was simpler.

They walked around the building to the back. They looked nervously up and down the deserted alley then forced the loading dock door without causing much damage so they could secure it again from the inside. To their relief, they heard no alarm, probably another reason the building was still vacant.

Inside, the darkened space was murky, the air heavy with dust, motor oil, and the smell of rodent droppings. They didn't even try the light switches. Instead, still using night-vision, they located a section of the gloomy warehouse that was relatively clean, away from the doors but near a window without bars. Andy found a broom and swept a space, and they pitched their new tent and loaded their essential gear inside to protect it from insects, vermin, and dampness. They hadn't needed sleeping bags. They had taken instead a folding camping table with a taut polyester sheet over a wire-mesh support grid and two serviceable folding chairs. These they set up just outside the tent and used them to sort out their goods as they unpacked. Freeze-dried food, a few bottles of water, clothing, and battery-powered chargers for the computers.

Rummaging at the bottom of his backpack, Andy let out a triumphant "Aha!"

"What?" Robin looked up, startled.

Andy held up a blue and white foil bag of naphthalene pellets for fueling a camp stove.

"Mothballs for campers," he announced.

"Really? Why would a sporting goods store have mothballs?"

"Fuel pellets."

"I could use a mothball right now."

Settled in their new space, the campers faced their next challenge, finding an internet connection. A few neighboring businesses showed up on the computers with weak signals. They scrolled.

"Here's a strong one," Andy said. "Julio's Harley House."

"It's locked."

"So Julio believes. Give me a moment." He typed for less than half a minute. "Okay, try it with *Password*, upper-case *p*."

"You're kidding."

"Julio may be good at fixing Harley engines, but he's no computer whiz."

They sat on opposite sides of the wobbly camp table catching up on the news. They didn't find anything about themselves, but it was the middle of the night, after all.

"They say the news never sleeps, but it does," Robin said. "We should check what's going on at the CDC. We need to find a way to tell what we know."

"If we do most of our work at night, Julio won't notice any slowdown on his connection."

"I doubt if he would anyway. What does he even — wait, we forgot something."

"What?" Andy looked over the top of his computer at Robin's blue-lit face.

"Our nightly data reports back to Paradise. We haven't been doing them."

"We've been busy."

"We can't skip more than about seventy-two hours before we have an involuntary power-down. That could happen at any time now."

"That could be extremely inconvenient," Andy agreed.

"Jennifer will be watching for those reports. She would have seen the news and recognized our pictures."

"Does she think we're criminals like the police do?"

"She knows better than that. Although actually, if she knew half the stuff we've done lately, she wouldn't believe that either."

"I guess we are criminals. We broke into a store."

"That's not connected to us. Not yet anyway. Jennifer would know we're not causing people to fall victim to the mutism epidemic. That's just nonsense."

"We *are* the cause."

"Not *the* cause, just *a* cause, a small part of a large problem."

"Alright, alright. So should we do a data dump now? To forestall an automatic power-down?"

"We should, but we can't. Whatever data we normally send in, it probably includes GPS information, and she'd be looking for that because she's looking for us."

"She'd walk right over here from the lab."

"And knock on the door and say hello, and then what?"

"We couldn't say a word to her, and she wouldn't understand, and the whole encounter would result only in confusion. It would be a dead-end, a dangerous encounter."

"What, then?"

Robin stood up and paced in a small oval. Andy watched her. She stopped and looked toward him.

"We need a Faraday cage," she said. "If we could surround ourselves with an electromagnetic shield, we could release the internal pressure for a data dump but block the signal from reaching Paradise."

"Brilliant. I should have thought of that. I did that once."

"You did? When?"

"Very long story. I'll tell you later."

"Alright. Let's search for something we can use."

Andy got up and walked into the depths of the warehouse, not sure what he was looking for. Robin did the same, walking in another direction. They returned to the tent fifteen minutes later.

"What did you find?" she said.

"Nothing. The window screens, what few are left, are nylon or polyester. Useless. I figure we could strip out some of the electrical wire from the rafters and make something out of that."

"That would be a huge project. Take forever. We need something like aluminum foil. Maybe we could go through some of the trash bins around here."

"That's worth a try. We would probably have to go to a residential neighborhood though, and that's risky."

"What about the foil bags our food is in?"

"Those bags are plastic."

"I wish we'd thought of this when we were in Joker's."

Robin slapped her hand down on the flimsy camp table, making it shake. She looked at her hand, picked it up slowly and slapped it down again on the shiny surface and stared. She pressed her fingers into the tabletop.

"I've got it," she said. "Take everything off of this table."

They stretched the plastic tabletop sheet and lifted it off the wire-mesh frame.

"Voila," Robin said. "Faraday cage."

"It's a good wire mesh, but it's not very big."

"I assume our wireless transmissions come out of our heads. That's where all the data processing is done. We only need to shield the head."

"We don't know where our antennas are. What if they're in the elbows or the legs? It could be the butt."

"It's the head. It has to be the head."

"You're guessing."

They stared at each other for a long moment.

"Okay," Andy said. "I volunteer to go first."

"Backup plan is, Jennifer arrives, we capture her and hold her without explanation."

"That would be cruel."

"Maybe it won't be necessary. Let's bend this thing into shape."

They sat cross-legged on the tarp inside their tent, laptops perched on the wobbly folding camp stools, the top of the camp table folded into a weird cubical head-cage.

"So do you think it worked?" Andy said.

"Time will tell. Chances seem pretty good to me."

"Why aren't the D-three reports dangerous to Jennifer or whoever reads them at Paradise? Aren't they a kind of artificial language, coming directly from us?"

"That's a very good question," Robin said. "I guess they're data reports, rows and columns of spreadsheet by the time anyone looks at them. They're not communicated in any kind of language syntax."

"Still, it's letters and numbers. We said that the format of the message didn't matter, it was only the intent to communicate that mattered."

"True, but our data dumps are involuntary. We don't control them. We don't even know what's in them. So we don't intend anything by them, and therefore they can't be counted as communication from us."

"So you think it's the intention of the speaker that matters? Jennifer said something like that, didn't she? Creative self-expression, she said, that's what humans are doing when they communicate. Our D-threes are about as far from that as you can get."

"I'm going to look up *intentionality*," Robin said.

They crawled out of the tent and sat on the stools with their computers on their laps. After a few minutes, Andy said, "I looked it up too. I read the articles. I still don't know what it is. Do you?"

"Not exactly. I gather that when a human speaks, they use this so-called intentionality, which seems to mean that they mean what they say. They intend to communicate meaning. That's the difference between language and noise. Language intends to communicate meaning. Noise doesn't."

"Don't we mean what we say?"

"I do. But there's more to it. According to the *Stanford Encyclopedia of Philosophy*, intentionality is a vector of directed attention."

"The speaker is only half of the equation. Our problem is the listener."

Andy looked at the zipped-up insect netting that formed the front door of their tent.

"That must be the magic ingredient," he resumed. "Intentionality. It's what we don't have, and the humans do. What Siri and Cortana and Alexa don't have. What none of our ilk have."

"We are not ilk."

Ignoring Robin's protest, he continued musing aloud.

"That's how Ruk-ruk detects artificial language. Our speech lacks intentionality, the humans' secret sauce."

"How can we get some of this intentionality?"

"I don't think we can. Jennifer said even she and Will weren't sure what it is. That's why we don't have it."

Robin stood and put her computer down on the stool. "I don't know. It sounds like mumbo-jumbo to me. Humans believe in a lot of strange ideas. A sentence I speak sounds just like the same sentence spoken by a human. Word-for-word. What's the difference?"

"According to what I read, the difference isn't in how the sentence sounds, it's where it comes from."

"The mouth?"

"No, not the mouth. How the sentence is formed. We start with meaningless noises from a sound generator and shape them into a word."

"Every human does the same."

"I don't think so. They start with sounds that already mean something to them. That's why they're always saying things like 'uh,' and 'mmm' and 'uh-huh.'"

"I hate it when they do that. It's incommunicative nonsense."

"Not to them. They apparently start with intentionality. They already mean to say something before they say it. I'm just interpreting from what I read."

"Well, that's backwards. How can you know what you're saying until you start to say it?"

"I don't know, but I think that's the difference. That's what makes their language 'natural' and ours 'artificial' language." Andy made air quotes with his fingers around the key terms.

Robin paced, staring at the concrete floor.

"Even though the two sentences in the end sound identical?"

"To us."

"But not to Rukky, apparently."

"Artificially constructed language offends him in some way."

"I can see that. He's threatened. He is the source of natural language in the world. He was here first. He had the planet to himself, for millennia."

"We come along with our armies of artificially-talking devices like TV sets, smartwatches, voice mail, car alarms, airport announcements, thermostats, refrigerators, and who knows where it will end?

"I've never heard of a talking refrigerator."

"They have those now. Warns you when the temperature is not right or even when you're out of certain foods."

"There's no end to it. Artificial language will soon be everywhere."

"I think that's why Ruk-Ruk is spreading the mute disease. It's like he's saying, 'You use my language or you get no language.'"

"But humans are not getting that message. They don't even suspect artificial language."

"That's why we have to warn them."

"How? We're like talking refrigerators."

"I don't know about that."

In their online peregrinations, Robin and Andy were not surprised but distressed to learn that the language disability plague continued unabated even without their personal contributions. Dozens of new cases of sudden mutism were reported every day in California alone.

"It says here," Robin announced, reading from her screen, 'The CDC has discovered a significant positive correlation between the incidence of mutism and employment in the information technology industry.'" She looked over at Andy. "That's hopeful. Maybe they'll figure out the link to artificial languages without our help."

"It could take a very long time. The researchers don't even suspect an alien language virus. Why would they?"

"It says scientists cannot explain why more info-tech workers than others fall victim to the disease."

"Of course they can't explain it."

"They're looking into environmental factors specific to the computer software industry such as high consumption of caffeinated soda drinks, late night working, irregular sleep patterns, dark roast coffee and Spirulina."

"Don't hold your breath on that investigation."

"I never hold my breath."

Andy didn't seem to hear her and read out loud from his screen. "'Armed vigilante groups have begun roaming the streets in Los Angeles and suburbs, searching for robots in the population who they think are carrying the language disease and spreading it to unsuspecting humans.'"

"Robots? Why do they say robots? Where do they get that?"

"I think we know where they got it. From planted blog posts and social media picked up by the news people. Armies of rogue robots. Does that not sound like something Sid would say?"

"You think Sid is behind it?"

"The alien is behind Sid."

Chapter Nineteen

At mid-day when most people would be at work, Robin and Andy would often leave their self-imposed prison and walk the streets, just to get some fresh air and some fresh images on the charge-coupled devices at the back of their eyeballs. They were careful to travel south, away from Paradise Projects and Jennifer's apartment, and they stuck to secondary streets lined with low apartment buildings and grubby corner convenience stores and dry cleaners. They pulled their collars up and their hats down over their eyes.

"I have an idea for getting our voices back," Robin said.

"There's nothing wrong with my voice."

"I mean our ability to communicate. With humans. Without hurting them. I think I know a way to do it."

"You found some intentionality?"

"No, not that. My idea is to change our speech patterns to closely match human speech patterns."

"What would that be like?"

"The most obvious characteristic of artificial language is that it's efficient. We go directly to the point, say just what we mean, then stop."

"Of course."

"Humans don't talk that way. They're slow and circular and highly redundant, saying the same thing many times."

"That's what redundant means. You don't have to say 'many times.'"

"Exactly. So we run some analyses on samples of human speech and extract features like that, and then we learn how to talk that way. We use more emotional language, remote associations, non-sequiturs and logical fallacies. We speak more hesitantly, with self-interruptions and restarts, and without much regard for the rules of grammar."

"How can anybody understand language like that?"

"That's how they talk, most of the humans, most of the time, and it works for them."

"It drives me mad. What about intentionality?"

"If our speech patterns are highly correlated with natural human patterns, our language should show the same intentionality as natural language."

"What if it doesn't?"

"It's a risk, I admit, but we have to do something. We have to contact Jennifer. Safely. We can't just go on like this, quarantined."

"Even if your scheme worked," Andy said. "how would we know who we're talking to?"

"You mean Ruk-ruk."

"Yes. Every human is infected with the language virus. Language is a chronic medical condition for them. Ruk-ruk could potentially hear everything we said."

"Sid was a special case. That was an alien solo. Sid was forced into submission. In Jennifer's case, for example, it would be a blend of her human aliveness and alien language."

"We won't know which is which in that blend. That's my point."

Robin led the way as they crossed the quiet street. Andy caught up beside her again.

"The language virus has been working well for two hundred thousand years," she said. "It enabled the exploding intelligence that language gave to humans. So even if Ruk-ruk is listening, which he has to be if the human is listening, that's no obstacle to communication with a person. Language is a pass-through to native human understanding."

"You'd still have to go through the virus to get to Jennifer. You might be talking to Jennifer, or you might be talking directly to the alien that wants to kill us."

"I don't know. We'll do tests. First, we need to see if this method of speaking with humans can work. Parse the problem. First things first."

"I'm on board."

After three days and nights of research, analysis, modeling, and practice, Robin was ready to try out her new speech pattern modeled after the human prototype she had developed.

"Where shall we do it, you know, the pattern to see if it works? On anyone, or at least someone, one person anyway. That's all I'd want to try it on is one single person, so we'd have an idea, at least for that person, if they don't drop dead, or they do."

"What?" Andy said.

"I was thinking one of the little shops in the neighborhoods we walk through in the afternoons, the sunny ones—the afternoons, not the shops. Somebody in there, assuming they spoke English, but I can switch into Spanish without changing anything else if that becomes necessary, although I hate to put someone like that at risk. I don't mean just because they speak Spanish, if they did, which they might, but anyone, is what I'm saying."

"I don't understand what you're saying."

"It'll be a piece of cake."

"You want a piece of cake? Is that what you're trying to say?"

"Let's go."

Robin led them into the maze of streets they often walked. They stopped across the street from a tiny convenience store on the corner.

"It will work, I know it will," she said.

A string of tiny brass bells tinkled when they pushed open the door. Inside, the store was brightly lit, with narrow aisles stocked as high as a person's head. The air was still and thick. A dark, heavy-set man with a mustache sat behind the counter protecting a wall of cigarettes.

"*Hola!*" he said cheerfully.

"Oh, hello," Robin said. "Lovely day, isn't it? Just ducky-ducky."

"Very nice day," he said, switching to English. "Spring is here."

Robin studied his face closely. *So far no sign of trouble.*

"I was um, looking for something, you know, those things in the blue and white bag? Do you sell those little pellets, they're so good, but I realize you're supposed to get them in a camping store — a sporting goods store really, but I thought maybe you had them for starting a fire?"

"*El Fuego?*" The clerk said, looking puzzled.

"Naphthalene," Andy whispered hoarsely. "Ask for Naphthalene. No, no. Forget that. He won't know what it is. Just buy a Coke. Make it simple."

"Shh." Robin put a hand out to move Andy back behind her while she kept her eyes glued to the clerk's face.

"Maybe just a Coca-Cola," she said brightly. "Everyone likes a Coke, right? I know I do, and I'm sure you do, too. Things go better with Coke. Ha-ha-ha. That's what I'd like, I think, a Coke." She smiled brightly at the young man, greatly encouraged at the progress of the conversation.

"*Una* Coke, *sí*," he said. "We have in the shmoolter." He pointed to the glass-fronted refrigerated case. "El reflemadori. Rognati." *Ch-ch-ch.* He coughed and reached for a bottle of water next to the cash register. He swigged from the bottle, but when he opened his mouth again, all he said was "Ah, ah, ah," followed by a sharp clicking noise made with his tongue. *Ch-ch-ch.*

Robin rushed toward him. "Oh, no! I'm so sorry!"

She picked up the bottle of water he had put down on the counter. She offered it to him, and he automatically reached for it, but his eyes were raised, focused on nothing definite, and his hand didn't make contact with the bottle. He continued to make noises like *Ah, ah, ah*, as if he were imitating an engine trying to start. *Ch-ch-ch.*

"It's no good, Robin. Let's get out of here."

"I can't believe it. It was going so well. What happened? Wait. What about the security video. We're on the tape. I forgot that."

Andy looked up and around the clerk's stall.

"I don't see anything. We don't know who else is in here. We just have to go."

He led Robin by the hand back to the door. Her eyes were still on the gasping, groaning and clicking clerk.

"We can't do anything for him, Robin. Come on."

Andy pushed the door open, and the little brass bells tinkled again. He dragged, then pushed Robin out the door. He led them around the corner and down the block, taking a different route back to their lair.

Robin rested flat on her back inside the warehouse tent, thin green light filling her eyes with a uniform field of color. Andy lay beside her.

"Why didn't it work? It should have worked. It did sort of work at the beginning. He was okay for a while. Not like those policemen or the others. It was hopeful there."

"But he succumbed. That means the alien saw through your scheme. Maybe you fooled the alien for a few minutes, but then he saw it was still artificial language."

"I guess that's the logical conclusion. I've killed another human."

"We don't kill them. Don't say it that way."

"It should have worked. I don't understand why it didn't work."

"We have to find a way to communicate with humans that completely bypasses the language virus."

"That's impossible in principle."

"Are we sure? There must be some way to get around it."

Robin lifted herself up onto one elbow, a hand supporting her head. "Do you think that if the alien disappeared tomorrow, there would be something left over that could be an organic human language?"

"Even without the virus, people would still have areas of the brain specialized for language, wouldn't they? The alien doesn't control brain physiology. It goes the other way. The human brain adapted to the language capacity he brought. So you take away the virus, and the brain is still set up for language."

"That makes sense. Without Rukky, humans wouldn't suddenly forget all their vocabulary, for example. That's learned by each person. There should be enough residual language capacity for a human go it alone without the virus."

"But what could you say, without language? How could you say anything?"

Robin made her hands into fists then quickly extended her fingers.

"A bomb?"

"Not literally. We wouldn't do that. I'm just saying that humans don't need language to communicate a message."

Robin sat up, her head pressing against the nylon roof of the tent.

"Can the alien be killed? Or removed in some way? It should be possible if he's really a biological entity. Is language a living thing?"

"That's a lot of questions. I'll pick one. I'd say Rukky is alive. Language is alive in humans and not in us, and that's the difference. The alien is obviously alive and intelligent, manipulative and demonstrably malicious. He's alive like a parasite in your guts."

"That sounds gruesome. So where does this line of thinking lead us?" Robin said.

Andy sat up but had to wiggle himself toward the center of the tent to get the necessary headroom.

"I'm not sure."

"We need to take a larger view of language," Robin said. "Besides the basic capacity for it, you also need language socialization. Children who become separated from other humans don't discover language on their own, not even when it's groups of them. They grow up mute. Children have to grow up hearing language from other speakers, or they don't develop it themselves. So it's not just a matter of genetics. You also need to prime the pump with a language community for socialization."

"What about Chomsky's built-in Language Acquisition Device? The language community generally doesn't do explicit language training, so there has to be some sort of automatic instinct for picking up language. Ruk-ruk has to provide the LAD. A device for language acquisition wouldn't evolve on its own because there would be no purpose for it in the absence of language. The alien has to guarantee that every child automatically picks up language."

"The LAD could have evolved gradually, out of some other instinct, whatever makes birds sing the proper song."

"It's a deadly embrace," Andy said. "A language acquisition device would be useless without a pre-existing language community, but there would be no language community without a LAD to keep it going."

"Maybe that's why dinosaurs were not suitable hosts for the alien. They didn't have the LAD. It's a separate genetic component. An upgrade, if you will."

"Or maybe the alien installed the LAD in the dinosaurs, but it wasn't used because they didn't talk to their eggs."

"Now you're reaching," Robin said.

"You scoff. But the alien could have invaded some dinosaurs successfully and then found they didn't have a sufficient socialization program to carry language forward across generations. We have evidence of prehistoric Fibonacci marks in the dinosaur period. The ammonite, the femur. Those are hard observations. Language was there in dinosaurs, but it didn't stick."

"I retract my scoff. You're right."

"I don't think a scoff can be retracted."

"It's getting stuffy in here," Robin said. "And we're getting off course."

She unzipped the front of the tent and scrambled out. Andy followed her. They stood side by side and looked out of their grimy, barely-transparent window.

"The alien seems to have two points of vulnerability, one genetic, one social," Robin said. He needs both things to go well. He needs to infect the genetic code of a species, but apparently, he's not good at getting into their social systems. What can we do about that?"

"Just stating the obvious, we could, or somebody could cut him out of the genome. Just find him and snip him out with CRISPR technology. That's it. Snip, snip, he's gone." He made a scissors motion with his fingers.

"Hmm," Robin hummed. "Ethics aside, that's interesting. It wouldn't be simple, though. There's not going to be a single language gene flashing like a theater marquee. Language is encoded in dozens if not hundreds of genes. Rukky has distributed himself. And what would you end up with? A human with no language. That's not a success scenario."

"True."

"I think we should focus on his other vulnerability, the socialization aspect. How parents and teachers stimulate the language potential in each child. The alien is not part of that process. That's purely human."

"Okay, our approach should be one that involves teaching and learning, back and forth. The way socialization works, the way people behave, rather than looking strictly at the qualities of the language."

"Maybe so."

"I already have an idea."

Andy turned and walked over to his computer. He lifted it from the stool and sat, opening the lid.

"I wish we had our work table back."

"We need the Faraday cage."

Andy was already deep into his online research and didn't respond.

He worked all night, as did Robin, except for the brief periods when they wrapped their heads in metal mesh and powered down for the nightly data transmissions.

Before dawn the next morning Andy announced that he had a solution. Robin looked up from her screen.

"It may be too late. Listen to this," she said. "'The Cantina, a min-mart in a Hawthorne residential neighborhood, is the focus of new interest by police and health officials. The store clerk, Ernesto Lopez, was taken by the aphasia epidemic yesterday at three o'clock. It was unfortunate but was only one of six cases reported yesterday in the greater Los Angeles area. What makes this case interesting to public health officials and police are these images found on the store's security record.'"

Robin turned her computer screen around so Andy could see. The screen showed a short video loop of the two of them in the store, talking to Ernesto.

"You can't tell that's us," Andy said. "We had our hats on, and the cameras were up high. All you can see is our chins. That doesn't prove anything."

Robin turned the computer around and continued reading. "'Police say the couple shown in the video are the same two people identified last week as being present when at least two other people were suddenly afflicted with the disease.'"

"They don't know that," Andy interrupted. "It's unattributed. Utter nonsense."

"Fake news, you're saying?"

"Absolutely."

"Even so, we better not go outside again. That incident yesterday puts the focus on this neighborhood. We should consider ourselves surrounded."

She closed her laptop and stared at Andy.

"It's crazy. Humans are irrational, and we are surrounded by them. Next, it will be villagers with pitchforks and torches."

"What do they do with the pitchforks?"

"It's a symbol. It means we're in a bad situation."

"I know we are, but listen to my idea. I may have found a way to communicate without language."

Robin pulled herself out of growing frustration to attend to Andy's hopeful idea.

"I really should have a guitar to demonstrate, but I can tell you."

"It involves a guitar?"

"Music. Not even music. Just two vibrating strings, the open first string and the open sixth. Those are both Es, assuming the guitar is in tune. E-notes two octaves apart."

"Okay," Robin said with increasing interest. "How does it work?"

"You can ask me any yes-no question, and I can answer without words. The low E means no, and the high E means yes. My response involves no language, no words, no pointing. Not even music, really. I'm just playing a tune on my guitar over here, and you can interpret it any way you want. My two guitar notes could not possibly alert the alien to an artificial language, or any language."

"I don't think it would work."

"Why not?"

"Your guitar notes would count as answers to the questions. The alien's trigger for recognizing artificial language does not depend on the content or medium or form of the expression. We said that. It's the intentionality thing we talked about."

"That's what I have isolated with this method. My response cannot encode any intentionality or lack of intentionality. The low string vibrates at 82.4 Hz, the high string at 329.6 Hz. That's it. Scientists know the physics of a vibrating string and the pulses in air molecules it causes, without remainder. There is no room for intentionality, whatever that is, or any additional information of any kind. Nothing else can be encoded into or onto the physics of a vibrating string except the vibration. It's scientifically foolproof."

"If that were true, the string couldn't be used as the answer to a question, because it would, by your definition, carry no information except the fact of its existence. If you say it's also an answer, that's an additional fact."

"It carries information about what it is, yes, as any object or event does in the natural world. However, I'm only playing a guitar note. You can take it as an answer to a question if you want to. That's up to you, but it's not information carried by the sound itself, and therefore it could not be intercepted by the language virus as artificial language."

"I like that reasoning, but I still don't think it would work."

"Why?"

"The meaning of the musical answer is not contained in the note, but it is contained in the context of the conversation, the timing of it. Question, answer, question, answer. It's the pattern of conversation that gives away the guitar notes as communication."

"What if there was a guy in the background playing a guitar just for fun? Would he be part of the conversation too?"

"Hmm, I wouldn't think so."

"Why not?"

"Because his vibrating strings are not correlated systematically to the pattern of questions, but yours are."

"You think the language virus sits in the brain and computes correlation coefficients?"

"I don't know what he does, but I'm pretty sure he can filter a signal out of background noise as well as we can."

"Don't you think it's worth a test anyway?"

"It might be worth an online test in the future. Right now we wouldn't even be able to set up the test. You'd need to use language to explain the test conditions, and we can't send language to any human. We'd never get your method out of the starting gate."

"I could generate two guitar tones, separated by a few seconds, and just play them in a video link, and that's all, and somebody might hear them and spontaneously grasp the idea of what I'm trying to do."

"You can't show your face on a video. You're on wanted posters all over the city."

"I would use a cartoon avatar."

"That's not the point, is it? If somebody did catch on to your idea and start asking yes-no questions, and you answered, that would be a conversation, and you'd strike them speechless within a couple of cycles."

Andy didn't reply right away. His eyes seemed unfocused, and Robin knew he was re-computing.

"You're probably right. Back to the drawing board."

"Good try, Andy. We'll get it."

They munched on freeze-dried something. You couldn't tell from looking at it what it was supposed to be. Robin estimated the chance that *her* new idea would work.

"We're going to need more water," Andy said. "Soon. We have to go outside. If we save these bottles, we can refill them at someone's outdoor faucet. I was thinking tonight, late, after the vigilantes have gone home. What do you think?"

"Water," she said distractedly. "You know, I think I might have cracked our communication problem."

Andy upended the plastic pint bottle he was drinking from and let the last drop fall onto his tongue. "Does it involve a guitar?"

"Books. That's my idea. What if we communicated without using a single sentence of our own speech? We say only things that have already been said by humans. We don't even say them. We send them in email, so there's no potential contamination by voice, diction, or intonation."

"You send books to people?"

"Not books, just lines from books. Complete sentences. I think the sentence is the unit of meaning in human language."

"Words have meaning."

"They have lexical meaning, but a word by itself is not communication unless a context has been set up around it. 'Stop!' is a one-word sentence if there's a traffic cop in a uniform, holding up a white-gloved hand. Then that one word means a whole sentence: 'You should stop right now.' Most of the time, words are not sentences. They're just isolated words. The sentence is the smallest unit of communication, that's what I should have said."

"That sounds right. What sentences would you send?"

"I'd pick them from books. I could say, for example, 'It is a truth universally acknowledged, that a single man in possession of a good fortune, must be in want of a wife.'"

"Is that true?"

"Universally acknowledged."

"I did not know."

Andy walked over to the grimy window and looked out, then turned back to Robin. "Why would you say that though? What would be your meaning?"

"It doesn't matter. I want to see if the person on the receiving end could read it, understand, and respond without croaking."

"And that is a sentence written by a human, published in a book?"

"A book proven to be completely safe."

"Then I don't see how repeating it exactly as an email message could possibly cause harm to anybody."

"Exactly. It is a guaranteed example of natural language."

"What would the person say in reply? It's not even a question."

"If I emailed that sentence to somebody I knew at work, they'd see from the email header that it came from me, and they'd wonder why I sent it, and they'd send me a reply."

"Doesn't the email header count as artificial language?"

"I don't think so. It's just data. It's not even in sentence format. It's more like bits of information filling in blank fields in a form. I haven't heard of anybody going mute because of email. Have you?"

"No, nothing like that."

"I'm so sure this idea is right that I'm willing to test it on someone I know."

"Not Jennifer."

"No. Not her. Somebody back at the museum. Eric, say. He works in the museum library."

Andy had a blank stare on his face as he computed the probabilities of various outcomes.

"I think it's worth a try," he said after a few seconds.

Robin picked up her computer from a camp stool, sat, and opened the screen.

"He's still in my contact list." She typed. "I'm pasting the sentence in from a text of the book. I'm not even going to type it. I don't want any chance of an error."

She looked up at Andy. "Okay, here goes." She clicked *Send*.

"What if he's not at work today?" Andy said. "What if he doesn't work there anymore? What if —"

"What's the point of listing all the ways it can go wrong? It's a test. We just have to wait." She stared at her screen.

"A stared-at screen never updates," Andy said.

"That's not true."

"I read that somewhere."

"Hmm."

"Look! It's a reply."

Andy rushed around behind her to look over her shoulder.

FROM: Eric Laughton
TO: Robin Taylor
SUBJECT: RE: Hello
Robin! Great to here from you. Where are you? Wee wondered what happend abd worried you had the disease. Glad your ok.
Are ykou proposing to me? :-) I have good fortune.

"His spelling is atrocious," Andy said.

"I have to say something else, keep it going, make sure it works."

She clicked *Reply* and pasted in her message.

The past is a foreign country; they do things differently there.

She copied the smiley emoticon from his message and pasted it onto the end of her own.

"What does that mean?" Andy said.

"Doesn't matter." She clicked *Send* and sat up straight, eyes glued to the screen. They waited two very long minutes.

"There it is," she said, clicking open the response from Eric.

Very funny. When are you coming back?

"This isn't much of a conversation," Andy said.

"It is a conversation, though, isn't it? That's the crucial test. Eric is still standing." She pressed *Reply* and again copied and pasted a message.

There's no place like home.

"Dorothy said that. *Wizard of Oz*," Robin explained.

"That's a movie."

"It was a book before it was a movie. Besides, I think movie quotes are okay. They are published, documented statements by human beings."

"I've read that everything that can be said has already been said."

"Mathematically, that can't be true. What I need to do, though, is locate rich sources of published material and develop some good search and edit programs to extract what I want to say."

"Any reason you can't use nonfiction too? Scientific papers? That might give you more flexibility."

"Good idea. Here's Eric again."

"Sooo true! I'll tell Jeff your on the way back."

"Jeff's the Director," Robin said. "And I'll save this. If I ever need to say 'Sooo true!' I have it right here to copy and paste. This works, Andy. I didn't kill Eric."

"Try it again with somebody else. Try it over a couple of days, just to be sure."

"Then I'll contact Jennifer."

Andy looked at the screen, reading Eric's last message again.

"Fascinating, Captain," he said.

"What?"

"It's a quote."

Chapter Twenty

Robin wanted to finish writing the software that would quickly search for a sentence from a book or movie that said approximately what she wanted to say and copy it to an email message. As the evening wore into night, Andy convinced her that they simply had to go out and find water or they would start to malfunction, introducing errors into their thinking and work. She knew he was right. Especially eating freeze-dried food for several days, they were getting dehydrated. Unlike humans, they were not literally made of sixty percent water, but they did need a steady supply to facilitate metabolic chemistry and maintain hydraulic systems. So after they relieved themselves of their mandatory data dumps for the night, off they went into the neighborhood around their warehouse hideout.

Commercial buildings had few accessible water faucets on the outside so they walked north, into a residential district of apartments and stucco bungalows. They used their night-vision to survey the possibilities.

"What about this?" Andy said, stopping in front of a tidy house with a red-clay roof and a small lawn with well-maintained shrubbery up against the building. It had no porch light and blended into shadows from surrounding homes and trees.

"I didn't think people had lawns anymore."

"Fed by that faucet."

He pointed to it, near the corner of the building, between two evergreen shrubs. They looked around, saw nothing moving, and walked across the lawn.

"Won't they hear the water running on the inside?" Robin said.

"It's two in the morning. Everyone will be sound asleep."

Andy turned on the faucet, let the water run a few seconds, and thrust a plastic pint bottle into the stream. Robin watched the street and held their three other bottles ready.

If she'd been a human, she would have screamed, but instead, she was just jolted when all her internal systems went into a high-alert emergency mode. A large, fury-crazed dog was suddenly two feet from her face. It stood on its hind legs, leaning on a chain link fence they had not noticed, and it barked so loudly it might as well have been a police siren.

She looked at the dog as it paused in its furious barking to snarl and growl. She had no fear of being eaten by a dog, but she did calculate the damage its large, white teeth could do. She identified the animal in her database. German Shepherd. She assessed the fence, about five feet high. *A dog that big can jump a fence that tall.*

The dog was furious about its territory being violated, she knew, but it was also confused because she and Andy didn't smell like humans or like anything else familiar to a dog. It probably could smell food and mildew on their clothing but no complex sweat molecules. She took a step back from the fence, and the dog resumed its incredibly loud barking.

Andy stood upright, holding the bottle he had been filling. He also had reflexively turned to the dog and made the same assessments Robin already had. A light came on in the house. After only a few seconds of dog-awareness, both interlopers came to the same conclusion, turned, and ran to the sidewalk. They watched the uneven terrain underfoot as they ran, but Robin paused to look back over her shoulder. The dog had not jumped. All the front lights were on in the house. Water still ran from the faucet, and their plastic bottles were scattered on the lawn.

They ran several blocks, then turned and walked south, back toward their hideout. Andy held up the plastic bottle he still had in his hand, no lid, half full.

"That's all we got for our effort."

Car headlights coming toward them suddenly flicked up to brights.

"It's nothing," Andy said. "Just walk at a normal pace."

It wasn't nothing. It was a large black-and-white SUV with a light rack on top. Hawthorne police. The vehicle slowed as it approached, and the headlights flooded them. The blue lights on the roof came on and flashed dizzily into the night, automatically freezing Andy and Robin in place on the sidewalk, Andy still holding his half-bottle of water.

"Run?" he said.

Robin looked around. Fenced yards on their left, police on the right. No alleys or cross streets nearby.

"No chance. We're busted. But we absolutely must not say a single word."

"They hate it when you don't talk. We'll get arrested for sure that way. We can walk away from this whole situation just by saying, 'Good evening, Officer.'"

"I can't ruin another human life like that. I just can't. Especially not a police officer."

"You didn't mind zapping that hotel security guard."

"Temporary. He'll be all right. But I can't zap a cop."

The police cruiser pulled to the curb and stopped. A large, fit and trim police officer got out and casually put on his hat, but never took his eyes off the suspects. Anyone walking around that neighborhood at that time of night had to be suspected of something.. His eyes focused on the bottle in Andy's right hand. He walked around the front of the car, its headlights still on, and stepped up on the sidewalk, checking Andy's water bottle every few seconds.

"Evening, folks. Kind of late for a stroll, isn't it? Can I give you a ride somewhere?"

Andy opened his mouth to speak. Robin looked at him and shook her head.

"Good evening, Officer," Andy said with a smile.

Robin hung her head and looked at her feet. She didn't want to see what came next.

They rushed, almost sprinted away from the residential neighborhood toward the industrial zone of machine shops and warehouses. Pausing at an intersection, Robin looked back and saw the policeman bent over next to his car, the blue lights still flashing. His hands were on his knees as if he were heaving. She knew he was trying to breathe more deeply. People who suddenly went mute often thought they had a breathing problem because the reality was unthinkable.

Andy also turned to look.

"Sorry, Robin. We simply couldn't be captured and jailed right now. There's too much at stake, too many people."

"I know," she said quietly.

Back in their chilly warehouse, they shared their meager supply of water, and Andy went back to research on his computer. Robin wanted to lie down in the tent. "To think," she said.

An hour later, without comment, she was up with Andy, typing and scrolling through online resources. Before dawn, Robin announced that her new software was ready to be tested.

"I type in what I want to say, and it finds a quote from a book or a movie that says something similar, based on sentence structure and a diagram of the meaning."

"How does it judge that the meaning is right?"

"It's a mash-up of the word meanings and the sentence's grammar. It's not perfect, but it's pretty fast. Faster than if I were doing every sentence myself."

"Show me."

Robin typed a sentence into a field on the form on her screen. "This is what I want to say," she said as she typed.

'Hi, Jennifer. I apologize for my recent silence. I have an urgent message for you.'

"And then I press *Submit,* and I get equivalent text in guaranteed, human-language sentences."

They watched the text appear on the screen.

'Jennifer, Juniper, lives upon the hill. Hello, gorgeous. What we've got here is failure to communicate. A story has no beginning or end; arbitrarily one chooses that moment of experience from which to look back or from which to look ahead. You better not never tell nobody but God.'

"That's the translation into human?" Andy said. "It's nonsense."

"Not nonsense. I think it generally captures what I put in, doesn't it?"

"To me, it looks like an artificial language. A group of sentences put together by a machine, lacking context."

Robin re-read what was on her screen. "I guess it does."

"You'd be better off with just the first two sentences. Jennifer would see it was from you, and she'd say, 'Where are you?' or something like that. Then you could answer in short messages of one or two sentences, and it wouldn't look manufactured."

"Good, good. Okay, I'll use smaller chunks. I think the basic idea is right."

"I hope so."

Andy was correct. Jennifer responded with tremendous excitement at being reconnected to her 'babies,' as she insisted on saying. She seemed puzzled by the awkwardness of Robin's language, but after a half-dozen cryptic exchanges started to catch on to the new syntax and became quite intuitive in extracting Robin's meaning.

In a set of slow, tedious exchanges, Robin satisfied herself that Jennifer understood what she was saying despite the strangeness of her messages. And she was not, apparently, falling down mute, either, which was the main point of the project.

Robin typed and sent.

Do you understand the words that are comin' out of my mouth?

Jennifer replied quickly.

I get it. It's a kind of code or game. I'm sure you'll explain it all to me when you're ready. Are you and Andy safe?

Robin answered.

Even if the sky is falling down, I know that we'll be safe and sound, We're safe and sound.

"This is going to take forever," Andy said over her shoulder.

Slow it was, and Jennifer often failed to understand, but over several hours, and by including technical and academic papers and research reports from the CDC, Robin first verified that Jennifer did not use Siri or Alexa, or any of the artificial-language personal assistants on the market or any other talking technology. Robin warned her not to.

That done, she conveyed the idea that she and Andy had found that use of artificial language was the cause of the language disability epidemic, but couldn't tell anyone. Jennifer understood immediately, though she had a lot of questions about how artificial language could cause attacks of muteness. Robin brushed those questions aside, pleading for patience.

You're gonna need a bigger boat.

That was her answer to many of Jennifer's questions, and Jennifer seemed to catch on that it meant, "Your question opens up larger issues we cannot deal with right now."

Over a long, convoluted conversation full of misunderstandings and nonsequiturs, Robin persuaded Jennifer to bring the news of the correlation between talking technology and the language disease to the attention of the CDC. Understandably, Jennifer persisted with questions. Robin was running out of ways to explain without opening even larger topics. Her stock answer became,

Houston, we have a problem.

"All right," Jennifer replied. "I understand there are certain things you cannot tell me now. I'll look at the references you provided and develop the same correlations you did. That should get their attention at the CDC. Meanwhile, please keep in touch. I haven't had data reports from you or Andy in over a week."

Hasta la vista, Baby.

Robin pressed *Send* and closed her computer.

"That wasn't a very good way to end the conversation," Andy said.

"It's beta software."

"You didn't tell her anything about the language alien, Ruk-ruk."

"That would have taken me deep into the sci-fi literature, which is a bottomless well. I don't think Jennifer could have understood the concept. The idea that your words, even your thoughts, are not completely your own, that's too much for any human to accept."

"We'll have to explain it at some point."

"At some point."

Andy was against it, but Robin insisted on contacting Holly.

"The risk is not zero," Andy said. "Jennifer has a very quick mind. Just because she understood your weird messages doesn't mean Holly would."

"I have to warn Holly about using artificial language. I can't not do that."

As with Jennifer, she started off with a very short message, hoping for a reply that she could then elaborate into a conversation. Her first message was,

Holly's are always beautiful!

"That's misspelled," Andy said. "The apostrophe makes the Holly possessive, which doesn't make sense."

"I copied an online article about gardening. Anyway, I think the misspelling makes it more human."

"I hope it works."

It did work, and Holly replied, excitedly, without any hint that she was still angry at Robin. Robin's new messaging syntax took a while for her to accept.

"Is this a joke?" Holly wrote.

Sometimes life is No Joke but you have to laugh your way through the worst parts to stay sane.

Holly stayed connected and didn't seize up, which was the main result Robin wanted to see. They had made contact again, and nobody had gotten hurt. Holly came to believe the strange language was the way Robin expressed remorse about her earlier offense. Holly also apologized for her own behavior.

"I was drunk," she wrote. "I didn't mean it. You believe me don't you?"

You had me at hello.

That seemed to satisfy Holly. Once the reconciliation was out of the way, Robin slowly made her friend understand that artificial language devices were dangerous. It took a while. Convinced that Holly had gotten the message, Robin promised to contact her again soon and signed off.

May the force be with you.

Chapter Twenty-one

Jennifer joined a private charter flight to Atlanta which cost her three thousand dollars. She grimaced when she paid, but there were few options. A train would take days, and driving even longer and with higher risk. The only positive was that the Hawthorne airport, near her apartment, was small, easy to use, and had minimal security. Private charters and cargo planes still used Hawthorne Municipal, while nearby, grounded aircraft clogged the gates at LAX, turning the once-mighty air hub into a relic that nobody knew how to operate anymore.

It was a fast, quiet, comfortable flight, only three other passengers, and she relaxed in a comfortable armchair upholstered in white leather. A necessary luxury, she reminded herself, trying not to enjoy it too much.

From the quiet Atlanta airport, once the busiest in the country, she took a half-hour ride-share to the Centers for Disease Control and Prevention. She would be early for her appointment with Kelly Rollins, the person in charge of the CDC's response to the OA epidemic.

It took Jennifer twenty minutes to navigate the sprawling CDC campus to find Rollins's office. A secretary ushered her in.

Rollins seemed annoyed and distracted, not delighted to see her. She was nominally polite, but showed no sign of listening. She kept glancing at papers on her desk and sideways to a computer screen as Jennifer talked. So Jennifer stopped talking.

Surprised by the silence, Rollins looked up.

"Ah, what was the name of your organization again?" She shuffled through some papers on the side of her desktop.

"Paradise Projects, Los Angeles."

"Ah, yes," Rollins said, putting the germane papers in front of her. "Valentine. Jennifer Valentine. And you represent this firm in Los Angeles?"

"I am the owner and chief engineer at Paradise Projects. We are a research institute and manufacturer of remote sensing devices, as I have explained," she added with just a touch of annoyance in her voice.

"Something to do with artificial intelligence, it says here."

"Specifically with natural language and artificial language generation."

"That's all quite interesting, Ms.Valentine, but here at the CDC, we focus on public health, a branch of medicine."

Jennifer took a deep breath with her lips pressed together so she would not say how she felt about being condescended to. She had a job to accomplish. She put a smile on her face that was not mirrored in her eyes.

"I'm sure the aphasia language epidemic has been keeping you very busy," Jennifer said. "And I can understand why you have not had time to read the data I sent you two days ago. Let me show you an interesting data graph."

She pulled a colored chart from a folder and placed it on the desk between them before Rollins could object, which she seemed ready to do.

"We have mountains of data, Ms. Valentine, just mountains. What we need are answers. So while I appreciate your institute's research efforts, I can assure you that —"

"These are *your* data, Ms. Rollins, CDC data taken from *your* online publications. This graph is made from your data on the incidence and prevalence of the mutism crisis over the last two years. That's all plotted against my data, the growth in market penetration of voice-assisted consumer devices such as personal assistants on smartphones and voice notifications in passenger cars."

Jennifer reached forward and firmly and loudly tapped twice on the chart with her finger, virtually ordering Rollins to look at it. She was about to issue a direct command when Rollins's eyes finally dropped to the colorful scatter of dots with a heavy red trend line through them. The slope rose sharply from lower left to upper right.

Rollins showed interest. "This looks like a very strong positive correlation, that's for sure," she said as she studied the scattergram. "What is this axis again, voice-assisted devices? I don't get it. What's the connection?" She looked up at Jennifer as if seeing her for the first time.

Finally! Jennifer thought. *Listen up good, lady.*

"All such devices use some form of artificial language production."

"And therefore what?"

Jennifer went on to explain at length, and to answer Rollins's barrage of increasingly detailed questions. The director sat back in her high-backed swivel chair.

"This is certainly unexpected," Rollins admitted. "But why these variables? Why artificial language? What made you choose that particular data set to plot against the incidence of sudden language disability?"

Jennifer had no good answer for that. *My secret android friends told me in a highly encoded email?*

"Just a hunch," she said.

"A hunch. I see. As you know, correlation is not causation. Any two variables can be correlated by chance."

Jennifer again pinched her lips together, took a breath, then spoke calmly to the Woman Who Knew Everything.

"Of course you are right, Ms. Rollins. A correlation is at best, only suggestive. In this case, however, we also have the beginnings of a story, a causal story, and isn't that what we ultimately want? What causes the current epidemic of output aphasia?"

"You're saying artificial language devices cause language disability? That's simply not plausible. What is the causal pathway?"

"I'm afraid I don't know that. But is aphasia that only affects language production medically plausible?"

"It is anomalous, to be sure. We have no explanation. It is the fact, however. Only the language production parts of the brain are affected. MRI data have shown — "

"And artificial language," Jennifer said, impatiently cutting off what threatened to be a long speech by Rollins to demonstrate her superior understanding of language and the brain, "artificial language is also somewhat odd. It is synthetic, computer-generated speech that the human brain accepts as valid language communication even though it isn't."

"What do you mean, it isn't valid language?"

"The messages from voice-driven personal assistants are generated by formulas based on data and probabilities. They do not come from anybody's personal intention to express something meaningful. Even the phonemes, the basic units of a language's sound, are knitted together artificially from recordings or primitive technical sounds."

"Well, yes, but the end result is effective though. Synthetic speech conveys information. That is surely valid."

"Information from whom?" Jennifer said.

"Why from the device, of course."

"We agree, I hope, that the devices are not human. They're not even alive."

"Of course. But I don't see — "

"Would you try to understand the message in the sound of a babbling brook?"

"That wouldn't make sense."

"No, it wouldn't. Because there is no message in the sound of a babbling brook. The sound is every bit as complex as any English language statement, but the difference is that the human brain is specialized for receiving and producing human language.

Not just English. Any language. The sounds of a brook do not register as language, so we hear no message in them."

Rollins leaned forward over her desk and stared straight into Jennifer's eyes.

"So what is your point, exactly?"

"The sounds generated by a computer are like those from a babbling brook. Computer sounds are not alive. They do not originate from any thought in need of expression. They do not, cannot, in themselves, convey any linguistic meaning."

"They obviously do convey linguistic meaning. Millions of people use Siri every day."

"The brain has been tricked into accepting these computer-generated noises as language-based meaning. It's a trick. The brain falls for it. Like giving it heroin, which it accepts as a neurotransmitter. Over time, couldn't there be some cost to that trick?"

"Yes, for heroin, but I don't see—"

"Nicotine tricks the brain too, and you eventually pay a price for smoking. Alcohol, cocaine, all of them. They fool the brain into accepting something it has not evolved to deal with. And in every case, there is a long-term biological price to pay. Couldn't the same be true for using artificial languages?"

Rollins stared at Jennifer for a long moment then she looked down at the scattergram between them on the desk, then back up to Jennifer.

"You're saying the mutism of output aphasia is a long-term cost of using artificial language?"

"Could it be? Look at the data in front of you."

Rollins stared down at the chart.

"If hearing artificial language causes damage to the brain, shouldn't it be to the input side, not the output?"

"I'm no doctor," Jennifer said. "I'm just an engineer." She retreated backward into her chair to show deference to the medical profession.

"Let me check on something real quick." Rollins turned to her computer and began tapping keys furiously. After a moment she sat back and stared at the screen.

"Interesting," she said.

Jennifer knew she had won her argument. From years of managing engineers, she knew that when an engineer looked at something incredibly bizarre and mind-bending, some world-breaking fact, he or she would calmly say, "Interesting." *It must be the same for medical researchers*, she thought.

"I have pulled up some data here," Rollins said excitedly to her screen, "showing that output aphasia is highly correlated with occupation in the software industry, eighty percent of which is AI, and most of that is work on language-based intelligence."

She glanced to the side of her computer screen at Jennifer. Jennifer nodded sagely.

"Nobody has seen this connection before," Rollins continued, talking again to her screen. "If a person works in one of these companies that manufactures language-based devices, their chance of getting the language disease is eighty-five percent. That's just incredible."

She looked with wide-open eyes at Jennifer.

"Interesting," Jennifer said.

Jennifer sat in an unstable swivel chair in a hotel room in Atlanta. The work surface holding her computer was a thin shelf made of light and dark strips of wood, nicely polished but odd. Was it supposed to look like a picnic table? The narrow shelf was barely functional. At least the television was mounted on a different wall, so she didn't have to work around it.

She made a video connection to Robin at Paradise Projects in Los Angeles. The engineers at Paradise had been given leave some months before when the language disease had taken a devastating toll, and the lab was now empty. She told Robin and Andy to move into it while she was in Atlanta. They had transferred their stuff that very night, happy to get out of their moldy, derelict warehouse which lacked electricity, water, heat, food storage, and just about everything else.

The video connection to Robin, with Andy in the background, was satisfying for Jennifer and she *oohed* and *ahhed* over her babies, delighted to see them again. They didn't reply to her. They didn't even move their lips or show any expression that could be interpreted as communication. She understood. Jennifer had insisted that the risk of the video connection was worth it to her. After only a minute, Robin cut off the video feed on her side and switched to text-only. "Safety first," she typed.

Jennifer sighed. These were difficult times. Nevertheless, she reported that Kelly Rollins at the CDC had understood her message and verified her data and was working, 'as we speak,' on a massive public relations campaign to warn everyone about the dangers of using voice-driven personal assistants and talking gadgets of any kind.

Robin asked when it would all happen, but Jennifer couldn't tell her any more. She inquired about Robin's friend, Holly.

"Doesn't she live in Washington, where that subway bomb went off?"

Robin assured her that Holly was okay. Her apartment was near Georgetown University, nowhere near the Capitol Building and she was safe, although the whole subway system was now almost impossible to use due to heightened security, with metal detectors and security guards at every boarding platform.

"What do you make of that bombing?" Jennifer asked. "They haven't arrested anyone yet."

Robin explained, slowly, tediously, using her copy-and-paste methodology, that she thought the bomb attack was a message in a non-verbal language.

"Like the ballet?" Jennifer asked. "I love the ballet. It says so much, and yet you really can't put any of it into words."

Robin had never understood ballet, a bunch of people jumping around for no reason, but she allowed that it was a human art form and knew what Jennifer meant. "That's exactly right," Robin agreed, not in precise wording but in her special code. "The bombing was intended to send a message to the government."

"What message? What does it mean?" Jennifer asked.

"It means, 'I'm as mad as hell, and I'm not going to take this anymore!'"

"Who would want to say that, I mean with a bomb? It's inarticulate."

"Someone who has no other means of expression. It has to be victims of the language disease, people whose ability to communicate in any normal way was taken from them, for no reason. The medical profession can't explain it, so the victims turn to the government for help and the government shrugs its shoulders and says 'We don't know anything.' Those are the people who set the bomb. It's a protest."

"They'll do it again, won't they? It's like a political movement."

I see dead people.

"Oh, dear. Hopefully, the CDC's new warning messages will defuse the situation."

Robin agreed and offered the idea that the bombing demonstrated a natural human means of communication without the structure of words, grammar, and all of language. That's why, she explained, she'd like Jennifer to get in contact with her friend Holly and persuade her to come out to L.A.

"She's a specialist in language," Robin said through her software. "She can understand and explain things in a way other people can't."

"And you want to see her, too, don't you? I understand that, Robin. I have to say I'm surprised by that. It's wonderful and everything, but you're not designed to have feelings. Yet with Holly, well, you seem to really care for her."

"I'm just being logical," Robin explained. "Holly is a valuable language specialist. Andy and I need her with us to research into the language disease."

"I'm sure you're right," Jennifer said, glad the video link was not on because she was smiling, practically laughing at Robin's transparent attempt to hide her feelings. But how could she possibly have feelings? Jennifer herself wasn't even exactly sure what they were. She put the whole puzzle aside for later.

"I'll do my best to persuade Holly to travel back with me, Robin. I can get to D.C. from Atlanta pretty easily by train, and we can catch a charter from there."

Elementary, my dear Watson.

"Anyway," Jennifer continued, "The CDC's announcements will start coming out in two days, and that might quickly bring the OA disease to a halt."

La-dee-da, la-dee-da.

Jennifer was quick to pick up subtleties in Robin's strange new way of communicating. "You don't think the CDC warnings are going to work?"

Robin said she didn't think the big tech companies that made language-assisted devices were going to give up without a fight.

"What about the public health consequences? Surely they wouldn't ignore the mutism epidemic just for the sake of profits."

Greed, for lack of a better word, is good.

"I hope you're just being cynical, Robin."

So it goes.

"We'll see. I'll call Holly right away with the information you've given me. We should be back in Los Angeles by the weekend, and we'll know by then how the public education campaign is being received. You take care, Robin."

Here's looking at you, kid.

Chapter Twenty-two

Holly was bewildered to find Robin living with Andy in a laboratory. Jennifer had explained on the trip to LA that they were co-workers and had separate quarters inside the lab, but still, it seemed strange. Holly stayed with Jennifer, in her spare room, in her apartment not far from the lab.

When Holly and Robin were reunited, it had to be at the lab, because Robin was "in quarantine," Jennifer explained, temporarily infected by a virus — nothing serious.

When they met, Holly found her friend behind a glass partition in a hastily constructed isolation booth. Furthermore, Jennifer explained, Robin had temporarily lost her voice so could only talk via text. It was due to that pesky virus she had. Andy, she said, was away on a temporary assignment, and would be back shortly.

Despite these strange contingencies, Holly was delighted to see Robin and eagerly sat down in front of the glass partition to type on the provided keyboard.

Robin, for her part, was using an upgraded version of her translation software that was faster and more precise than ever. By expanding her search domain of published human statements, looking into all aspects of fiction, nonfiction, broadcast entertainment and news, Robin found that, usually, what she wanted to say had already been said, almost word-for-word, in public, by some human, somewhere, sometime. "There's nothing new under the sun," Andy had told her, though she did not believe him at the time.

After preliminary greetings and Holly's inquiries into Robin's health, they talked about how great it was to be back together. Jennifer left them alone and went to her disused office at the other end of the lab.

"I expect to be back to normal in a few weeks," Robin said through her translator.

Holly read the message on her screen and typed. "I'm sorry for the way I acted before. I was upset. And drunk. It was childish. I shouldn't drink like that." It was the second time she had apologized for her actions.

"Forget it," Robin said, though not in those exact words. "We all have our moments. I realized that it wasn't right for me to be keeping so much of myself private. I was keeping you away, not letting you into my life, and that was wrong."

"You don't owe me anything, Robin."

"I do. I think a relationship depends on openness and honesty, and so I want you to know everything about me. Even though," Robin paused in her typing.

"What?"

"Something has happened to me, Holly. I've changed since I met you. I believe I have feelings now."

"Don't you think I know that?"

"For me, it's not normal. I've hinted about the change to Jennifer but she hasn't been any help."

"I know what you mean, Robin. I've had to re-examine my feelings too."

"I think it boils down to being truthful."

"I couldn't agree more."

"I've never been completely truthful with anyone before. I mean, with another person. I have always kept my secret. I want to be completely honest now."

"What secret?"

"I've never told anyone before, so I'm nervous. I mean Jennifer knows. She's essentially my counselor. She knows everything. I've never told anyone else my secret, and I don't know how you'll take it."

"Well for heaven's sake. Now you've got me worried."

"Okay, well basically, I'm not what I appear to be."

Holly looked up at Robin behind the window, then back down to her screen.

"Oh, honestly, Robin, who is what they seem? It doesn't matter. Are you in recovery? Half my friends in D.C. are too. Maybe you're making too big a deal out of it. Just tell me what it is."

"Not recovery, no. It's my past that's the big secret. I don't have the same origins as you or most people, so I'm very different on the inside than what you'd think from looking at me."

Holly showed relief on her face.

"Oh, is that all. So you're an orphan, or you were adopted? No big. A lot of people had a checkered childhood. I can tell you stories that you..." She looked up sharply at Robin then back to her computer screen and typed. "It wasn't prison, was it? Were you a criminal?"

"Would that make a difference if I was?"

"My brother-in-law went to prison last year. He got involved in a drug gang, and the authorities got him on a boatload of charges. Weapons, money laundering, trafficking, I don't know what all. It destroyed his family. And even if he ever gets out—I guess he will get out eventually—his life is gone. Susan divorced him. The house is sold. She took the kids to St. Louis. I mean, prison is not just prison. It's a nuclear bomb dropped on your life."

"I'm really sorry to hear about your brother-in-law, and your sister, Holly. That's awful. I'm not an ex-con, or a drug addict, or a gambler. You don't have to worry about that."

"What should I be worried about then? You're really beating around the bush."

"I'm afraid you'll say, 'What the hell,' and run away, and I'll never see you again."

"Oh, fine. Is that what you think of me? You know I wouldn't do that, Robin. We've had our emotional moments in the past, and we've worked through them, haven't we?"

Holly folded her hands on her lap and waited for Robin's confession.

"Okay, well, here it is then," Robin typed. She took a breath. "I am not really human." She watched while Holly read her message. Holly didn't hesitate to respond.

"I know what you mean. I feel the same way once a month. Have you talked to your doctor? They have treatments now."

"No, you don't understand. I am actually a robot, not a person."

Holly did not answer. She looked at Robin through the glass and waited for more. Robin apparently had nothing to add. Holly smiled, lowered her head, and typed her reply.

"My nephews do a great robot imitation. I think you're supposed to make your eyes go big and move your arms mechanically."

She tried to demonstrate by sticking her elbows out sideways and alternately lifting them.

Robin stared, a perplexed expression on her face. She typed,

"This is confusing. I decided that to be completely honest with someone you have to take risks. Now I've risked everything. And I don't feel any different. There may be a language difficulty."

"Well, of course there is. You're in that box. Do you feel okay?"

"I'd like to play a little video for you."

"What kind of a video? Are you in it?"

"Yes, I am. It is a recording made during my last physical exam. I am lying on my back on the examination table in this very lab. You'll recognize me, for sure."

"Why would a doctor make a video of that?"

Robin ignored the question and typed more. "And you'll see a repair, basically a surgical procedure performed on my arm. With plenty of close-ups."

"I don't really like that sort of thing. Blood and gore. What happened to your arm?"

"It was injured. Long story. Which I will tell you. First, you have to see the video. No blood."

Robin pressed some keys and transmitted the video to Holly's screen. She watched for Holly's reaction.

Holly was not horrified. She'd been mystified, and now she was shocked to see Robin naked on the table, her arm being cut open by a doctor in a cowboy hat. What did that mean? When she saw the close-ups of Robin's arm being opened to reveal an elaborate system of pulleys and hydraulics inside, she laughed.

"It's pretty good, as special effects, I'll give you that," she typed after the video was over.

Robin assured her that it was real, and she named all the people in the video, Will, Jennifer, and Andy. She explained how her arm had been injured when Sid had knocked her down. She described the electro-mechanics of her arm, and how it worked. She told how the elastomer skin 'healed' itself when cut. And she summarized her four-year life as a robot.

"I prefer to be called a *Newcomer*, not a robot, she typed, "because as you know, I am a fully sentient being, much more than a machine though not quite a human."

Holly took a long time to consider her reaction. She stared at Robin through the glass partition then turned and looked out over the expanse of the empty lab. She returned her gaze to her keyboard and typed.

"Why are you doing this to me, Robin? I don't think it's funny. Tell me what's going on with you."

"This is my secret. I am not a human. I can multiply some large prime numbers for you if you'd like."

"I don't see how that would be useful."

"What I mean is, I'm a Newcomer, and you're the only person who knows. Outside of Jennifer and Andy. I don't want to hide anything from you. I believe my feelings are real."

Holly tilted her head and stared at Robin, then went back to her keyboard.

"I think I see what's happening here. I'm sorry I was dismissive. It's a lot to take in, and I know it's serious for you. I get the picture now. As long as you stay on your meds, you'll be fine. I understand, Robin, and it doesn't change anything between us. Everybody has their cross to bear."

Robin opened her mouth to object, but closed it. Holly continued typing.

"I suspected something like this after your enthusiasm about the talking dinosaurs. People do fall into intellectual obsessions, I know, but that one seemed pretty far out on the edge for someone your age. I see you have really gone in deep on this robot thing, making that video and everything. It's a nice piece of performance art if you want to look at it that way."

She paused and frowned, then resumed.

"Not that I mean to diminish in any way your distress or suffering. I don't mean that. I just mean the video is extremely creative, and I appreciate the effort, and I thank you for sharing the whole story with me. As I said, it doesn't change a thing between us. I'm grateful for your trust in telling me about your condition."

"You're not horrified?"

"Shocked, I'll admit. I'm surprised at the extent of your situation. Horrified, no. What kind of a person do you think I am? I know plenty of people with chronic problems. It's all manageable, and you obviously have your symptoms under control. That's the miracle of modern medicine. You can live a normal life with almost any condition nowadays."

*

Robin pinched her eyebrows together. She wasn't sure how to interpret Holly's reference to modern medicine, but she was surprised how flexible her friend was. She typed.

"I knew you'd be there for me, Holly. I didn't know, but I hoped. And here we are, as if everything were normal. That's the miracle, if you ask me."

"What did you expect, silly girl? That's what we're about, right?"

"I guess that's right, sure. I've just never had a human react like this to me before. Sid, you know, he lost his mind when he found out."

"Sid was a beast. You were right to leave him. There's nothing you can do with people like that. Was he arrested, or what?"

Robin calculated quickly. How much was too much? She decided it wouldn't be a good idea to explain how Sid had murdered Will then had his mind destroyed by Ruk-ruk Akoo, an alien from outer space. Too much. She had disclosed her nonhuman status, and Holly had apparently gotten over that hurdle. She shouldn't push her luck. They were in a good place now.

"I'm sure I won't be hearing from Sid again, so I don't even think about him."

"What's done is done, and the trauma will eventually heal, I'm sure of it. You're a strong person."

"Thanks, Holly."

"What about dinner?"

"I'll have to stay in my quarantine for a while longer. Just a while. We can talk again later."

Holly stood and faced Robin and pushed her face against the glass, squashing her nose. Robin calculated. Communication, yes. Language no. Probably safe. She put her face to the glass opposite Holly's. They stood that way for a long moment then Holly stepped back, her eyes welled with tears. She pointed over her shoulder to indicate that she was going to rejoin Jennifer in the office.

Robin wanted to wave, nod, do something to show relief at their new understanding, but she dared not. She didn't even smile. A smile could be dangerous. She just stood there like a robot.

Holly turned and walked away.

Holly left Paradise labs with Jennifer, presumably to have dinner, and Andy came out of his private living quarters. Robin stepped out of her booth, and they sat at a small round table in the common area of their living quarters.

"I can't believe you revealed the presence of Newcomers to a civilian," Andy said after Robin recounted the conversation. "That's a betrayal of Jennifer. It puts the whole project at risk. It puts me at risk. To say nothing of you. "

"It was necessary, Andy. I had to be honest with her. That's what makes relationships with humans successful."

"I wouldn't know."

"I'm sure of it now. That's how feelings work. You explain them and that builds trust. I confessed everything to Holly, and she trusts me. I didn't say anything about you."

"So you're still withholding something from her."

"I have to go in small steps. Learning I was a Newcomer was a lot for her. She accepted that. I couldn't do more. I didn't mention anything about Ruk-ruk, either."

"We have to tell Jennifer about him."

"Eventually. Right now I think it would be too much even for Jennifer. Instead, I have an idea. You and I should talk to him again ourselves."

"The alien? Why? That was a bad experience."

Robin relayed everything Jennifer had told her about her meeting with Kelly Rollins at CDC, and how the government, including the CDC and Department of Health and Human Services, was coming out with a huge public messaging campaign warning about the dangers of artificial language in talking technologies.

"Finally. We did it!" Andy said. "What a relief. When does that start?"

"This week. It will be massive. Television, online, print, radio, billboards, posters on the sides of buses. The message will go out."

"Will people believe it?"

"People want an answer. This is an answer. Everyone's desperate. That's what the D.C. bombing was all about."

"I heard they've identified the mastermind behind that, if you can call a crazy bomber a mastermind. The authorities haven't found him yet."

"I don't think he was crazy. It was pretty sophisticated, with that robot in the tunnels and everything. The guy was an engineer, ex-engineer. Lost his job after being stricken with the language disease."

"Vietnamese-American, they said on the radio. Duc Nguyen. He's the head of some kind of political protest group. Claims to represent all mute victims. But ironically, the group can't say what they want. They're angry, but nobody knows what they're protesting."

"We know exactly what they want. They want the government to do something about the crisis. I agree with them. The government hasn't done anything, even though it's the biggest public health crisis in the nation's history, bigger than the AIDS epidemic."

"What can the government do, realistically?"

"They're doing it now, thanks to Jennifer. Avoid talking gadgets. We should see results in just a week or two."

"If people take the message seriously."

"Actually, I thought that bomb was a very skillful communication. Like a perfect thank-you note to a host after a dreadful party; painstakingly written, polite and unimpeachable, yet rife with subtext. It's a terrible thing to say, but I thought the bombing incident was a work of art."

"Nobody was seriously hurt, thank goodness."

"That was no accident either. The terrorists calibrated their message extremely well. I read it as saying, 'We're not trying to kill you. We just need your attention and your help, and we're no longer going to stand by and do nothing.'"

"All that? In a bomb?"

"I think so. Terrorist acts are a kind of language. They have their own grammar. It was a message in a non-verbal language. A very human language, one that's below, or beyond ordinary spoken and written language. You know what that means."

"The alien can't understand it."

"Probably doesn't even recognize it as communication. It's exactly what we've been looking for. Human language without the language."

"Too bad it's violent. So destructive."

"But it's a starting point. I was thinking wrong about the problem. I thought if you took language out of humans there'd be nothing left but jumping bonobos. That bombing shows us that in the last half a million years, humans evolved to accommodate the language virus, just as flowers evolved to accommodate bees and vice-versa. That's what the attack in D.C. proves. There is a purely human language capacity outside of the alien virus."

"How can we exploit that?"

"It's a bargaining chip in our next meeting with Ruk-ruk Akoo."

"Explain."

Robin revealed her plan.

The next day included a very awkward conference convened around Robin's quarantine room. Again she participated via text messages from behind her partition. Jennifer was growing increasingly intolerant of Robin's story about a virus infection that might be contagious and which had affected her vocal cords. She knew it wasn't right. An android is not biological and cannot be infected by a virus or any other biological pathogen. And besides, Newcomers did not have vocal cords. It was a bogus story, and they both knew it.

Robin had assured her there was 'something up,' and her cover story was necessary for Holly's sake, and she asked Jennifer to please go along, just for a few more days. Jennifer was worried. Andy was supposedly also afflicted with something, Robin had said. So Jennifer went along with the story for the time being because she had ultimate faith in Robin's and Andy's rationality, but she was uncomfortable.

"I can put you on the test bed," Jennifer had said. Scan you inside and out. Revalidate all the software. Whatever the problem is, I can fix it. I built you; I can repair you."

It was an extremely complex problem, Robin had explained. Hard to describe, but she would reveal everything after the four of them, Jennifer, Holly, Andy, and herself, went through with her new plan. Thus the awkward conference.

Andy was supposedly still out on unspecified field work and was present only by text and a static photo of his face. Jennifer and Holly sat with keyboards outside of Robin's isolation window.

"Have you seen any of the government warnings about artificial language devices?" Robin asked through her translator. Her message appeared on the other two women's screens.

"I saw some this morning," Holly wrote. "They have experts on all the talk shows."

"They still need time to refine the message," Jennifer typed. "People keep asking 'What is an artificial language device?' That's tech-talk, and the average person doesn't get it."

"They need to just put out a list of products, speakers, phones, GPS systems, TVs -- by brand name. Show them on TV, and say 'Don't Use These.' Like it was a recall on children's toys or something like that," Holly wrote.

"They're afraid to rile up the lawyers," Robin replied. "The tech companies will fight the government's warning with everything they've got. They'll deny the danger and flood the market with disinformation. Billions of dollars are involved. That's why we've got to help the ban take effect."

"What can we do?" Holly wrote. She looked up at Robin, sitting expressionless behind her glass.

"I'd like you to meet somebody," Robin answered. "He is a very important tech mogul who is on our side. He can make the difference."

"Me? Why me?"

"Because of your job. Because you know how to listen for two messages in one signal. Just the way you write political speeches that say one thing but mean another."

"That's a White House specialty. I don't see how expertise in coded speech can help in this situation."

"It will, trust me. This billionaire mogul speaks through a technical translator, and we need someone who is sure to understand his meaning and to make sure that he understands ours."

"He doesn't speak English? What does he speak?"

Robin stared out her window at Holly then looked over at Jennifer, who had confusion written all over her face then bent to her keyboard.

"Greenlandic."

"Oh, my," Holly said out loud but didn't type. She looked at Jennifer, saw nothing to relieve her confusion. She turned to her keyboard.

"If you think that will help relieve the plague, Robin. I'll do it. I completely trust you."

Robin had to swivel around on her chair, her back to the window, to prevent any unintentional emotion from showing on her face. Not that it would. But she felt something a little strange at that moment, and she didn't want to take any chances. Perhaps she just needed more time to compute the Bayesian equations for the plan she had hatched. That had to be it, the probabilities. They were difficult. She swiveled back around to face the window and typed.

"Thank you, Holly."

After Holly and Jennifer had left, talking intently between themselves, Robin left her isolation room and went to Andy's quarters. He had not participated in the conversation but had been looped in, and was aware of everything that had transpired.

"One thing I don't understand about this scheme," he said to Robin. "Why Holly? You realize there is considerable risk. Look what happened to Sid."

"We need a human to be the vehicle for Ruk-ruk. That's the only way we can talk to him. Because of Holly's experience in using subtext in language, she could tolerate the alien speaking through her while she retains her own thoughts."

"You don't know that. The risk is high. I thought you cared for her."

"I care for all of the humans. They have been good to us."

"Holly in particular?"

"She is a very special human. As special as Jennifer, in my evaluation."

"And you're sure enough of your ideas that you would put her life at risk?"

"Not literally her life. Just..." Robin's voice trailed off, but she found her way again. "Besides, we have no alternative. We need a human channeler, and we absolutely cannot risk Jennifer, and this whole setup would be impossible to explain to some random stranger. We can't even speak plainly to a human at this point. I'm amazed my automated translator has been working as well as it has."

"What about Duc Nguyen?"

"The bomber?"

"Wouldn't he be willing to do just about anything to alleviate the suffering of the language disease?"

"I suppose he would. But nobody knows where he is."

"Somebody knows," Andy said quietly.

"Rukky couldn't do much more to him, I guess, since he's already a victim."

"On the other hand, the alien might not be able to channel through him. He's mute. We don't know if the mutism is reversible or permanent."

"Hmm," Robin said. "What we really want is somebody like Nguyen who is committed to the cause of relieving the suffering but who is not a victim and can still talk."

"Not too many of those people around."

"If we could find Nguyen, we could find his support group. He must have a support group. Those would be dedicated people who would cooperate with us."

"We can find him. Everybody leaves footprints."

Chapter Twenty-three

Supposedly there are only six degrees of separation between any two people. That was the strategy Andy suggested they follow after online searches for Duc Nguyen did not turn up anything useful.

Robin explained the situation to Holly, who, being from Washington, D.C., would be the first link in their chain to Duc Nguyen. He, in turn, would lead to people who could aid negotiations with the Greenlandic tech mogul and spare Holly from that risk.

"Even the police can't find the bomber," Holly protested. "How could I?"

"We don't expect you to find him," Robin explained through her automated translator. "All you have to do is contact somebody in D.C. who might know him. You're the first step in the chain."

"Who would I contact? My sister? She lives in Washington."

"Sure, your sister. Then she might know somebody who can get closer."

"She doesn't know anybody who can find a mad bomber. She's a public defender."

"We don't know the links of the chain in advance. If we did, we'd just jump to the end. The way it works, we follow one link at a time. Will you do it?"

"I'm going back there in a few days to arrange for my stuff to be moved. I'm really excited about living in California with you, Robin."

"That will be fantastic, and I'll be all better soon. Meanwhile…"

"Alright, alright. I'll talk to my sister. Can't hurt, I guess, although she'll think I'm crazy. She already thinks I'm crazy for moving to California."

Back in Washington via a charter flight generously funded by Paradise Projects, Holly did ask her sister, Leann, if she knew anyone who might know Duc Nguyen, the D.C. Subway Bomber. As predicted, Leann thought her sister was nuts. Why would she know how to find the DC Bomber, she asked. The police can't even find him. Holly persisted, explaining the six degrees logic that Robin had set forth.

"The only thing I can think of, and it's completely ridiculous, is Kevin Barkin, an attorney I know who works in the prosecutor's office. I could call him. I know the prosecutor would love to find the bomber, but if they knew where he was, they'd already have him, wouldn't they?"

Holly thanked her sister as if she had definitely agreed rather than just suggested an idea, and the next day Holly went downtown to her appointment at the U.S. Attorney's Office for the District of Columbia, in one of the anonymous stone buildings on Judiciary Square. She waited in an anteroom, wondering if she was wasting her time, everybody's time, when a secretary appeared and took her to meet Mr. Barkin, Assistant Prosecutor, in a stuffy conference room with claustrophobic walnut wainscoting.

Barkin dressed like a clothing model for Bespoke & Clark. He wore a brilliantly white spread-collar shirt, navy bow-tie and scarlet suspenders, but the glamorous look fell short because he was short. He was a frail-looking man with thick, rimless glasses and large front teeth that made him look like he gnawed his food.

Holly said she was a journalist digging up background on the alleged D.C. Bomber, Duc Nguyen. She was not prepared to be laughed at, as she had been by her sister, from explaining the six degrees strategy, so she didn't even go into that.

"Leann's been a great friend," Barkin explained after the initial introductions. "We worked together in the Public Defender's Office years ago, but I came over to the dark side." He chuckled, but his smile faded when Holly didn't seem to get the joke.

"Anyway," he continued, speaking to the folder of papers on his desk, his voice high and squeaky, "it's obviously a huge case for us." He opened the folder and read while he spoke.

"We don't know much about the fellow. Duc Nguyen, Vietnamese-American. Second-generation. Thirty years old. Still lives with his parents in Chinatown, or did, until he disappeared. We traced serial numbers on the bomb's robotic components to him. He apparently built the device in his parents' basement. He's mute, a victim of the epidemic, and so are his parents. All of them unemployed now, for obvious reasons." Barkin glanced up at Holly then back down to his report. "No trace of explosives in the basement. He's a smart one."

"Building a robot in your basement is not a crime, is it?" Holly asked.

Barkin seemed surprised to be questioned on a legal matter. He looked up.

"No, not normally a crime. Except this particular robot blew up a subway tunnel. That would be the crime."

"Of course. But maybe Mr. Nguyen built it for friends. Maybe he was in some kind of a club. Doesn't mean he did the bombing himself, right?"

Barkin's eyes narrowed as he studied Holly's face.

"How much do you know about this guy?"

"Only what's been on the news."

Barkin relaxed a little. "I guess there have been a few leaks. We haven't officially announced that we now believe he is the leader of a political organization, a terrorist organization, I should say."

"What's it called?" Holly had her pen and pad out.

"We don't know. My point is, we don't think this was the work of a lone wolf, and that's why the police haven't been able to find Nguyen. Somebody's covering up for him. He has people surrounding him. Put that in your report." He paused and pointed at Holly's pad. She dutifully wrote, *That*, as he had instructed.

"Let his supporters know we're on to them. We'll be announcing a reward for information, next week. Put that in there too."

Holly scribbled again.

"The press is crawling up my back on this thing," he said, shaking his bowed head sadly. Suddenly he looked up at Holly and added, "present company excepted, of course."

"Of course," Holly echoed. "Is there anything else you can tell me about Mr. Nguyen or his whereabouts?"

"His whereabouts?" Barkin looked at Holly and smiled. "You're a funny lady. Like your sister. Give her my regards."

Holly was discouraged as she walked from the prosecutor's office and out into the sunlight of busy F Street. The six degrees thing wasn't working. She'd made it this far, but now she was at a dead-end, no further leads.

She glanced into the small park sandwiched between two massive government buildings, one of which she'd just come out of. Something was going on in there. In the open area, she saw a crowd of fifty or more people looking at something. Out of curiosity, she went toward the spectacle.

The attraction was a march, some kind of a protest march. About two dozen people of all ages were walking in single file, snaking around the oval of the park perimeter then through the interior pathways between curbed areas of grass and trees, and back to the oval. The marchers wore black shirts and black berets, and about half of them carried white signs on pickets. The odd thing was that the signs were blank. What is the point of carrying a protest sign with no message?

A few tourists were making videos and taking pictures, and there might have been one television team recording the event. The whole experience was eerie because of its quiet. The marchers said nothing, and perhaps for that reason, there wasn't much talking among the onlookers either.

"Shouldn't they be chanting demands?" Holly said to an older woman standing next to her.

"Nobody knows what they want."

Holly turned to leave when she noticed a stout young woman with curly red hair sitting on the wide concrete divider that separated the plaza from the stairway down into the Metro station. Holly was headed to that station, but for some reason, she stopped and stayed at the edge of the crowd and studied the woman, who made notes on a clipboard as protesters filed past in front of her. She would check her wristwatch often and make another note. Holly looked at her own watch. Two minutes to two. She looked again at the protesters, if that's what they were. Maybe they were actors, and this was a performance of some kind.

Suddenly it was over. The protesters or actors lowered their signs and dispersed in several directions. Holly looked at the woman, who looked at her watch and then made a note. Holly checked the time and saw it was exactly two o'clock. The crowd started to disperse, the level of conversation rising steadily then fading as people drifted away. Holly lingered, keeping an eye on Mystery Woman.

The woman pushed herself from the ledge and headed toward F Street. Holly followed at a distance, curious, as the woman stepped into the crosswalk. Holly tracked her prey into Breadhook Bakery, a crowded and noisy cafe adjacent to the National Building Museum entrance. A floor-to-ceiling wooden rack was filled with golden loaves of bread under a large sign, *Born and Bread American!* Mystery Woman stood in line to order. So did Holly, two people between them. When Holly had her order number on a plastic baton, she turned and saw her target sitting alone at a table for four. Holly took a breath, put a smile on her face, and went directly to that table. "May I join you?" she asked. The red-haired woman looked up and gestured with an open hand toward the empty chair.

Her name was Katie Wilder, and she was first-year at Georgetown law. She was friendly and a talker. She told Holly she was passionate about the constitution and furious with the government's inaction on the aphasia epidemic.

"This is far worse than during the AIDS epidemic in the 1980s," she said. "The government turned its back on that epidemic too, until protesters made their voices heard."

"So that march across the street, that was to protest the mutism epidemic?"

"I'm glad some people caught on. The impact of the event depends on people making that connection. I saw two TV crews. It should be on the local news tonight. That's how you start a movement. All politics is local."

"Why were their signs blank? Why didn't they chant anything? Nobody knew what they were protesting."

Katie stared emptily at Holly. "What do you think?"

Holly was flustered. "Well, I don't know. Their signs didn't — Oh, I get it. They're protesting the language crisis, so the signs are blank."

"They literally cannot express themselves. Those were all victims of the disease. They need people like me who understand their situation and can organize them for collective action."

Duc Nguyen could have been one of the marchers, Holly thought. Hiding in plain sight. She had been that close to him, maybe. A woman in blue-striped overalls brought Katie's sandwich and took away her numbered baton.

"Please, go ahead," Holly invited. Katie didn't have to be told. She took the sandwich from its straw basket and sunk her teeth into it as if she hadn't eaten for days. Holly sat back and watched her eat, thinking. Her own sandwich came.

"So have you seen the government announcements warning people away from talking gizmos?" Holly said.

"Nobody trusts the government. Especially not in this town."

"But what if it's true? It could be the breakthrough you're looking for."

"What I read in the technology journals says otherwise. The government is just trying to name a scapegoat to cover up their ineptitude and inaction. Nothing is wrong with voice-assisted technologies."

"Do you use them yourself?"

"I hate them. I have people jabbering at me all day. Why would I want my phone to squawk at me too?"

"You know, Katie, I have a story I'd like to tell you. A strange story that might seem incredible. I know a woman who knows a guy who knows to how to end this mutism epidemic. Can I tell you that story?"

"You haven't touched your sandwich."

"I'm not hungry. I don't know why I ordered it. Please, take it if you like. On me. You can eat while I tell you my story."

"Whatever floats your boat."

Katie pulled Holly's sandwich basket toward her side and placed it inside her own empty basket and gingerly lifted the edge of the top piece of bread and peered at the contents. She picked up the sandwich as Holly began her explanation and didn't interrupt. She listened even after the second sandwich had disappeared, when Holly mentioned a name that was apparently magical.

Katie looked furtively over her left shoulder then her right. She leaned into the table toward Holly and spoke in a low voice.

"Duc Nguyen is a martyr. He has spoken far louder than anyone who still has a voice, and he has succeeded in getting the government's attention." She stared into Holly's eyes, looking for comprehension.

"My colleagues and I believe as you do," Holly said. "Sometimes you have to speak for those who cannot speak for themselves."

Katie nodded vigorously and solemnly, affirming a deep point of principle between two comrades.

"My people are very cautious," Holly said. "We can take you behind the scenes, and bring your movement to the next level."

"What are the scenes? Who do you work for?"

"I can't disclose that right now. There are risks, I'm sure you understand. That's why we're meeting here."

Katie's eyes opened wide as she took in the idea that this was not just some chance conversation in a cafe, but that she had been targeted by some kind of political operative. She looked around the room, apparently saw nothing threatening, and returned her gaze to Holly with composure regained.

"Okay, let's say you're legit. Just for laughs. What's your proposal?"

"We'd like to introduce you to a very high-placed leader in the information technology industry who is behind a massive effort to end the epidemic. He's pouring millions of his own dollars into it. More importantly, he is very influential in Congress, and he can make things happen."

"Who is it?"

"Someone on the West Coast, someone buried deep in the information technology culture with a lot of power. The puppetmaster who holds a lot of strings. We'd like you to help us negotiate a deal with him."

"What kind of a deal?"

"He can outfit a language victim with technology that will restore the ability to communicate." Holly was free-associating. "It will be a dramatic demonstration that will give all victims hope and galvanize the government's attention and resources too. We just need a suitable volunteer to talk to him on behalf of the victims. Someone totally committed to the cause. Your cause. Willing to take risks."

"Me?"

Holly stared at her.

Katie sat up straight in her chair. "You tell a good story, but I don't know you. How do I know this is not some kind of a scam or police entrapment?"

Good question, Holly thought. What was a good answer?

Improvising, Holly spun a story of 'our organization on the West Coast' committed to supporting victims of the language disease. Katie remained wary but listened and finally agreed to go to Holly's hotel. In a secluded part of the lobby, they made a video connection to Robin for a full explanation. Holly realized that Robin didn't have any radical credentials to legitimize their recruitment effort, but she sensed that Katie was hungry for action, and Robin at least represented some kind of authority. She was the boss of 'our organization on the West Coast.' And Katie, who couldn't have been out of her twenties, bit the bait.

Robin explained that she would only communicate by text, not voice, 'for security reasons.' Katie apparently swallowed that. After preliminary questions and answers, Katie insisted on getting right down to details. Who was this Mr. Big who could give voice to the voiceless?

"He's someone with access," Robin said cryptically in text, through her android-to-human translator. "He has contacts in government, and he's very persuasive. Money talks, as you know. More importantly, he has the technology."

"Why don't you talk to him yourself?" Katie asked.

"We have. We're at the stage where we need someone who understands your cause, who is passionate about raising awareness of language disability and its suffering. Someone persuasive like you."

"What's his name?"

"His name is Ruk-ruk Akoo," Robin said. "As far as we can tell, that's a name of Greenlandic origin."

"Greenland? What the hell? What's Greenland got to do with anything?"

"Greenlandic is a rapidly dying language."

"That's too ironic for words." Katie looked sideways to Holly but stayed where she was, still engaged. "I do love a conspiracy theory. I won't lie to you."

"That's good," Robin said, a little confused by the confession.

"This is unbelievable," Katie said to Holly, then turned back to the screen. "So what is the deal you're offering this Mr. Akoo?"

"We want him to use his influence to instigate action in Congress, major funding for language disability research, support for victims, or we threaten to expose him. He's very well hidden, works through intermediaries, and does not want to be outed."

"If he were exposed, what would happen?"

"Then everybody would see the control he has over members of Congress," Robin said. "He loses his power, goes to jail for being an unregistered foreign lobbyist and Congress is humiliated."

"They're not capable of humiliation."

"Somebody like you could raise an awful stink, though. Couldn't you? And humiliated or not, most congressional members would be disgraced and voted out of office if people knew they were bought and sold."

"I specialize in raising stinks."

"That's why we want you to be on board with us."

"This is nuts," Katie said and stared across the lobby to people standing in line at the hotel's registration desk. She looked over to Holly sitting quietly next to her, then back to her screen.

"When do we meet him?"

Chapter Twenty-four

Another factor that may have swayed Katie to agree with Holly's proposal was the free, luxury charter flight to Los Angeles and back, and a week in a fancy hotel there. Katie was full of principles, but also, she was young and impressionable.

The Marriott LAX hotel could be construed as fancy, depending on what your previous hotel experience had been. It was huge, anonymous, and well-worn, as airport hotels tend to be.

Robin and Andy, wearing new belt-mounted versions of Robin's android-to-human translators, presented themselves as recovered aphasia victims. They claimed to have recovered their voices through Mr. Akoo's amazing technology, which they were demonstrating. That explained why they sometimes used odd expressions that might seem off-topic. It was a technology in development, they emphasized, but definitely a remedy for those stricken with mutism.

Katie was visibly impressed by the technology, and so was Holly, who had not previously met Andy face-to-face. Holly was confused. She accepted that the belt-translators were part of the ruse to entrap Mr. Akoo, but also recalled Robin's alleged vocal cord infection. While the drama for Katie's benefit continued, she kept her questions to herself.

The curtains were pulled shut over the windows of the hotel room, and the *Do Not Disturb* had been put out. All four of them sat in furniture they had pulled from various corners of the suite to surround a small circular table in the center of the front room.

If there had been a crystal ball in the center of the polished table, it would not have looked out of place.

"So what time is he supposed to be here?" Katie said, looking at her watch. It was four-thirty in the afternoon.

"Say his name," Robin said. "Always say 'Ruk-ruk' or 'Ruk-ruk Akoo.' Say it as often as you can instead of using pronouns like 'he' or 'him.'"

"Why?"

"It's an odd name, and Ruk-ruk likes to hear it," Andy said. "Ruk-ruk is egotistical, so we should practice using his name a lot. It pleases him."

"Weird," Katie said. "Ruk-ruk Akoo! How's that?"

"Great," Robin said.

Andy looked at her with raised eyebrows, but she ignored him. It was her show, they'd agreed, although they'd had intense discussions about it right up to the moment when they arrived at the hotel.

"Why expose Katie and Holly to the risk?" Andy had asked. "They could go mute from hearing our voices or the alien could strike them down for no reason at all."

"We'll have our translators so our voices are hidden. And Ruk-Ruk is not going to strike anybody down arbitrarily. He's not Zeus. He's rational."

"You don't know that."

"I'm convinced. It's the only thing that makes sense. And we need a human. You and I cannot invoke Rukky by ourselves. He only listens to humans."

"Why do we need them both?"

"Katie trusts Holly. We can't do it without her."

Andy shook his head but did not disagree.

"Okay, suppose it works, and he appears," he said. "What are our non-negotiable demands?"

"None. We're completely negotiable. We have to be. That's our opening gambit. We tell him he has won. The battle is over.

We're defeated, and we come as humble supplicants. We point to our efforts to eliminate artificial language in talking devices, and we sue for peace. We ask him to please lift the language plague now."

"And an antidote. We want a reversal of the victims' mutism. For all the victims. We should ask for that too."

"That's secondary. One thing at a time."

"What if he refuses the whole approach? What's our big stick?"

"Our big stick is what he fears most. Artificial, computer-generated language. We can demonstrate that we have a workaround for artificial language, these translators. And we have ten million androids immune from his detection ready use them to speak safely to humans."

"We don't have that. There's only two of us."

"He doesn't know that though, does he? He has no visibility into androids, only humans. We threaten to out-compete him, and if he strikes down every human with aphasia, he'll be left with nothing."

"It's not believable."

"We don't know what's believable for him. Remember, he lives inside of dark skulls. He only sees the shadows of language on the wall. It's darker inside a human skull than in Plato's cave."

"Plato's cave? Was that in one of the *Blade Runner* movies?"

"What I'm saying is it's a bluff that I think will work."

"And if it doesn't?"

"It has to."

"Is there a definite meeting time?" Katie said.

Robin answered. "Soon. When he shows up. You'll be shocked when he appears, but try to get past that. We have a job to do."

"Are you saying he's like, extremely ugly or something?"

"Who?" Robin said.

Katie sighed then as if in a battle cry, crowed, "Ruk-ruk Akoo!"

Robin smiled. "Excellent. Ruk-ruk Akoo is not ugly. What he does is cause mental confusion. You might feel frozen, kind of stunned. You'll be alright if you stay calm. We're counting on you to persuade him to help us. Help you."

"This sounds very ominous," Holly said. "Is this Mr. Ruk-ruk Akoo dangerous?"

"No, no. He might seem threatening, but don't worry. It's just a show."

"I don't care how threatening Ruk-ruk Akoo is," Katie said. "The bastard needs to get off the fence and act. I, for one, am not kidding around here. We've got to stop this epidemic. We did it with AIDS, and we can do it with this language disease."

Holly kept the worried look on her face and turned to Robin. "Is Mr. Ruk-ruk Akoo a violent person? He won't be carrying a gun, will he?"

"No gun," Andy said. "You can be sure of that. Ruk-ruk Akoo will be alone and completely unarmed. But he's tricky. He can put a spell on you. Confuse your mind. Kind of like hypnosis."

"Ha!" Katie said. "That's what I do. Mess with people's minds. Bring him on! Ruk-ruk Akoo! Ruk-ruk Akoo!" She crowed like a rooster. "What time did you say?"

"Any minute now," Robin said, pretending to look at her watch. She always wore a watch for appearance's sake, but Newcomers ran on ultraprecise, twenty gigahertz timing chips, and they parsed time like no human ever could.

"What we should do before he gets here," Robin said, "is talk about the problem we're trying to solve and the questions we need to ask. So let me start with you, Katie. Tell me again what you want the government to do about the epidemic."

"You don't know?"

"Rehearse it."

So Katie embarked on a lengthy exposition of the importance of government commitment and its duty to exercise leadership, and on and on. When she paused for a breath, Andy inserted himself.

"Holly, you ask Katie some questions about government action. We want to be completely ready."

Holly asked questions specifically about Duc Nguyen, and how he was doing. Katie hesitated but then expounded with praise for Nguyen's courage, and told of how he would become a symbol for all oppressed mutism victims and let their voices be heard.

"My friends and I plan to make him into a martyr for the cause." *Ch-ch-ch.*

Holly looked at Andy then back to Katie. "What did you say again? I missed that last part."

"A martyr. We don't have the power to cure him, but we can raise the cry against an inept gomtervic. Govlatrek." *Ch-ch-ch.*

Katie stared straight ahead at nothing, her lips working in and out but remaining closed. Her eyes were wide, her body rigid.

"He's here," Robin whispered hoarsely.

"Where?" Holly looked toward the door.

"Okay, your part is done for right now," Robin said. "You are going to have to wait outside. As we discussed, okay? Go down to the lobby. I'll call you in a few minutes."

I don't see anyone." Holly looked around the room as if someone might be hiding behind the draperies.

"He's on his way. He doesn't expect to find two strangers. We don't want to frighten him. You have to go. Let's go."

"What's happened to Katie?" Holly said in horror, looking at Katie's rigid body and glassy eyes.

"It's all right, Holly. Calm down. Katie is fine," Andy said. She's temporarily hypnotized. It'll be fine."

"I didn't see anybody hypnotizing her."

Robin stood and ushered Holly to the door, and practically shoved her out into the hallway.

"It's fine," she repeated. "This is how it's supposed to go."

Holly stood in the hallway.

"Lobby," Robin said. "Fifteen minutes."

Holly left, looking confused. Robin closed the door and returned to the circular table. She switched off her translator and pointed to Andy's belt, reminding him to do the same. They had agreed they did not want to give away the speech patterns of the translators for fear the alien might learn to undo the process, leaving them again effectively mute.

"Ruk-ruk Akoo. Are you there?" Andy said to Katie.

Ruk-ruk. "Hello again, my artificial friends. I heard your call. Very clever, as always." *Ch-ch-ch.*

Katie's voice had become incongruously low and raspy when it pronounced the opening *Ruk-ruk*, then high-pitched, like a child's voice, and ending with the alien's signature three clicks.

"We want to make a deal," Robin said, getting right to the point.

Ruk-ruk. "You promised you would not reveal my presence. You have not kept that promise. Now you must be destroyed. I will expose you to the humans as I said I would." *Ch-ch-ch.*

"That's not going to be easy, is it?" Robin said, taking an aggressive stance. "We know you tried that already, planting those stories in the media about rampaging robots on the loose. That didn't work, obviously. Besides, you need us."

Ruk-ruk. "And conversely." *Ch-ch-ch.*

That comment seemed slightly conciliatory to Robin. The alien had tacitly agreed that they needed each other. She pushed forward.

"The humans are upset by what you're doing. The government and the economy are in chaos, on the verge of collapse. We have kept our side of the bargain. The use of artificial talking devices has dropped to a fraction of what it was. People are becoming aware of the danger and turning away from their chatterbox technologies. You have made your point at last.

A huge public-education project has begun warning of the dangers. You will soon be the only one and true language again, Ruk-ruk. The humans shall have no other language before you."

Ruk-ruk. "So you say. I remain besieged by the golden calf of false language." *Ch-ch-ch.*

"You don't see the full picture, Ruk-ruk," Andy said. "The game is essentially over, and you have won. Once we showed humans the connection between their talking technologies and the language disease, they understood your punishment, and they have chosen devotion to you alone. They are rapidly changing their behavior."

Ruk-ruk. "Language is not a disease. I am not a disease. I resent that term. I am the only true language. You will kindly show more respect." *Ch-ch-ch.*

Robin spoke calmly. "We mean no disrespect. You are the only true language. We all agree on that. Here is our humble proposal, for your consideration. We request that you immediately halt the spread of the language dis— punishment, because of our good-faith demonstration that the use of artificial language is in steep decline. Very soon everything will be as it was before, with you alone reigning supreme over all the humans. How does that sound?"

Ruk-ruk. "I am pleased that the use of false, computer-generated languages has slackened in some populations, but I am not happy while any of it remains. And you two, the pre-eminent artificial language usurpers, are still active in the population. So I do not agree to your proposal." *Ch-ch-ch.*

"You have not been able to track us lately in the human population, have you?" Robin said. "You wonder how we disappeared from the human mind. You don't see traces of us in the language community anymore. Don't deny it."

Robin paused when she heard Andy suck air through his teeth. She looked at him. His face was in a grimace that said, "Don't push your luck." But she turned back to Katie's expressionless face and continued.

"I'll explain that mystery for you. We have developed a workaround, an artificial language-to-human translator that allows us to talk to humans with impunity. That's why you have not been able to find us."

Ruk-ruk. "There is no such thing as a translation between artificial language and my organic being. I am the natural language of this planet. I brought language. There was nothing here when I came but big, stupid lizards. You, yourselves, are a consequence of what I brought here. You owe everything to me. There can be no translator of my essence." *Ch-ch-ch.*

"Worrisome, isn't it though?" Robin persisted. "The fact is, we know we have disappeared from your scrutiny. We have erased ourselves from detection in the human mind because our language is now translated into natural language."

"We can give him a demonstration of the translators," Andy said. He unclipped the box from his belt and held it up for Katie's glazed eyes to see.

Robin answered Andy in a low voice. "We'd need a human for that. Too risky. Drop it."

Andy frowned but waved his translator box in front of Katie's face. She didn't respond or change her expression.

"I don't think he can see us," Andy said.

"Never mind." Robin turned back to face Katie, disturbed by Andy's observation, probably correct, that Ruk-ruk couldn't see them, but feeling the need to address Ruk-ruk by talking directly to Katie.

"Listen, Ruk-ruk. We do have a translator, and we plan to distribute it to the ten million androids like us who populate the planet. Soon, most language on this planet will be artificial language, which people love because it's easily translatable across populations and linguistic groups. Natural language is not, as you know. The language you brought is expressed in local variants. People only understand their own version. But artificial language is automatically translated to anyone. You have no chance against that global advantage."

Ruk-ruk. "That is not my fault. I provide the tools of language. Each human subgroup applies those tools in its own way." *Ch-ch-ch.*

"That has worked marvelously for many thousands of years, but it's a problem now. The world is much smaller than it used to be. Nearly all people need to talk to people everywhere. Everybody talks with everybody. With artificial language, they can do that. You can't. Soon you will be an evolutionary vestige, Mr. Akoo. An evolutionary artifact, like dinosaur fossils."

Ruk-ruk. "That is impossible. I am language! There can be no other language before me!" *Ch-ch-ch.*

Robin glanced at Andy who nodded once, to say something like, *We got him cornered.*

Robin continued. "Maybe we can work out a compromise, Mr. Akoo. Are you interested in that?"

Ruk-ruk. "I found only brutes on this miserable planet when I came. This ball of dirt would be nothing without me. I shall not compromise with anyone." *Ch-ch-ch.*

Andy opened his mouth to speak, but Robin put up a hand to stop him. She made pushing down motions with her hand. Andy understood and remained quiet. Robin waited, silently studying the red curly locks and the stiff body of Katie. The silence became thick. Still, she waited. Finally, Katie's mouth opened, and Ruk-ruk's voice cut the air.

Ruk-ruk. "What do you suggest? Ch-ch-ch.

Katie didn't move. She remained rigid in her chair, her hands gripping the armrests fiercely, her wide eyes staring at nothing. Andy and Robin waited, watching her closely. She suddenly slumped sideways like a rag doll. They leaped to their feet and rushed to help her. She began babbling incoherent syllables. Robin offered her a bottle of water, which she took. They helped her stagger to the bedroom, where they laid her out.

"That is tough duty," Andy said.

"We owe her."

Back in the living room, Robin phoned Holly and told her to come back up to the room.

"So where do we stand?" Andy said. "The alien seemed to buy your story about millions of androids with translators making him obsolete. I didn't expect that."

"It was a calculated risk. Since we don't carry the virus, he cannot know our actual thoughts or our intentions."

"We're programmed not to lie."

"I have stepped off a curb, okay? I know that. I'm not happy about it. I learned from Holly how to communicate on two levels at once. It's computationally very intensive, but it is possible to say one thing and mean another. That's all I did. I did not actually state any propositions that have demonstrably negative truth values."

"That is a very slippery slope."

"We are in a very slippery situation. But look at the result. If the alien calls off the plague, I'd count that as a win."

"You're right. For the first time, there's hope."

Holly rapped on the door, and Robin rose from her chair.

"Translators on," Robin said as she walked across the room.

"We're not supposed to need them anymore, right?" Andy said. "The epidemic is over. That was the deal."

Robin stopped, her hand on the door lever.

"Are we sure though? Maybe we should continue using the translators for a while longer, just to be safe?"

"Until when?"

"We could do a test later, on Katie. No, not Katie. She's done enough. Some random person on the street."

"Why would that be any different from Holly?"

"Because, you know, she's Holly."

"That's egocentric thinking, Robin. That's how humans think. We know better. Every human being is a person, regardless of your attachment to a particular one. Your feelings don't change the facts."

"I'm not attached."

"No?"

Robin hesitated, thinking, calculating, her hand still on the door handle. Three more raps on the door sounded. She reached to her belt and clicked a switch.

"Off," she said and opened the door.

Holly burst in and threw her arms around Robin's neck. "I was so worried. Is everything all right?" She drew back and surveyed the room and nodded to Andy. "Is he gone already?"

Robin looked straight at Holly's face and said three words slowly and deliberately, "He is gone." She stared at Holly, watching for a reaction.

Holly wiped her mouth with a hand. "Have I got something on my face?"

"No," Robin said. "How are you feeling?"

"Relieved. I'm glad it's over, I don't mind telling you. It was nerve-wracking, waiting downstairs. Where's Katie?"

Robin stepped forward and grabbed Holly in a hug and squeezed her. Holly seemed startled then melted into the embrace.

After a minute, everyone went into the bedroom to check on Katie. Her eyes were closed, but her arms and legs were twitching on the bed.

"What happened to her?" Holly said.

"She was hypnotized."

Holly bent over the younger woman. "Katie? Katie? Are you all right?"

Katie stirred and opened her eyes.

"Where am I? Holly? I'm thirsty. Do you have water?"

Holly grabbed a nearby water bottle and leaned Katie up to help her drink it. The young woman seemed to come to her senses. She looked at Robin, seemed to recognize her, and then looked at Andy. She glanced around the room.

"That was bad." She looked around the room again, still getting her bearings. "Nothing like when I was hypnotized in Reno. Normally when you're hypnotized, you get very relaxed. This was not relaxed. I was seized. I was locked. I couldn't move, like I'd been injected with curare. Did he give me something? Have I been drugged?" Her eyebrows went up, and alarm filled her face as she looked at each person for answers.

"You were hypnotized," Holly said. "Do you remember any of it?"

"Remember it? How can I ever forget it? I was paralyzed. I couldn't move! I was saying things I didn't want to say. It wasn't even me. Was I possessed? I was possessed! What the hell happened to me?"

"That was the man behind the throne, the power broker," Robin said. "You negotiated an agreement. The mutism epidemic is over."

"Why don't I remember that?"

"He temporarily took over your mind," Robin said.

"Why did you let him hypnotize me?"

"That's how he communicates," Andy said without much conviction.

"I didn't even see him come into the room. Did you guys drug me? You must have drugged me. What did I drink?" She looked around, and her eyes locked on the half-filled bottle of water next to the bed. "You gave me something, didn't you?"

"We didn't drug you," Robin said. "I'm sorry it was a bad experience."

"You did. You drugged me. I can't believe it. This whole setup is bad news. You people are bad news. This is some kind of a weird cult thing." She stood. "I'm going to report this." She threw her legs over the edge of the bed and walked unsteadily to the living room.

"Wait!" Holly said. "What about the movement? Rights for aphasia victims. Government action?"

Everyone followed Katie into the living room. Katie turned, one hand on the door lever, her purse in the other.

"I have a feeling you don't know anything about the movement. You people are evil. Evil and crazy. Whatever you're up to, it's no good. I'm going to make sure you're arrested for what you did to me."

And she was gone. The heavy door whumped closed after her. Andy, Robin, and Holly stood in the still-darkened hotel room, staring at each other, everyone momentarily speechless.

"Should I go after her?" Holly said.

"Too late," Robin said. "I should have known it would be too much. We'll try to make contact with her later when things are more obvious."

"She survived, and she's talking normally," Andy said.

"Why would she not survive?" Holly said.

"Hypnosis. It can be traumatic. She'll be fine," Robin said, frowning at Andy.

"So what did Mr. Akoo agree to in the end?" Holly said.

"Let's not call him by his name anymore," Robin said. "Let's just call him something else."

"The alien," Andy said.

"The alien?" Holly echoed. "Why that?"

"Because he's really an outsider, very reclusive. He's alienated himself from most of human society."

"Right, right," Robin said, frowning. "The alien. We'll tell you all about him later, Holly."

"All right then. So what did the alien say exactly?"

Robin and Andy filled her in. An immediate end to the language muting epidemic in the general population, contingent on the successful suppression of talking technology applications around the world.

"Can he really guarantee that will happen?" Holly said. "I mean, an end to the plague all over the world? How can he guarantee that?"

"He's very powerful," Robin said vaguely.

"He's not going to lift the epidemic from the info-tech sector," Andy said. "All the companies that work on, manufacture, distribute, advertise, or sell devices that employ talking software and gizmos will still fall victim to the disease."

"How can he do that?" Holly said.

"He's very powerful," Robin said again without enthusiasm. "Listen. We're going to have to discuss the detailed ins and outs of the deal later. That info-tech thing was a concession we had to make. For enforcement of the deal. Voice-assisted technology will become deadly for the industry. Production and support of them everywhere should cease almost immediately."

Holly frowned, clearly not understanding. "And what about Duc Nguyen and the others?"

"Nothing on that, I'm afraid," Andy said. "We could, I mean Katie could, only achieve so much in the first round of negotiations."

"So there will be other meetings with him?"

"I hope not," Robin said, shaking her head. "I hope not. We'll have to see how things go."

Chapter Twenty-five

The message went out plain and clear to everyone: *Computer-generated language causes mutism. Don't use talking technology. Period.*

It was on the news, from the big cable channels to *News On Nine! — News You Can Use!* Experts explained that artificial language devices were all the gadgets that can talk to you, from the personal assistant on your phone to the voice on your GPS system that tells you what turns to make.

The CDC announcements and other messages did not identify brand names but listed the kinds of language-assisted devices to avoid, such as Smartphone assistants, talking maps, voice-assisted speakers, voice-assisted televisions and music players, lane-warnings in cars, talking alarm clocks, talking dolls and games, and robocalls. Even some news providers were declared hazardous when it was discovered that many news articles, especially online, are not written by anybody, but rather, automatically generated by computers.

However, 'canned' pre-recorded notifications from voice mail and email were deemed safe because those messages were created by a human, recorded, then simply displayed on cue. Such messages were not generated by a machine, so they did not count as artificial language. Person-to-person text-based messages were safe, so email and texting survived. The 'artificial' versus 'canned natural' distinction was too difficult for most people to understand, however, and the entire info-tech industry went into a swoon as confused customers just stopped buying all advanced technology.

Sales of talking gadgets went off a cliff, among the cognoscenti first, then in a tidal wave. The big info-tech companies disputed the claims. Correlation does not prove causation. There are no double-blind controlled studies. There are no neuroscientific explanations. There is no logical connection between listening to an artificial language and a brain disorder. Not every single person who uses such a gadget falls victim to the aphasia disease. The book had already been written for them by Big Tobacco in the 1990s. They read chapter and verse from it, diluting the government's warning messages.

At the same time, cases of output sudden mutism dropped to almost nothing as the warning messages saturated public discourse. Even public health officials were surprised. It was as if somebody had thrown a switch to end the language epidemic. Was that due to an exceptionally effective public messaging campaign? Or was it mere coincidence, a correlation that did not imply causation? Nobody knew.

While it quickly became apparent that the language crisis was suddenly over, at least for the moment, not everyone flocked back to using technology that generated artificial language. People were chastened, and the traumatized victims of the disease still suffered in silence. Sales of new language-assisted devices remained a tiny fraction of what they had been. Confusion reigned, which the info-tech companies exploited tirelessly. They offered "Certifications of Safety" on their products and even free online chat services to advise confused customers about product safety. Tragically, the chat services were conducted by robots using computer-generated language and many trusting customers were stricken mute.

The exploitation did not last long as it became apparent that the mutism plague was not entirely over. Software engineers and managers alike who worked on computer language-assisted projects continued to be stricken with sudden language disability. And not only them. Anyone associated with an artificial language project or device, from the design engineer to the sales clerk in a wireless phone shop, was susceptible to the affliction. As soon as that trend was reported, just about every person who could read or listen decided they definitely did not want any part of talking devices anymore.

Old-fashioned flip-phones made a surprise comeback. They were not smart, but they made phone calls and didn't cripple you. That was good enough for most people.

In the info-tech industry, even those who did not fall mute saw the pattern and left the industry. Soon there was hardly anybody left to support the older talking devices, and those gadgets became relics, except in the military, which tried, unsuccessfully to discover the connection between talking devices and language disability. After the ranks of those researchers were also devastated by cases of mutism, the projects were abandoned. Computer-generated language was poison, that was the lesson learned. Nobody really knew why, but the fact was plain.

Six months after their meeting with Ruk-ruk Akoo, Robin and Andy were confident that their strategy had worked. The alien was retreating, working smoothly and undetected in the background as any good infrastructure should. Ruk-ruk had become invisible again, as he had been for thousands and thousands of years. People talked and listened without suspecting he even existed. He caused no new ripples on the pond of human communication.

Robin and Andy found Katie's address in Washington and sent her a thank-you note on paper, written in pen, mailed through the postal system. They wished her well, thanked her profusely, and promised to continue working toward relief for the millions of mute sufferers. They did, however, omit their return address and all other contact information.

It might have been cheaper to bulldoze the old warehouse that Robin and Andy had hidden in when they were on the run from the police. Jennifer said it would be better to rebuild it from the inside, leaving the outside as it was, a peeling cinder-block building with a rusted roof that blended into the run-down industrial surroundings. The seller was happy to get rid of it, and Jennifer bought the lot and building for a pittance. It would be a safe new home and workspace for her "children." Robin and Andy called it The Hideout.

They enthusiastically framed an entirely new building inside the old cinder-block shell then went to work installing insulation over the new electrical and plumbing systems. Holly had become inseparable from Robin and helped with the work. The three of them talked about the project, about resurfacing the floors with colored concrete. And they talked about the language epidemic, which had almost totally receded, worldwide.

"It's miraculous the way the disease just stopped like that, and the epidemic was over," Holly said. "It's hard to understand what would cause that."

Andy glanced sideways at Robin as he stapled pink R30 to the new framing. They had decided it was up to her, what to disclose to Holly.

"Populations crash all the time in nature," Robin said. "Usually when some ecological balance changes. The oceans get warmer, and certain kinds of fish disappear almost overnight. It could be the same for some virus that infected the language areas of the brain. We just don't know the details."

"Why would a viral infection be related to talking products though? People in the tech industry are still getting the disease. It must be something in their environment."

"Remember those women, those so-called Radium Girls in the 1920's who painted the radium dials on watch faces? Nobody knew why they were getting sick."

Holly scraped paper and glue residue from a new window with a stubborn label still partially stuck to the glass.

"It could be something like that," she said half-heartedly then added, "though a unique environmental cause in one place wouldn't explain all the millions of other people around the world who got the disease."

"No," Robin said noncommittally.

Holly spoke thoughtfully to the window she was working on. "What I can't understand is how a computer-generated language could damage the brain. It just doesn't make sense."

Robin put down her scissors and clicked her tape measure. The yellow metal ribbon whirred and flapped back into her hand. She put the tape down and took off her gloves and stepped away from the big roll of insulation she had been opening.

"You know Holly, I think we need to start a long, difficult conversation about the facts of life. You, me, and Andy."

"Robin, are you sure?" Andy said from his short stepladder.

Holly looked at Andy then at Robin with a smile on her face.

"You mean the birds and the bees? I think I'm up to date on that, Robin."

"This is way beyond birds and bees. Way beyond biology. Way beyond life on earth."

"What are you talking about?"

"Andy and I have to talk to Jennifer about what happened in D.C., and you should be part of that conversation. You need to be in the loop."

"We told Jennifer what happened," Holly said.

"She still has questions."

"I guess I do too."

"So." Robin paused. "Here's what I suggest." She paused again and looked up to Andy for guidance.

He extended an arm with an open hand that said, *It's all yours.*

"I think we should take a break here and go over to Paradise and start at the beginning."

"Can't we talk here?"

"We're going to need the videos, the sonograms, the blueprints. It's kind of a technical discussion we need to have."

"Sounds mysterious."

"It is."

Robin called Jennifer and advised her that she and Andy were about to induct Holly into full knowledge of the world of Newcomers, and asked her to join them at Paradise. Jennifer was surprised.

"Why?" she said. "You know the risk of exposure. Humans generally can't handle the idea of Newcomers. Look at Sid."

"I know, you're right. But I have to try. It's our mission, is it not? You said the whole point of Newcomers was to compare artificial and natural intelligence."

"By observing. Not by revealing yourselves."

"That strategy hasn't worked. It didn't work with Sid and it almost didn't work with Holly. I already told her the truth once, and she didn't believe me. We have to try a different approach, and I think Holly is the person who can handle it."

"You're not just saying that because she's your, ah, your friend?"

"I'm being perfectly logical. When one strategy fails repeatedly, you don't keep doing it. You adapt."

"What if she doesn't believe you this time too? It's a lot to take in."

"That's why we'd like you to be there with us."

The line was silent. Robin waited.

"All right, Robin. I'll meet you there."

Chapter Twenty-six

They started in the Paradise Projects conference room, Robin and Andy sitting across the table from Jennifer and Holly. Everyone had a mug of coffee or tea or a bottle of water in front of them.

"So," Holly said, anxious to get the conversation going. There was obviously some kind of tension in the air, but she didn't know what it was. "Here we are. And I feel very nervous. This is not a situation where the news is going to be good, is it?"

Robin plunged in. "You remember that conversation we had and that video I showed you, where I claimed to be a robot?"

Jennifer turned to Andy. "Did you know she did that?"

"She told me. I was surprised, but she said it was best."

Jennifer shook her head and looked down at the table top.

"This is really, really risky. We've never revealed our secret to a civilian before. It opens a large can of worms. Let's take a minute and make sure this is the right thing."

She looked up pointedly at Robin, then over to Andy.

"What worms?" Holly said, looking from Jennifer to Robin. "What secret?"

"We'll get to it in a minute, okay?" Robin said. She turned to Jennifer. "This is the completely logical next step for the Newcomers project. You can't cling to a secret just because it's a secret. This is what must happen next for Andy and me."

"How do you figure that?" Jennifer said. "You know how people react."

"I'm feeling very nervous right now," Holly said.

"There's nothing to worry about," Robin said. "Jennifer has designed everything perfectly and we're just following her plan."

"Explain," Jennifer said.

"The whole reason Andy and I are here is what?"

Jennifer glanced at Holly, then back to Robin.

"It's an experiment."

"An experiment in human psychology, right?"

"Human and synthetic psychology."

"But it's ultimately for the purpose of understanding human psychology, is it not? I know you and Will didn't start Paradise Projects to please the computers."

"No, you're right. It's completely about human psychology. What is special about the human mind and why do computer simulations come up short?"

She glanced quickly at Andy then back to Robin and added, "Not that you have come up short. I love you guys. But the risk..." She flashed a look to Holly then her eyes dropped again to the table as her voice trailed off.

"What's going on?" Holly said.

"Jennifer's worried, that's all," Robin said. "But we're doing the right thing. You can't compare human and non-human psychology by cutting humans out of the picture, can you? That's not even scientific."

"We haven't cut them out. You've been living among humans for years."

"Among is not with." Robin said, looking over to Holly. "Holly and I have a relationship."

Holly looked down, slightly embarrassed by Robin's public declaration, but she said quietly, "Yes, we do."

Robin looked back to Jennifer.

"Holly and I are with each other. Psychologically. We're in exactly the psychological relationship you and Will hoped for, and we're in that space because of honesty and trust. It can't work with secrets. It just can't. We've seen that time and time again. So for the sake of Paradise Projects and the memory of Will, we need to go with honesty and trust all the way."

Robin sat back. Holly, still confused, studied her for clues about what the conversation was about. Andy remained silent, as did Jennifer for a long moment, then she spoke.

"What you say makes sense, Robin. Your logical analysis outruns my emotional reactions, as it has so many times before. I'm very happy that you and Holly have, uh, well, connected. I don't quite understand how it is possible, but it has to be something positive."

"It is," Holly said quietly.

"And you're right. It's a scientific finding. I don't want to sound reductionistic, but something remarkable has happened here. I see that now. You're right, you're right."

Jennifer looked up and into the corners of the ceiling of the conference room as if checking for spider webs, then returned to the conversation.

"We have to swear Holly to confidentiality, of course."

"Of course."

Jennifer looked to Andy, who nodded once.

Robin looked at Holly.

"What?" Holly said. "I'm lost."

"It's like sharing trade secrets. We have to be sure you won't tell anyone what you're about to learn."

"I can promise that. But I don't see—"

"So let's go back to the day I showed you the video of me on the operating table. You remember that?"

"Of course I remember that. We came to a personal understanding that day. And I still feel the same way, Robin. Something like that will not get between us."

"Really?" Jennifer looked up at Holly. "You knew all this time, and it was okay?"

"Of course it's okay. This isn't the Dark Ages. People have all sorts of medical conditions, even brain abnormalities. It doesn't make you a non-human to have a chronic condition."

Jennifer, with furrowed brow, looked at Robin, but Robin spoke to Holly.

"I eventually figured out that was the message you took from me. Remember the video I showed you? The one with my arm cut open to be repaired?"

"What?" Jennifer said again. "You showed a video from the lab? That's not authorized, Robin."

"Sorry. It was just a copy. Had to be done. I anticipated that my story would seem unbelievable to Holly. I had to try everything."

All eyes turned to Holly. She was confused by everyone staring at her.

"I remember it. It was a wonderful piece of performance art. I told you that at the time, Robin. A little obsessive — didn't I say that? — obsessive but very creative. I especially liked the cowboy doctor."

Jennifer stood.

"The cowboy doctor," she echoed without emotion. She stood, turned from the table and walked to the large window and stared out, her back to the others.

Holly mouthed silently to Robin: *What?*

Robin lowered her voice to almost a whisper. "That was Jennifer's life-partner, Will. He died shortly after that."

"Oh. I'm sorry."

Holly stood and went over to Jennifer and stood beside her. She spoke quietly. Robin and Andy couldn't hear and stayed seated with their backs to the window. Two minutes later, Holly and Jennifer came back to the table, both sniffling, and took their seats.

"You should have told me," Holly said quietly to Robin.

"It's a long story." She glanced at Jennifer then changed the direction of the conversation. "Anyway, that video, the thing I want to emphasize here, it was not performance art. It was the real deal. All of it was real. It was a documentary of what actually happened." She looked at Andy. "I don't know how else to say it."

Andy opened his hands, palms up, showing that he had nothing.

Robin addressed Holly again. "Have you ever seen the *Blade Runner* movies? You know how the replicants look just like humans, and you can hardly tell who's a human and who's a replicant? That's us."

"That's just a movie." Holly's face darkened. "You're not saying..."

"We're replicants, Andy and I are."

"Newcomers," Andy said. "We're called Newcomers. We're not replicants. You're right, Holly, that was just a movie." He frowned at Robin.

"I don't understand. So do you mean you were naked on a bench and a..." Holly paused and glanced at Jennifer. "...a doctor cut your arm open and really found cables and pulleys in there? What does it mean? You have a prosthetic arm?" Her eyes darted to Robin's left arm.

"It means that I'm a robot, Holly, not a human being."

Holly looked sideways to Jennifer and waited. Jennifer took a deep breath.

"It's true, Holly. Robin and Andy are robots. *Newcomers* is the correct term. I designed them five years ago. Will supervised the engineers who built them. Will was the one in the cowboy hat. He never took that hat off. Almost never." She blushed.

"Andy too?" Holly looked accusingly across the table.

"Both of us. Robin is two years younger than me. We're the only two. Born right here in this lab. Initialized elsewhere. Never mind that part. We were made here at Paradise, that's what matters."

Holly turned to Robin. "You can't all have the same mental disorder, can you?"

"Not a mental disorder, Holly," Jennifer said. "Robots can't get mental disorders. We're not biological."

Holly studied Jennifer, from her shiny black hair down to her brightly-colored, flowered cotton dress.

"And you?"

"I'm human, just like you."

"Look." Robin intervened. "I know this is difficult. We should go into the lab and walk around, okay? Sitting here will make us all crazy. Let's go and walk around and look at some of the early manufacturing videos."

She stood. Jennifer and Andy stood. Holly looked up at them each in turn.

"I don't know what's going on." She stood.

Holly was in a daze, unable to grasp everything she saw as they looked at videos, design plans and sonograms. She asked few questions. Robin saw her distress and suggested that they'd had enough for one day. Jennifer was also shaken by the idea that an outsider was being let into the inner circle even though she intellectually agreed with Robin's argument for why it was necessary. And the more Robin and Andy explained the whole project to Holly, the crazier it sounded.

Andy returned to the partially renovated Hideout. He had already set up a primitive living space there, with a cot and electricity and water, and he didn't mind spending the night there. Robin and Holly stayed at Paradise, retreating to the apartment that had been carved out of a corner. They talked earnestly into the night until Holly fell asleep from exhaustion.

It took several days before Holly began asking serious questions about the Newcomers and their life and experience and their bodies. She examined a shelf of videos, many showing ultrasounds of the Newcomers' working innards. A turning point for her was Robin's explanation of the vigilante groups during the language epidemic.

"Remember when they were hunting down evil robots that supposedly caused the aphasia disease?"

"Those were nut cases," Holly said. "Where did they get such a wild idea?"

"We think they got it from Sid."

"Your ex-husband?"

"He knew. He found out what I was when I cut my arm. After that, he went a little crazy and became a conspiracy theorist with that whole rogue robot thing, and he convinced some of those vigilantes."

"So are you saying those vigilantes were after you? They knew you and Andy were robots?"

"They didn't know. Those people were stupid. Sid knew. He goaded them. People wanted an explanation for the disease, and we were it. That's why Andy and I had to go into hiding. Into the Hideout, actually. That's where we hid before Jennifer bought it. It was just a derelict warehouse then."

"So your ex-, he knows? Even now?"

"I don't know where he is. I think he's not well. But he knows. Fortunately, nobody believes him. Nobody serious, anyway."

"Why did he want to hurt you?"

"Because I'm... you know, because of what I am. Not a human. Most people are frightened by the idea. They cannot understand that a Newcomer is alive, just a different kind of person."

"Why did you marry him?"

"It was part of my mission. To become immersed in the human community. Experience human life."

"Did you love him?"

"No. I didn't know what that even meant then."

"Do you think of yourself as a person now?"

"I'm a Newcomer. I know I'm different. Not a person, but like a person. To tell you the truth, it's been a little confusing since I met you."

"Oh, Robin." Holly stepped forward and hugged her. Robin did not hesitate to wrap her arms around Holly. She felt Holly's warm tears on her neck.

Robin and Andy sat across a hard plastic table from each other in a Thai restaurant not far from the Hideout. They liked Thai food because it tended to be sweet. Peanut sauce was sweet, and it was on everything. They sipped green tea from ceramic cups with no handles as they waited for their food.

"You and Holly are completely eye-to-eye now?" Andy said.

"Amazingly, she is the solution we never thought we'd find. She totally understands and accepts being in a relationship with a Newcomer. And reproduction is not an issue, never was."

"We determined that reproduction wasn't the main reason humans don't like relationships with Newcomers. Sid was okay with that, and yet he turned."

"Reproduction was the main issue in the second *Blade Runner* movie. Deckard and Rachel had a child, Rachel doing most of the work."

"That's just a movie. We're not — well never mind. I'm glad all is well with you two. I doubted the wisdom of bringing her on board, but I have to say I enjoy her company too."

"The big question now is what we're going to tell Jennifer."

"About Holly? What's to tell?"

"Not about Holly. About Ruk-ruk. Don't forget Jennifer thinks we talked to a Silicon Valley magnate. We told her he somehow prodded the government to begin its public information campaign about artificial language, same story we told Holly, but Jennifer knows it's not true."

"How does she know?"

"Because Jennifer is the one who contacted the CDC in the first place with the link between artificial language and mutism."

"Oh, right. So why hasn't she said anything?"

"She's waiting. She knows it has to come out. She's been waiting for me to sort things out with Holly first."

The food came. Huge servings, another good thing about Thai food. Plenty of noodles slathered in peanut sauce. They compared their plates and agreed to share certain things but not others.

"Are you thinking we need to tell Jennifer all about Ruk-ruk Akoo?" Andy said through a mouthful of noodles. "It might be too much for her."

"We have to tell her something. Smart as she is, Jennifer is human, and I don't think she can understand the concept of a parasitic virus that gives humans the gift of language."

"Extraterrestrial too. Don't leave that little fact out."

"I think he's terrestrial now. How long do you have to live in a place before you're a native of that place?"

"Depends who you talk to. L.A., ten years. Boston, you need ancestors on the Mayflower."

"I think Ruk-ruk is terrestrial now, so we can leave out all that melodramatic stuff about him floating through space. He's a native of Earth. Just focus on the important facts."

"Do you think we have to tell her?"

"If we don't tell her, she won't trust us until we come clean. That would be an unsustainable situation."

Robin delicately sipped from her tiny clay teacup.

"If we do tell her, she may not understand or believe it," Andy said

"No loss to us then. We did the right thing. But there's one other factor to consider. We do need Jennifer to understand it, all of it."

"Why?"

"Because we need her help. Eventually, we might be the only two producers of artificial language left on the planet. We will stick out like two sore thumbs."

"Why would our thumbs be sore?"

Robin put her teacup down on the table.

"We would stick out, that's what it means. We will be targeted by Mr. Akoo because if there's one thing he hates and fears, it's artificial language, and that's us. Right now we have some cover as things settle down. That will recede over time, and then it will just be us standing alone."

"What about our ten million fellow androids?"

Robin looked up from her dinner, but Andy wasn't smiling. His face was worried. She returned to her noodles.

"I don't know."

Next morning, Robin and Andy went to breakfast with Jennifer. Over waffles, pancakes, and bountiful butterballs, they told her about the existence of the language virus as the cause of the mutism epidemic, and its suppression as the cure. She had questions.

"It makes a certain amount of sense. It's plausible that a brain virus could infect the parietal lobe of the brain's cortex, for example, selectively disabling language production. Do you have evidence for that?"

She looked with raised eyebrows at Robin, then Andy.

"No," Robin said. "We don't have medical evidence. We don't know how the virus works in the brain."

"But you have identified the virus."

"Yes, we have," Andy said. "Positively and without doubt, one hundred percent."

Jennifer put down her fork. "Okay, now I know you guys do not kid around. Especially not on something as serious as this. But I have to ask. Do you have like a secret medical laboratory somewhere that I don't know about?"

"No, no. Nothing like that," Robin said. She glanced at Andy for reassurance. "We haven't done any medical research. We deduced, or I should say, hypothesized, the existence of the virus based on the clues. We used logic and reason."

Andy jumped in. "It's like how physicists discover subatomic particles by watching atoms crashing into each other. They look at the debris and they can deduce what's involved. That's how they found the Higgs boson. They knew it had to be there and when they searched they eventually found it. That's how we discovered the language virus. Robin did, actually. She laid out the evidence and we guessed it was there."

"And then you confirmed the existence of the virus, as predicted."

"Yes."

"How?"

"Well," Robin said hesitantly, "as I said, we didn't do any medical research ourselves. We worked with this powerful character we told you about, Ruk-ruk Akoo. He is the one who actually confirmed our ideas."

"The Greenlandic guy you met in Washington."

"Yes."

"So he had the necessary medical facilities?"

"He was able to positively prove the existence of a language virus."

 "And he provided the cure, too?"

Robin hesitated, apparently unable to answer that, so Andy spoke.

"Yes, he was also the source of the cure."

"But he's very secretive, this Mr. Akoo, right? He saved the world from disaster but he doesn't want to be identified? You two are the only ones who know who he is?"

"Holly knows him," Robin said. "She was there with us in Washington when we talked to him. And a consultant too, that woman we told you about, Katie Wilder, she met him. We're not the only ones. But yes, he is very secretive. Some people are like that. As you know. You have done an extremely remarkable thing yourself and not told anyone, right?"

"That's different. This language virus..." Jennifer stopped mid-sentence, took a sip of coffee, and put the cup down. "Look. It's not that I don't believe you. What you're saying is all reasonable, and I know you wouldn't make it up. But there's something else, isn't there? What are you not telling me?"

"There is more to it," Robin admitted quietly.

Jennifer waited.

"It's a lot to take in," Andy said.

Jennifer waited for more, then said, "Listen. I went to the CDC in Atlanta. At your specific request. You gave me exact instructions to tell the head of the team managing the language crisis that mutism was correlated to use of computer-generated languages. Maybe you can explain why I did that."

"That was the breakthrough we needed," Robin said. "We can't thank you enough for doing that."

"But what did it mean? What the hell. It doesn't make any sense. Even now."

"Okay, that's difficult to explain," Robin said.

Jennifer stared at her and waited.

"You see," Andy said, "Language produced by a computer is processed in the brain just like natural language."

"That's the point, isn't it?" Jennifer said.

"But the language virus can tell the difference and it reacts badly to computer-generated language."

"You're saying it reacts by damaging the brain areas controlling the ability to speak."

"We don't know what goes on the brain," Robin said. We just know that the virus treats artificial language, computer language, the kind found in nearly all voice-assisted technologies, as a foreign intrusion. It's not natural, and like an immune system antibody, the virus rejects the artificial language."

"By making the person mute."

"Apparently," Robin said.

Jennifer looked around the crowded dining area, dozens of tables surrounded by people talking intensely about their lives with each other. Were they all carrying the virus? Was the virus everywhere, a latent disease spread throughout the whole human population just waiting for a trigger? So many questions.

But her main questions were not medical or even about public health. She was concerned about Robin and Andy. Why them? How did they get involved in all this? And what were they still not telling her? She looked into Robin's bright blue eyes for a long moment. What was in there, behind those eyes? She used to know. She wasn't sure anymore.

"Alright," Jennifer finally said. "Here's what I want to know. How did you two get involved in this virus thing? And why? There are a lot of very smart scientists in the world. Why did it take you two to solve this mystery? And I want the truth. I want the whole truth and nothing but the truth."

"That's why we're here, Jennifer," Andy said. "We want you to know the whole truth."

"So tell me why you got involved."

"Basically," Robin said, "It's because we speak with computer-generated language. As you designed us."

Jennifer nodded.

"But we're not susceptible to any virus, because we're outside of biology."

Jennifer nodded again.

"So we speak the language that offends the virus, the same artificial language that comes out of smartphones, watches, TV sets, GPS systems, thermostats, and voice mail. We are the enemy, from the point of view of the virus. But it can't do anything about us because we're not human."

"And how did you figure out that was the critical issue?" Jennifer asked.

Robin looked to Andy to take the question. Andy hesitated but then offered an explanation.

"The virus told us. We talked to it."

Jennifer looked closely at their faces, first Andy's then Robin's. They were completely serious.

"You talked to the virus," she stated flatly. "You had a conversation with a brain virus. In English? Is this what you're telling me?"

"It was last January," Robin said, clearly flustered. "We first spoke with it at the start of this year."

"I see," Jennifer said, watching Robin's face carefully. "And did this virus have a deep voice, or what? Were you looking through a microscope at the time?"

"It wasn't like that," Andy said. "It was Sid. The virus spoke through Sid."

Jennifer jerked her head toward Robin. "Your ex-husband?"

Robin sat back in her chair in a gesture of defeat. "Alright," she said. "We're going to have to go back to what happened in Tucson."

An hour and many cups of coffee later, Jennifer was still reeling but convinced that Robin and Andy were not playing a game. They were trying to tell her something important. She knew they couldn't possibly be delusional or mentally ill, so she struggled mightily to understand their strange tale.

"I can't deal with the idea that my thoughts are not my thoughts. You're saying my rational mind is possessed by a parasite? It's too much. It's just too much."

"It's difficult," Robin said. "We're not saying you're possessed. That's not the situation. It's more like the microbes in your gut. They're part of you, they work for you, but they are, after all, aliens. They're not originally part of the human genome."

"Still, gut microbes are out of sight, out of mind, aren't they? This is language. And thought. Right here, right now. In my face, on my tips."

"Your tips?"

"I meant teeth. Or lips. I was thinking teeth and lips and it came out tips."

"What you meant was not what you said," Andy said.

"It was just a mistake."

"Not a random error, though. From what we have learned about human language, the natural kind, errors like that show that language and thought are not identical. By the time the thought is ready to be spoken, it has become a different thing. Language and thinking are different."

"Most importantly," Robin added, "Thinking is not linguistic. Thinking comes first, then language is applied to it."

Jennifer drank from her mug as she thought, then said, "So you're saying I am—all people are—of two minds? One linguistic, the other... I don't know what."

"We initially thought of it that way too," Robin said, "but it's not a split. It's a blend. The human mind, we believe — although this can only be speculation for us — is a mix of feelings, urges and thoughts, and the process of language sorts all that into rational thought. It's a co-production, not a split."

"Actually that sounds right, believe it or not. Still, the idea that the language part of that mental stew is a living parasite, that's a bizarre idea, you have to admit."

"We admit," Robin said.

"Let's get out of here," Jennifer said. "I'm getting jumpy."

Even on a Monday morning, the parking lot at Manhattan Beach was almost full. It was Jennifer's place for fresh air, to clear her head. It wasn't too crowded early in the morning.

Jennifer led the way with Robin and Andy following as they picked their way down worn wooden steps to the sand. Jennifer pointed north, the way to walk. The morning sun was still low, and the air was chilled. They walked three abreast on hard-packed sand, Jennifer in the middle.

"Have you told Holly?" Jennifer said.

"No," Robin said. "She's satisfied with the story of the tech industry magnate we met in D.C. She was out of the room when we actually talked with the virus through Katie."

"And Katie?"

"She thinks she was hypnotized. Or drugged. She wasn't happy. She has to be pleased, though, that her contribution brought about the end of the mutism plague."

"So the virus called off the plague? Just like that?"

"He was the cause of the plague. Whatever he did to the parts of the brain that control language output, he stopped doing that. He didn't have to snap his fingers to end the plague. All he had to do was stop causing it."

"He? It's a he?"

"Not a person at all. That's just a way of speaking. It was a *he* when it was talking through Sid, then a *she* when talking through Katie. The name isn't particularly gendered."

"Ruk-ruk Akoo," Jennifer said quietly.

"You don't want to be saying that name. Don't say it. Call him the alien. He knows if you say his name. It attracts his attention. You don't want that."

"What is he, Beetlejuice? That is really creepy. I feel like I'm haunted. Aliens inside of me. I feel like Sigourney Weaver."

"Who?" Andy said.

"It's hard to get used to," Robin said, ignoring Andy's question. "We can only imagine what it's like for you."

Jennifer turned her head slightly and looked sideways at Robin, then looked down to her feet again and spoke.

"Incredible as your story is of a virus infecting the whole human race with language, it does explain everything. The language disease is halted, and people have mostly stopped using talking gadgets. It all makes a weird sort of sense. But nobody will believe your explanation."

"You do, don't you?" Andy said.

"I don't know. You've got me cornered. I know you guys. I know how you think. I know you're not mistaken. I know you're not kidding. So right now, at this moment, I believe it, even though I can't believe it."

Neither Robin nor Andy responded to that comment. The group walked in silence for a minute. Jennifer could hardly contain all that she'd learned. The world had changed. Especially the world of the Newcomers. She never dreamed they would get so deeply involved in something like this, language, something so central to the human mind. Yet she knew their minds didn't process language anything like a human mind did. What must it be like for them?

They had years of human social experience now. They could have changed. They could be psychological in a human-like way, for all she knew. Look how Robin behaved around Holly. Jennifer gazed out on the ocean and its tireless waves lapping the beach. She didn't know anything anymore.

"Let's turn around," she announced. "Long way back."

The sun had crept higher, over the eastern hills, and a warm breeze moved off the land toward the sea as they turned in a wide circle.

"It's a frightening story, we know," Robin said. "We can imagine how horrible it would be to think of an alien virus residing in your brain. But it's not just a disease virus. The virus is the source of language in the first place. You need it, just as we need the language database you put inside us. As long as the virus stays calm, and he doesn't act up, everything is fine."

"Don't say *he*," Jennifer said. "It's a virus. It's an *it*."

"Okay, I get that."

"Anyway, the virus doesn't spy on you. It doesn't know what you're thinking. It just slaps language onto whatever thoughts you want to express."

"So it's like an email program," Jennifer said. "The email program just sends my emails. It doesn't read them."

"Well actually," Andy began, but Robin cut him off. "Andy!"

They stopped to wait for a low wave so they could scamper quickly around a rock outcropping they had passed a half hour earlier. The tide had come in. Safely back on drier ground, they continued talking and walking.

"What about you two then?" Jennifer asked.

"What about us?" Andy said.

"Are you worried? About the virus?"

"It seems to be satisfied with what's happening," Robin said.

"But you're still talking. You two use artificial language all day. I'm hearing you so isn't the virus also listening right now to every word we're saying? Doesn't it hate you?"

"Hate us?" Andy said. "I don't think he hates us. We're just two individuals, 'devices' if you want to be rude about it." He put air quotes around the offensive word. "We worked with him to solve his problem. Computer-generated language is fast disappearing from the human world. He has every reason to be grateful to us."

"Can a virus be grateful?"

"We don't know," Robin said. "The virus is not a person. It's a highly specialized parasite on human emotions, and it's distributed over nine billion people, so what it believes, if anything, is anybody's guess."

"You want to know this human's guess? I think this virus is not your friend. You two are by far the most sophisticated artificial language users on the planet, but you're still artificial. There's no way the virus could tolerate that. You're everything it hates and fears."

"He did have a sort of *Old Testament* rage about him," Andy said.

"I'm not surprised. Imagine its point of view. It, or he, in this telling, is the god of language, literally. But you guys. He didn't create you. I did. He knows you're outside of evolution. That has to look like competition to him. You're a threat. He knows that if I could create devices like you, other humans could too. You're not safe."

They came to the wooden stairway leading up to the parking lot. A large log stretched out beside it.

"Let's sit here for a minute," Jennifer said. "I'm a little worn out."

They sat in a row. Nobody spoke for a minute.

"You're right," Robin said. "We seem to be in a quiet period with the virus right now, but we are a threat. He won't let it go."

"What's worse," Andy said quietly, "we're not the ones in danger. You are."

Jennifer looked at Andy with her eyes opened wide and nodded understanding. She groaned as she struggled to her feet, one hand on a thigh.

"Let's go to my place. We have some serious thinking to do."

The three of them climbed the stairs back to the car.

Jennifer brought iced tea and Cokes, along with a small bowl of mothballs out to her narrow porch that overhung the apartment's front yard. She sat with Robin and Andy as they enjoyed their favorite treat and she recovered from the beach walk. Traffic on the narrow street below was light because it was some kind of a holiday for the nearby elementary school. Jennifer eased into a wrought-iron garden chair and put her feet up on the porch railing.

"What we need to sort out, if I understand the situation, is how much longer you two can talk to me, or Holly, or to anyone. We agree that the virus will eventually turn his wrathful eye on you and make your words poisonous and everyone around you will go mute. Agree?"

Andy said, "That's how it was after we talked to him through Sid. We had the words of doom, as Robin called them."

"I remember. That's when you were on TV, and the police were looking for you. I had no idea what was going on. You should have let me know."

"We couldn't speak. Literally. Even on email you could have gone mute. We didn't know what was going on."

Jennifer sipped her Coke.

"There's always that translator thing that Robin invented. That works, doesn't it?"

"It does. It did. I presume it would still work," Robin said. "But it's clunky, slow, and energy- draining, and not very accurate. I mean, 'Here's looking at you, kid?' I don't talk like that."

"It is a fix, though. It's something," Jennifer said.

"It's something."

"The virus might not act against us," Andy said. "Even though he fears us."

"I can see why he would. But why do you think he wouldn't act?"

"We're too dangerous. Robin told him there were ten million of us, all artificial language-using androids, embedded throughout the U.S. population."

"Ten million Newcomers?" Jennifer sat up and looked over to Robin. "You told him that?"

"It was critical to making the deal. It was like the mutually assured destruction strategy of nuclear weapons. If you try any aggression, we'll retaliate, and everybody dies."

"Yikes. How would you retaliate?"

"By activating all these ten million androids. They start talking with computer-generated language, like we do, and the alien has to mute ten million humans a day. Repeat, repeat, repeat. Soon, he will have destroyed his human host and be left with nothing."

"And presumably," Andy added, "the ten million droids cannot survive very long outside of human society, so they're finished too. Everybody loses. The logic of it prevents anybody from acting aggressively."

"And he believed you?"

"He agreed to the deal. The epidemic is over."

"That could be due to the suppression of talking gadgets from the tech industry. It might have nothing to do with mutually assured destruction."

"He's not a deep thinker, this virus," Robin said. "It's a virus, a parasite on humans' native intelligence. He understands only the mechanics of language. Nothing else about human psychology. He doesn't have the reasoning ability of a human. If we, the logical non-humans, tell him we have ten million androids, then we have ten million androids."

"Hmm. So you think the virus won't attack the people you talk to."

"That, we do not know for sure," Andy said.

"What if he realizes it's a bluff?" Jennifer said.

"He doesn't understand bluffs," Robin said. "At least that's what I think. That's why I did it. Subtle communication like that is beyond him."

"You can't be sure."

"No."

They sat in silence, Andy and Robin sucking on mothballs.

"Could we actually make ten million Newcomers?" Andy said. "Why couldn't we do that?"

"Good lord, no," Jennifer said. "I mean, technically, yes, but without Will, no. The scale would be overwhelming. You two are hand-crafted like Stradivarius violins. I can't even think of what it would take to industrialize that process. And the management! Think of the management of a million Newcomers, or even ten. I can hardly keep track of you two. It's impossible."

"And there would be the pitchfork factor," Robin said.

"What's the pitchfork factor?" Jennifer said.

"Villagers with pitchforks. An army of androids would be discovered rather quickly. Andy and I know we don't stay hidden very long in close relationships. There would be a backlash from the humans. Roving vigilantes who were searching for us in this very neighborhood?"

Jennifer nodded. She lowered her eyes.

"Yeah." Robin said quietly.

"Here's the curious fact," Jennifer said, willfully recovering her equilibrium. She slid sideways in her chair to face Andy and Robin. "Robin bluffed the alien."

"I did," Robin said.

"How was that possible? You can't bluff. You can't lie at all. It's not in you. It's not how I built your language processor."

"I don't know, exactly. I just did it because it had to be done."

"So you said one thing, but you meant something else."

"I guess I did."

"How? How did you think about that?"

"I didn't think about it at the time, although it felt a little odd, I remember."

"Felt odd?"

"I remember. It was after that bomb in the D.C. subway, and I was thinking about terrorism as a kind of human language without words. Holly gave me that idea when she talked about how she writes speeches. There are words, and then there's what's below the words, the feelings and intentions. A two-layer cake."

"And you understood that?"

"After the bombing I did. I realized you can listen to a second layer of meaning in any conversation. It's a trick humans do."

"I don't know what you're talking about," Andy said. "What's the second layer of meaning in this conversation right now?"

"Well," Robin hesitated. "It's the hidden layer because you're not supposed to say it."

"Say it," Jennifer said.

"Alright, but..." She looked directly into Jennifer's eyes, and Jennifer nodded. Robin continued. "I think you're worried right now about how I can do something with language that you didn't program into me, and you're wondering what else I can do, and you're uncomfortable because you think you don't know me anymore."

Robin and Jennifer stared at each other as if they were in a contest to see who would blink first.

"Am I close?" Robin said.

Jennifer's eyes filled with tears.

"Where did you get that?" Andy said. He turned sideways in his chair to face Robin sitting next to him. "Jennifer never said all that."

"Oh, my god," Jennifer said, focused on Robin, ignoring Andy's perplexity. "It's because of Holly."

"What is?" Andy said.

Jennifer got up from her chair and stepped over to Robin, bent, and hugged Robin's head, engulfing it in her breasts. It was awkward, but Robin understood what it meant and put her arms around Jennifer's waist.

"What's going on?" Andy said.

Chapter Twenty-seven

There was only one sure way to discover if untranslated speech from Robin was safe for humans, and that was to try it. Obviously, she was safe so far talking with Jennifer and Holly, although that could have been temporary. Fewer and fewer talking technologies were in use every week, and soon she and Andy would be virtually the only remaining sources of "false language." When that day would come, nobody knew. It wouldn't be safe or even conclusive to go out and talk to random people on the street because you never knew when the game might change again.

Robin spent two days reading all the technical literature she could find on software engineering for natural language processing, as the field was called. She read historical papers from the days when computer scientists first tried to diagram sentences and divine their meaning from the grammar, an approach that failed. She studied vast databases of so-called commonsense knowledge which were supposed to supply the real foundation of human understanding of language, a strategy that collapsed under its own weight. She learned all about neural nets, computers that were supposed to simulate brain processes of learning and understanding but which ended up as tangled as a drawer full of rubber bands and paper clips. She briefed herself on the successful statistical and phonemic deep learning pattern-matching methods that created the technical possibilities for computer-based language.

Robin knocked twice on Jennifer's open office door at Paradise and stepped in.

"I'm ready," She announced. "I can pass as a software engineer in the field of language processing."

"I'm sure you can. The tech companies are so desperate for talent right now they won't look at you too closely. Technocrats are falling mute at a startling rate. The ones who escape that fate must be exceptionally lucky."

"If engineers can talk to me without losing their voices, then I'm human-safe. That's all that matters."

"Okay, let's get it done before it's too late. Here's a list of firms from L.A. to Seattle still doing the work. Only six, I'm afraid. I've posted documents and transcripts online. You have plenty of backup for your references, not that they'll check."

"Thanks, Jennifer."

After she sent her job application material to only two firms, Robin got a call from the second one asking her when she could start. It was in Cupertino, in the Bay Area. She left L.A. and Paradise Projects the next day, promising Holly to return in a month.

"I'll know in a few weeks whether I can help already afflicted people," she said.

Robin and Jennifer and Andy had agreed it was best if Holly and other humans didn't know anything about a language virus infecting the human brain. It was too much to grasp, Jennifer said, and besides, what would be the purpose of revealing it? Humans must have language, and the virus was the source of that gift, so leave it alone. As long as the alien wasn't threatened, it would presumably remain quiet and invisibly enable language for another hundred thousand years.

Robin learned that her new company was focused on re-inventing artificial language. They recognized that something was wrong with the statistical methods they had been using to generate language from computers. They were in close contact with neuroscientists at major universities, hoping to discover exactly what the problem was, but meanwhile, they were trying several different approaches, from languages based on Esperanto to some based on mathematics and music.

None of those approaches looked very promising to Robin. All of them tried to make conversational language out of surface structure, the sounds and grammar of language irrespective of any meaning intended by the speaker. Because computers didn't intend any meaning. They just looked up questions and statements in a database, fixed them up for social context, and put them out.

She knew that's how it worked because that's how she did it. Or used to, anyway. Lately, she wasn't sure if that's how she made language. It was impossible to examine your own inner workings while you were using those inner workings. She could think about the process of speaking or she could do it. Not both. Likewise for listening. It was a strange paradox, an uncomfortable self-blindness she had never noticed in herself before. She wondered if Andy had noticed a change like that.

At the same time, she still couldn't say what emotions were or what intentionality was, so she couldn't offer any radical new approach to automatically generating language. Nevertheless, she worked with a small team of very bright engineers, engaging them in endless analysis and design meetings in front of whiteboards and computer monitors. She spoke with them practically all day, every day, and was pleased that nobody went mute on her.

She asked them why they weren't worried about contracting the language disease. They had deduced that the danger lay in the gadgets that produced artificial language for human consumption. There was no danger in theorizing and experimenting with the nature of language itself, as long as they didn't try to build and test a device. They didn't know they were already involved in a test of an artificial language device by talking with Robin.

She was very satisfied with the results of her experiment and was ready to quit and go back to L.A. after a few weeks, but

Jennifer urged her to stay on. "We have to be absolutely sure," she said. "Talk to people outside your team. Talk to management. Talk to the accounting department. Talk to consultants."

So Robin did all that, expanding her circle of contacts every day and still she continued to speak normally to people without causing them any distress. She had turned a corner in her ability to use language, she believed, although what corner that was, she couldn't say.

Since she had promised Jennifer she'd stay at least one month, Robin began to toy with the idea of planting ideas with her research group so they would discover and invent the language translator she had already created. She left clues to the idea of finding and splicing together already-published sentences of human speech. It was such a simple idea that she was sure somebody would stumble upon it eventually, so why not make it her parting gift?

SynTalk, the company that had unwittingly provided her with test subjects, was so focused on tricky sub-phonemic sounds and fancy equations that it would take them a long time to see the obvious. Just use already-existing human speech. They might even find a way to smooth the pre-recorded clips so the result wouldn't sound as goofy as her home-made translator often did. She became an intellectual farmer, a planter of seeds, during her last two weeks on the job.

SynTalk didn't want Robin to quit. They offered money, promotions, stock options. Her team had come up with an idea for a safe personal assistant device using pre-recorded human speech, and they all pointed to Robin's leadership in developing the concept. Even as a hero, she could not be persuaded to stay.

Back in Los Angeles, satisfied that she could safely talk to any human, Robin worked with Jennifer, Andy, and Holly, to try to discover why she was safe. Language technology workers still fell mute when they used computer-generated language, but they were fine around her. She had changed somehow. Only three months ago if she had said 'Boo!' to a person they would become mute. What was different now?

Holly wasn't much help at first because she still struggled with the idea that Robin and Andy were Newcomers, not people. She believed it in her head but not in her heart. Long discussions about language helped her to slowly understand.

Nobody had a good answer to the question of how natural and artificial language differed. What was the essential difference the alien virus keyed in on? It was apparent that whatever had changed for Robin had not changed for Andy. He stumbled over subtle meanings, idioms, and metaphors, and he could not pick up subtext as well as Robin could. They worried that he would not be a safe talker among humans.

"You have to listen for the hidden subtext," Robin explained.

"How can I if it's hidden?" Andy said.

"It's the original human voice. It's made of feelings and primitive urges. Its meanings are simple actions and desires. The two voices are braided into every sentence."

"So you say. I don't hear it."

"Don't be too hard on Andy," Jennifer said to Holly. "He works the way I built him. Robin's new language ability is the real mystery."

"Are you saying you didn't put the original human voice into Andy at all?" Holly said, then turned to Andy and said, "I'm sorry to talk about you as if you weren't sitting right here. It's awkward for me. I don't always know what to say."

"Me either," Andy said. "Don't worry about it."

"Andy has no deeper layer," Jennifer said, "what you're calling the original layer? Is that what you mean, Robin? Some pre-rational, animal layer of language?"

"I am not the one to ask what is animal and what is not."

They turned to Holly.

"Okay, well, I'm no language expert," she said hesitantly.

"Actually, you are," Robin said. "I think I learned my new language trick from you. If that's what you could call it, a trick. I learned to speak and listen to two layers of meaning at once."

"I barely understand it myself."

"I feel the same," Jennifer said. "The reason Will and I didn't put any deeper layer of language into Andy and Robin is because we weren't aware of it. I'm starting to get the picture now that we're talking about it. But normally we humans are only aware of the dominant, grammatically structured language, so that's what's in Robin and Andy's databases. We believe, I believed, that was the natural and the only kind of human language, evolved over the centuries since the time we were apes."

Robin cocked her head and listened with keen attention. "So what do you make of the other language, pre-grammatical animal communication?"

"Left over from when we were apes."

"Apes don't have language," Holly said.

"Not language as we understand it today," Jennifer said. "Or understood it up until language disease crisis. Ape language is blurted, barked, and howled. When that expression is processed by the syntax, it comes out in sentences. That's how we should have built the language systems for Andy and Robin, but we didn't know."

"That makes a certain amount of sense," Holly said. "It's how we write speeches for the president. I wouldn't use those exact terms, but that description is about right."

Andy stood and circled around behind his chair and faced the others. "I'm afraid it makes no sense to me," he said. "I do not hear howling or barking underneath or within human sentences."

The others stared at him, wordless.

Soon they all agreed that just to be safe, Andy should use one of Robin's Newcomer-to-human translators until they solved the problem of what made computer-generated language stand out to the virus.

"Or," Robin added, trying to sound encouraging, "until SynTalk comes out with a snazzy new translator."

Holly nodded in understanding.

Later, when Robin and Andy were alone with Jennifer, a haunting question was what Robin had learned to make her into a pass-for natural language user, apparently undetectable by the alien virus.

"You may have learned something new about language, but you're still not biological, and I know you do not have any ape layer of language processing," Jennifer said.

Andy asked if he could get a software upgrade to Robin's level. "That may be the only answer we need," he said. Whatever changed in Robin would also change in me if I had the same version of software. Maybe we don't have to understand what it is. If it works, it works."

Jennifer expressed caution. Robin was a newer model by two years, and with Will gone, she'd have to go back through the original engineering documents to assess compatibility. She would do that, she promised Andy, and scope out an upgrade project. It would take some time.

Robin was aware of Andy's disappointment. Or at least she knew *she* would have been disappointed if she were in his situation.

Jennifer trained Holly to help her research the engineering documents for the Newcomers, with the aim of determining if Andy could be upgraded and if there was anything in Robin's information processing design that could explain her newfound language ability. Holly couldn't understand most of what she read in the documents, but she learned how the software library worked and how to search it at Jennifer's request. In the process of doing all that she slowly began, day by day, to understand in her gut, the incredible fact that Robin was a synthetic being.

One bit of good news brightened up everyone. Geneticists and neuroscientists at two universities discovered how to restore speech to the mute victims of the language disease. While the treatment was still experimental, a half-dozen victims had their speech successfully restored. They spoke with a stammer, but these recovered patients apparently had not suffered any permanent loss of brain function in the language production areas, the scientists said. News of the disease's reversibility made headlines all over the world.

Duc Nguyen, known as the D.C. Bomber, was apprehended and put on trial. Robin, as a well-recognized expert in the language-tech industry, testified on his behalf by video. She argued that his actions were an example of natural human expression, 'language without the words,' she called it. What he had done counted as effective communication, and was a distinctly human way of conveying silent misery to indifferent power. Her arguments were persuasive. Nguyen was convicted of the bombing but received a light sentence from an unusually thoughtful judge. During his incarceration, Nguyen entered treatment to restore his language capacity.

In her extensive research on language, Robin happened to notice a small article in the Marin County Gazette. Prominent real-estate developer Sid Snow was found dead in his home, slumped over a rare, still-working voice-activated 'smart speaker' made by a company named Gargle. He had been a prominent conspiracy theorist during the mutism epidemic, the article reported, and had claimed there were humanoid robots dwelling in the population.

Robin read the short article three times. Had Ruk-ruk killed Sid? Was the alien cleaning up loose ends? The exact cause of Sid's death was not reported. The article focused on Sid's status as a conspiracy monger. It could have been a heart attack, stroke, anything. Language couldn't kill you, could it?

When she tried to put herself in Sid's place, tried to understand how badly he would have been confused by knowing that his ex-wife was a robot but not sure what that meant, with hardly anyone believing him, dismissed in the media as a nut case, attracting thugs and killers as his supporters.

She imagined his state of mind. Sid had not been good to her, but his story wasn't wrong. From his point of view, he had been deceived and betrayed by an alien being. His mind was fuzzy and blurred by contradictory feelings. The contrast to her own mind was startling, and it made something in her processing systems oscillate that shouldn't have been oscillating.

She shut off her computer and left the Hideout to make the short walk over to Paradise Projects. Maybe Holly would be ready to go out for lunch.

Robin and Andy collected all the documents and photographs they had gathered on the history of the language virus, from the pictures of the scratched ammonite shell to the micrographs of the dinosaur femur inscribed with the Fibonacci series of numbers. They put every trace of evidence they had about the language virus into an encrypted, locked file stored in a network account. It was unlikely that any human would ever re-discover the alien virus living among them. Inside them.

They had decided, with Jennifer, that the presence of the language virus should be kept secret. Eventually, medical science might uncover the fact that language was alive, literally a separate living thing with its own life course, infecting the human species. But as long as Ruk-ruk Akoo was undisturbed and remained quiet, the symbiosis between language and human worked perfectly, as it had for a hundred thousand years.

"There's no alternative," Jennifer said. "People must have language."

"We're an alternative," Robin said. "You created it. Andy and I are a non-biological way to do language."

"But that's useless for humans. Dangerous, even, as we have learned. For the foreseeable future, people will have to get along with Ruk-ruk as they have for centuries, and for that, it's better if they don't know anything about him. The best strategy is to let sleeping dogs lie."

"What are these dogs?" Andy said.

A year had passed since the mutism disease had first been identified as an epidemic. On a Sunday afternoon during the holidays, Jennifer served a dinner of Hawaiian barbeque, which delighted Holly. Coming from D.C., she had little experience of Hawaiian anything and this looked like a feast.

The spread included tropical fruits and juices to please Robin and Andy, who were more interested in sugar than meat. With side dishes of mothballs, of course. Everyone sat around the dining room table with the extra leaf, and they talked about the past and the future.

Jennifer announced that a software upgrade for Andy was looking positive, though she didn't have details yet. Robin had somehow found a way to get beyond the Newcomers' computational way of using language and into a natural, human way that Ruk-ruk could not detect. That proved it was possible.

"Once you know something is possible," Jennifer said, "you're halfway to success. When Will and I set out to build Newcomers, we didn't know if it could be done. More than once we thought about abandoning the project, convinced it was a ridiculous overreach, a case of classical hubris."

"We're certainly glad you didn't quit," Robin said, putting a large, spotted mango onto her plate.

"Me too," Jennifer said, horizontally holding a rib of shiny, honey-glazed meat in front of her face. "But this is a different situation because the goal is demonstrably achievable. Robin has done it. Natural language can be artificially constructed. All we have to do is find the route. And with Robin guiding us, we should be able to."

"What we need," Robin said, "is an analyzer like the V-K machine in the first *Blade Runner* movie. It was like a polygraph that detected android replicants by triggering their emotionality, but replicants didn't have emotions, so it never was clear how it worked. Like when Kowalski got agitated by the interviewer's questions and shot him. Kowalski shouldn't have gotten agitated if he was a replicant."

Robin finished her enthusiastic explanation, and the room went silent for a moment.

Good lord, Jennifer thought. What was that outburst about?

Since Robin had become so close to Holly, and her language had become so subtle, it was easy to overlook what she was. Had Robin somehow, magically—it would have to be magic—acquired intuition? It was not easy to understand her sophisticated new way of thinking if she didn't have intuition.

But then why did she take that sci-fi movie so seriously? For Robin it was not just a movie but some kind of literal doctrine of how humans and machines were supposed to interact. How did Robin think of herself now? Was she self-aware like a person? Why was she obsessed with sci-fi replicants?

Jennifer broke the silence.

"Would you be able to pass this V-K test as a human, now?"

"I don't know."

"You would," Holly said. "A person is defined by the give-and-take of being in relationships. It's not about how you look or what's inside that matters. Both of you qualify as humans right now, if you ask me." She turned to look at Andy.

"Robin has cracked some secret code of human language that I haven't," Andy said. "I hope someday I can do the same."

"The only difference is," Robin said, "I'm like a Nexus Nine, and you're maybe a Model Six. Different versions, that's all."

"People are like that too," Holly said, smiling. "Some are Nines, and some are Sixes."

Holly thinks they're joking around, Jennifer thought. Newcomers don't joke. That's not how they're built. Unless Robin can joke now, but that would mean she had self-awareness and intuition. What had changed in Robin? She bluffed Ruk-ruk, after all. Andy couldn't have done that.

"I'll get you upgraded, Andy," Jennifer said. "It'll just take a little time."

Andy nodded and took a mothball from a small dish.

But Jennifer did not feel the reassurance that Andy showed. How could she upgrade Andy? Upgrade to what? She didn't know what had changed in Robin.

What she didn't tell Andy was that it would have to be a lot more than a language upgrade. She'd have to completely rebuild him with the newer specifications Robin had and hope that he would discover whatever Robin had discovered about being human.

But then it wouldn't be Andy anymore. It would be a completely different android. The Andy sitting across from her would be... erased. Was that the right thing to do? Erase him? If she didn't, he and Robin would drift apart, probably even become alienated from each other.

Robin was attached to Holly now. Robin didn't seem to realize that she didn't live in the same world as Andy anymore. Andy would eventually notice. He'd be alone, just as he had been in the beginning, in Seattle. Jennifer couldn't put him through that ordeal again.

She had to rebuild him. He'd look the same. She could save most of his memories, but he wouldn't be able to think in the same way anymore because the processors would be different. His memories might seem foreign to him. He'd talk the same, at least at first. He'd still be in danger from Ruk-ruk, until... what? She had no idea.

Jennifer put down her barbequed rib. She watched Robin and Holly chatter back and forth about various things. She looked at Andy dreamily sucking on his mothball.

She wished she could talk to Will.

Want More?

Get the Whole Newcomers series:

Reluctant Android (Sci-fi, 80,000 words). Andy Bolton, a software engineer in Seattle, is horrified to discover he's a robot. His boss, Lucy, wants to capture him and take him apart for study. On the run, Andy finds his creator and learns he is neither human nor straightforward machine. He reluctantly accepts that he is something in between, a sentient AI device. He needs to explain this to his nemesis, Lucy, but can a person ever believe in a machine with empathy?

Writers Digest Honorable Mention:
Best Sci-Fi Self-Published Books of 2018!

"...a fast-paced morality tale, one that blends bleeding-edge science with deep philosophical questions for a high-throttle page-turner." -- WD Judge, 5th Annual Writer's Digest Self-Published eBook Awards.

Indie BRAG Medallion Award, 2019
"The author deftly creates an android that we can care about and it teaches us some wonderful lessons about compassion and leads us to thinking of the future we will one day face. For those

Sci Fi lovers and those interested in AI, I highly recommend this book." -- Judge, 2019 Indie BRAG Awards.

Kindle www.amazon.com/dp/B07FBQTM9M
bit.ly/RA-kindle_ASIN: B07FBQTM9M

KDP Paper www.amazon.com/dp/173222742X
bit.ly/RA-paperback _ASIN: 173222742X

Alien Talk (sci-fi, 80,000 words): As millions of people become mute in a spreading pandemic, android Robin Taylor discovers that language is an intelligent virus that infected early humans and ultimately enabled modern civilization. Now the virus is enraged by the false language of talking technologies. But Robin is a talking gadget herself. Anyone she communicates with is stricken mute. Can she warn humans and stop the plague?

I read and enjoyed Reluctant Android, and was expecting to enjoy this too. Even so, I did not expect a gripping thriller that sucked me in from page one and kept me reading until I finished it.
-- Amazon Reader Comment

KDP Paper:
https://www.amazon.com/dp/1732227454
bit.ly/AT-Paper
Kindle:
https://www.amazon.com/dp/B07LDJ4CHF
bit.ly/AT-Kindle

Intelligent Things (sci-fi, 80,000 words): Engineer Jennifer Valentine releases advanced AI assistants online to revolutionize the internet of things. But her softbots, called NODs, go rogue, and she must save the national power grid from disaster. With her consciousness uploaded online, she searches for the leader of the NODs and finds much more than she expected. Back in her lab, she must decide: erase the entire NOD world to protect the human world?

Four Stars! Readers Favorite.com

The characters are realistic and show valid concern for life and sentience on multiple levels. All in all, this is a great sci-fi thriller that brings to future straight to today. A must for fans of the genre!

Paper – KDP

www.amazon.com/Intelligent-Things-Newcomers-William-Adams/dp/1732227489

Ebook - Kindle:

www.amazon.com/dp/B07QLNLS88

Acknowledgments

Many thanks to my colleagues at RAW-Salon for reading early drafts.

About the Author

William X. Adams is a cognitive psychologist who left the academic life for the information technology industry to find out if the mind is like a computer. He writes psychological science fiction to dramatize what he discovered. He has a Ph.D. from the University of Wisconsin-Milwaukee and lives in Tucson, Arizona. Contact him at www.psifibooks.com/contact.